S0-CQR-282

A CHAIR BETWEEN THE RAILS

Vaulan Cycle, Book I

KENT, OH

RIPENING BOOKS

2013

Dear Phillip,

I hope you enjoy these novels! This one may surprise you. All the best,

George

© 2013 George Anderson. All rights reserved. This text may not be reproduced, in part or in whole, without the express written consent of the author, with the exception of short passages used for reviews, in which case written permission is not required. For guidance on obtaining written permission, please contact the author:

author@gtanders.com

First edition produced by Ripening Books.

ISBN-10: 0985652217

ISBN-13: 978-0-9856522-1-0

Cover design and interior typesetting by George Anderson.

Title set in Adec 2.0, a free typeface created by Serge Shi, available at:

http://www.behance.net/gallery/Typeface-Adec20-(free)/2075950

Ripening Books

THE VAULAN CYCLE

by g. t. anders

Author's Note

There has been some confusion about the order of books in the Vaulan Cycle. This story is chronologically the first, despite the fact that *The Tower of Babel* was (unfortunately) published first.

However, the books can be read and (largely) enjoyed in any order.

A CHAÏR BETWEEN THE RAÏLS

g. t. anders

VAULAN CYCLE, BOOK I

By James Feckidee
The steel planet
Year 1946-to-the-side

PART I
Events on Earth
Year 1945

1

YOU SEE, I FIRST discovered the poet William Blake, that man chosen by whomever God thinks God is to relieve me from the agony that it is to think and feel—first discovered him when I was twelve, sitting in Uncle Phil's study. I will always remember that day. The fire was so warm (winter, you know—a great room for winters, and wrought-iron window-framed). His voice was warm, too. And now this: Uncle Phil, dead; the funeral, tonight, in half an hour; and myself, hapless James Feckidee, a little more dead inside than I'd been yesterday, waiting to fill up the old Ford and watching the slow-turning clouds of young October.

My boy Austin was only four, but sometimes I let him roam. He stood now on the other side of the gas station gravel, holding the payphone up to his ear and listening. I must have listened like that in Uncle Phil's study, when my mind was still malleable. Austin must be listening now to the dead phone, like his imagination was more than reality, like he knew something I didn't—like he *heard* something I didn't. He probably did.

The gas station attendant came out. He had a big scar above his left eye. He was still drunk, or maybe you would say already drunk, seeing as how it was almost dusk, and that would be a mighty hangover. Regardless, this guy needed a razor and a cup of coffee.

"Need a fillup?" he asked.

"Yes," I muttered.

"How about a wash and a wax?"

"No thank you. We're off to a funeral, so it doesn't matter."

"I'm sorry, sir." He pumped my gas.

I stood kicking at the gravel. Austin smiled at me across the drive, holding that dead payphone up to his ear.

"The kid hears something, you know," said the gas station attendant.

I blinked and looked at the guy. His hand was clamped on the pump, but his vacant eyes watched my boy.

"Excuse me?"

"That's a rare ability." His empty face turned toward me, and the scar above his left eye seemed to throb.

"I don't know what you're talking about."

The man shrugged. "But *I* do, and so does your son." His speech was strangely clear for the bleariness of his eyes. He shut off the pump and crossed the gravel. "Hey, little guy. What do you hear in that phone?"

I dashed after him. I swept up my boy just as the creep's hand went for him. The payphone fell hard, clanging gray against the gray metal, colorless—always colorless, this deep morass, this wading through.

"Telephone—telephone—" My boy kicked, scrambling over my shoulder, but I held him.

We stood breathing and staring at each other, the creep and me. Alien colors passed under the man's face. At last he murmured, "You have no idea what he can do."

"Listen." My terror, my rage. "Tell me what I owe you, and leave us alone."

Now the creep raised both hands, shaking his head. "All right. You're not ready. Now, I can't stop what's been set in motion—though I *can* protect you, if you'll trust me."

"What do I owe you?" I didn't care that he hadn't filled the tank up all the way. He'd given us enough gas to get away from him.

"Sixty-seven cents," he said.

"I'll meet you inside." I glared at him, holding my boy, waiting for him to leave. At last he lowered his gaze and nodded and walked past me toward the door.

"Telephone—telephone—" My boy was still throwing a tantrum.

"You can't stop him," said the creep as he went inside. "You can't stop what he is."

"What he is," I muttered. "He's my boy, *that's* what he is."

With the gentle force of fatherhood, I put my struggling ball of limbs into the car. Though it hurt me, I locked him in. You see, I had to. He sobbed and pounded on the window as I walked away, but it was for his own good.

Inside, I paid the creep. He measured out my coins with exacting idiocy. At last he said, "You're a penny short, but who's counting?" He threw all the money into the same compartment in the drawer. "Listen." He leaned over the counter and took me with those broad, bloodshot eyes. "Something is happening which you know nothing about. Something has been loosed which you can't stop. Your boy is special. See? You can't keep him away from his purpose." The creep's gaze wandered past me to the window. I spun. My boy was at the phone again, listening.

"Shut up!" I left the idiot and stormed outside. I swept up my boy.

"Daddy, no! Telephone—"

I caught the receiver as it fell. I put it to my ear. Not a sound, not a hum, even after I dropped in a nickel as an experiment.

"Daddy—daddy—"

Back to the car. I would have to hold him in my lap. If he had figured out how to unlock the car door, there was no telling what he would do to get back to that phone while we were moving.

"Daddy—daddy—"

I clutched him to my chest with one arm and wrangled the ignition and the gearshift with the other. He was still struggling.

"Calm down. I need you to behave. We're going to Uncle Phil's funeral."

But I don't think he even knew who Uncle Phil was to me.

We were just shuffling past the knees of relatives, just settling into the pew, when the minister began to intone his dirge of comfort. I guess we were late—but couldn't we be forgiven? What a battle, just to get there.

"Dearly beloved, we are gathered here today to remember..."

Oh, I could remember. I remembered how Uncle Phil used to look up over the desk at me. The lenses and their thin film of opacity somehow rendered him inverse professorial, like he was the antithesis of the unapproachable scholar, though still retentive of all the knowledge.

He wasn't even my grandfather in archetype, but more like a brother-fellow-conspirator who happened to have white hair. It must have been brown once; we're a brown-haired family.

The minister's gaze revolved slowly around the congregation. "When a brother in the Lord passes on, we gather…"

Uncle Phil came to all the family gatherings when I was really young. If only I could have given Austin the same opportunity to get to know him. But Austin had barely even met Uncle Phil, what with the sickness that taken my uncle four years ago, strangely coinciding with the boy's birth. Now Uncle Phil had been taken from Austin forever, just as he had been taken from me for a few years, when he had mysteriously disappeared…

"…who reigns now with Jesus Christ in the fields of eternity—*that* is the true Phillip Feckidee. *That* is the man as God made him. But *that*—" the minister pointed down from the pulpit to the open casket and the glorious white shock of hair—"is just the withered shell. No, do not weep for Phillip Feckidee!"

But they wept anyway, all around me. It was a quiet sound like dead leaves rustling in some abandoned gymnasium of the woods. Likewise, it had no meaning. I don't weep, you understand; so I just sat there. I pitied them, really. To be so lost, so weak, that you can't maintain your steely humanity. Never find me doing that.

Of course, Uncle Phil *did* find me that way once. He came to the diamond near sundown, driving that old jalopy bounce-banging through ruts as if on wagon wheels. I'd been catching, and I'd taken a foul ball to the cheekbone. I'm still not the same shape there. That was such a dry summer, and dust and blood makes this sort of dough. If you could feel it, like I still do. I was weeping then; don't know if I have since. Of course, all the pains after that have been nothing but amplifications of the original, of the first time it was shown to me that I was paper and not a god, that I was flesh and not iron eternal spirit. From then on, the universe has been diligent and relentless to remind me of its arrogant superiority, and this is no exception.

The minister got down after making an open invitation. I, who read and write and don't speak publicly, as a rule, got up and stood between the whitewashed walls from which a thousand declamations of fire and brimstone had come. I stood looking out across the flat and opaque and mundane body of the Lord, who were black-dressed and daub-eyed and ready to ring with my words; and I, reader, writer, and mock-theologian of nothingness, began to speak.

"To me, he will always be Uncle Phil. Economy of speech assumed the dropping of *great*. Great was a mere technicality. The fact that he was great was so fundamental that if you had to say it, if you had to call him my *great-uncle*, you didn't know him at all. I just called him Uncle Phil. But you know, he always felt more like a brother than a man fifty years my senior. He never came at me with that superiority complex so natural to a writer of his intellectual and artistic prowess. He was just incredibly normal."

My voice rang in glorious cadence across the room. I seemed to hold their emotions, these foreign things, in the palm of my hand.

"Above all, Phillip Feckidee was a mover, a man who might have changed the world. He was a man who looked elsewhere. He insisted that if we follow him into his dance, we go elsewhere with him. For that, I loved him dearly."

I probably didn't speak that magnificently, but you know how we represent ourselves. I got down from the podium then, something like caring and triumphant.

Then I stood in the casket line among the black-backed shapes that I should have known all my life—among those things still shuddering, still beset with that particular affliction that I do not know. I stood mingled, but walled off and outcast and safer that way. That was me, then, there. The sidelong light of the dusk-brown sun made the women's left ears glitter and the men's watches shine. One by one they came to the point of flowers and solemnity and lacquered wood where they got stopped up. From there on out, it was all flow, sweet forgetful flow into scattering and disintegration.

I was perfectly lucid.

Now swept up in the inexorable push of the line, I came upon him. O, the long daring face and the hardset jaw carved for derision but accustomed only to laughter. The same glasses and their opaque film, like they were dimly misted—but they were dry, it was only the light—and the eyes shut in eternal mystery behind them. That same brazen wash of white hair, unchanged in death as it had been unchangeable in life. The hands of a giant folded in wrinkled wisdom like poetry, like Blake's hands as they must have been when Blake had lain like this, floating in flowers and white satin, as he must have, floating, just atoms now unencumbered with the higher mysteries of will and consciousness and emotion, a part of the earth now prepared for disintegration, just atoms, as they tell us, just atoms, and the rest is atom bombs.

Oh, my memories—

"Read to me, James."

Uncle Phil leaned ravenously across the desk. Firelight flashed on his lenses, but it could not dim the hunger in his eyes.

Why do I always read? I asked. *Why don't you read?*

"I can't, dear James. I've lost the ability."

How? Are you going blind?

He laughed. "Of course not! Just read to me, James. My soul is starved for words."

Chapter one. I read to him. I loved him. *Dark Urizen prepared; his ten thousands of thunders, ranged in gloomed array, stretch out across the dread world...*

"Blake has a way with words, doesn't he, James?"

Yes.

"Sorry, keep going."

I shifted the musty book and found my place. *Voices of terror are heard, like thunders of autumn, when the cloud blazes over the harvests...*

Maybe Blake had meant that to refer to a late summer storm, but now I would always hear in it the Japanese cities decimated, the Japanese sky ablaze. What would Uncle Phil think of us, of our country? He would never tell me now, for he had taken sick years before the bomb.

"Take pen and paper. Take this on dictation, if you don't mind, James."

I never minded hearing his voice or feeling his swift winged words infuse my pen with universal vibrations.

"Do you ever think about how these are just words, just letterforms, just swept ink illegible on the page?"

No, I said.

"It's true, James. These forms have only the meaning we've learned to give them…"

I never thought of that, I said.

"So pay attention to the context of anything, of everything. That's how we pass it down. That's how we preserve intellect and meaning. Remember: without our efforts, these letters are just ink on a page."

Just ink on a page. Just atoms. He was just atoms now, and the rest was atom bombs. They had done it over there, and it didn't make a difference metaphysically where or who, even though I couldn't fulfill my duty to my country. It had been done. We had done it to our planet, to our race, to ourselves.

I love you, dear uncle.

All around me, the black-clad forms moved in reverent pantomime. Mine was a timeless salutation before the casket, and no one dared interrupt me. I gazed. The stillness of his waxy face did not move. Floating in a garden of fragrance and color, he did not respond to me, and he never would again.

"What do you mean incompetent?!" Uncle Phil shouted, jumping up from behind the desk.

Mentally incompetent, I said.

"And how did the Army determine—"

Ask them!

"I don't see how that could affect soldiering. You're a strong lad. You're intelligent. You have a mind both creative and logical."

I'm not strong, I said. *I barely passed the fitness exam.*

"I've never heard of this mental incompetence business. You should be serving your country."

I can't! That's what I'm saying!

He turned and left the room then.

"She's really leaving?" Uncle Phil shouted, spinning to face me across the study.

I said that.
"There's no—"
She said the word.
"My God, James. What about the boy?"
What about him? I'm not sending him to an orphanage. I'm his father.
"Doesn't she want—"
No. And if she did, I'd tell her to—
"So you'll be the one who—"
Yes. He's my son.
"And why? Did she tell you?"
You know her. The damn floozie magazines—as if those were real people, as if I ever touched any of them—
"But you were looking."
What difference does it make? It's just art. Just paintings and photographs. I never said I didn't love her. I never told her that.
"I think you did, James."

He looked out the window then, doubtless at the June flowerbeds devoured under careless grass that I had forgotten to trim.

Now I would never finish the gardening for him; and even if I ever patched this up into something like a life, he would never find out. The last version of James Feckidee he had known, which he would know forever now, was the divorced, the violent, the perverted.

I told you that I didn't want to talk about this thing, even if it's just in my own mind and just a conversation between selves. You know, I preferred childhood, when there was no self but only that which I took for an emerging self called me. And now this, and these, and *we*. I don't like it.

My time before the casket was over. I worked my way outwards through the line and pool of these black-weighted things all penitent and mourning. I carried my son. No sense making him tag along; if I was tired, he must be even more so. At least I had the sense to see that.

I stood now in the lobby. The mood was strangely serene. I suppose it usually is after funerals of the old. It's only the fallen young and the heartland boy soldiers that can elicit true grief from men. The women, sure, every time; but the men know the degrees of death, the hierarchies. They know when they can weep. This wasn't that time. He was a great man: brilliant, internationally known, long-lived, white-haired; and he was wearing a fine waistcoat in the casket.

In the photos on the board in the narthex, I found an alarming picture. A young Uncle Phil stood in sepiatone with his arm around the same man who had tried to touch my son at the gas station. While the creep looked no younger in the photo, Uncle Phil was in his twenties.

"James!"

An arm spun me and a hand shook my hand.

"Yes. Yes." I blinked rapidly. "Good to see you again. Yes. He was a great man." The words rolled out of me like a page punched up on a typewriter—like a script—like the funeral script. There is one, you know.

That was why I couldn't empathize with them. That was why I couldn't even tell you who was shaking my hand.

"Glad you're home safe, James. Those damn Japs! I bet you have stories to tell. At least we got 'em. My boys helped load the bomb."

How dare he. As if my country had let me serve—as if I even supported the atrocity. I yanked my hand out of his and stormed away.

The people cleared out slowly. I stayed for the photo board. I'd assembled the images myself, of course, both from my own meager collection and from the box of dog-eared prints at Uncle Phil's house. Funny, you know, that that photo should dodge my notice. But wait: I hadn't seen the gas station clerk yet when I had put the pictures together yesterday.

"Jimmy."

I turned. I recognized her: aunt-on-mother's side who had never understood "sides" and had adopted the whole Feckidee clan, including Uncle Phil (of no blood relation) into her heart of hearts. She enveloped me and shook a little. I patted her back.

"I know," I said. "He was a great man."

"Yes…" Her voice was tremulous, her broken spirit lifted heavenwards. "Yes…"

I patted her back. I almost envied her weakness.

Then they were all gone. The minister stood alone at the door with hands folded. He wore a gentle smile which he hoped showed sincerity. In reality, he was only doing his job. In reality, he couldn't wait to get home.

"Did you collect the photographs?" He must have been talking to me, since we were the only ones left in the narthex.

"Yes." I took the board down.

"You did a wonderful job putting that together, son."

"Thanks." As if it took any kind of talent to arrange and tack them.

I looked again. The odd photo sat smack dab in the middle. The other photos stood apart from it, as if they feared it.

"Mr. Feckidee was a well-loved man."

I looked at the minister over the top of the photo board. "Right."

"I'm so sorry for your loss."

I nodded.

"Have a good evening, my friend."

I didn't say anything. He wasn't my friend. Who was?

We drove in the cool dry October dusk. Uncle Phil had always wanted it at this time of day; and since he couldn't control the time of year (though he had died in his favorite month anyway), we had given him as much as we could. They were burying him now, somewhere in the night. He was a strange man, wanting to be buried in the dark without lamps; but we had honored his wishes.

Well, he would go into the ground in the dark whether I was there or not. We were going home.

Austin was placid now. The disappointment about the payphone, the weariness of a grownup event, had all drained out with the stillness of this long night drive on churning country roads. I think he was even sleeping. How could he not, with the gentle bob and sway of soft Ford suspension and the endless rise and fall of the engine whine?

Out of true night, I came blinking with a start. Awake, awake. Was already awake, driving. Do you sense it? Of course. Oh, my neck. Trees rolled back, gray marks on night's ticker-tape. Feel. *Feel.* It is the most unsafe. A presence, a mind without breath.

Swerving—stick to the road.

My breathing was short and shallow. Was I afraid? Yes. There was a *thing* out here. It could be the woods themself, like they formed some sort of collective organism, I don't know; but something was watching me, and the pavement was rough and buckled like it *meant* to.

If I'd been sleeping at the wheel—

Around the bend, a dead end wall of trees. I slammed on the brakes. The tires screamed in the woods. We slid, stopped, rocked back, rocked into stillness. Wrong road. Wrong turn. Lost in the woods. Where are we? You're his father, you son of a bitch. You gotta take better care of him than that. She didn't, so it falls to you. He's already in the red with it, and you have to overcome that first, like an overdrawn bank account. So this can't happen.

Breathing, breathing. Was that my breath, or the breath of something else?

Idiot. You missed a turn. Study yourself: yes, tired. Yes, losing it. Losing your mind.

But straight ahead, there was something *out there.*

Go back. Turn around. You can do this. Get him home safe. He's your son. *She* would have left him out here. *You're* his savior.

I drove a half turn—almost got into the ditch—backed a half turn, almost got into the other ditch. I couldn't have driven through that wall of trees on the way here, which meant I was now backtracking to get back to backtracking. Almost funny, if it didn't implicate me so much, if it didn't set me in comparison to her.

My Ford carved out the dark night again. Now Austin tossed and whimpered in sleep. I had broken the circumscribing peace. I had done this to him. I had turned his young dreams into nightmares in this cool fall drive now fallen from the heights. I had spoiled his paradise, nearly as much as she had.

I drove.

Pursued.

Wait, why that word out of nowhere? Was it the sense of mindless hunger on the back of the car, on the back of my head?

I drove faster.

Strangeness times two today. The gas station clerk, who thought it was all right to touch my son, to encourage his antics with a dead phone as if the boy had really heard something in that earpiece. The same guy in a photo that I, unnoticing, had tacked to the board. In the photo, the creep the same age as today, and Uncle Phil forty, fifty years younger than the body in the casket. And now this—this inexplicable *whatever* in the woods. I guess that's times three. There you go, I'm losing it.

It's not your fault. You're just stressed and you're hurt because Uncle Phil is gone. But that feeling hasn't gone away. So keep driving, and get him home. Watch for the turn you took wrong before.

Again I slammed on the brakes. We had passed a dark lane on right and left. I backed up till the headlights showed it all. But there were no road signs, just trees marching down, naked-trunked and silent. I calmed myself and breathed. I knew this was my turn; the lane crossing my path was better paved and a little wider. The only question was which direction to take. Instinct said go left, so I did. I couldn't imagine having turned like this, but I must have.

In ten minutes I was passing half-remembered landmarks: a grotesque tree on the right, a little bridge over a creek. We were going the right way again.

My brain, and this noise in my head, this ebbing flowing rising sinking. They say the insane never question their sanity. Where does that put me?

I had told myself that something was following me home from these hills.

At last, from back road to half back to ambling main street, we came again to that college town where I lived and worked and studied. The swept fenders gleaming under streetlights and the neon sign glowing above the Slovakian Club spoke softly of safety, of Americana, of the dream that we're all pursuing. In that moment, I knew that today and tonight were just a minor setback. I was still in pursuit. If the wife was gone, at least the house and the money and the professorship and the security for my son would come, would come—even if we had to drop atom bombs to make this thing work, to make the land of the free a fortress.

5

I was renting a little house back then. It was tucked away in a quiet neighborhood where the trees trailed ivy and sagging branches into the disheveled drives. I fit right in, being too preoccupied with my thesis on Blake and my night hours at the diner to cut the grass. Besides, it wasn't like I owned the place, and it hadn't looked any better when I had moved in. But I did feel bad about that grass.

I pulled in there now. Getting to the back and the garage, I found that I had forgotten to leave even the porch light on. Everything was incredibly dark; and when I shut off the car and got out, I found it incredibly quiet too.

I got Austin inside. I do remember turning on the porch light and giving the stark yard a long look. But I didn't see anything other than trees and bushes and garage, all sleeping in a mental photograph.

Austin never woke up. His face was so peaceful when I laid him out on his little bed and tucked him in. I tested the metal railing. It would hold again tonight. He could roll every which way in some nightmare, but he sure as hell wasn't going to fall out of bed. I was his father, damnit. I would protect him.

Downstairs, I switched on the TV and got a Pabst from the fridge. I knew I shouldn't drink tonight, and I wasn't going to have even a second one; but I just wanted the taste, and I wanted to relax. The stuff helped, that was all; I just wanted it—didn't *need* it. I was going to bed in an hour or two anyway, so it didn't matter. It wasn't like I did this all the time. It wasn't like I ever bought more than a case. And sometimes Matt came over and helped me with them. So it wasn't like I was an alcoholic.

I do remember the shapes on TV. Blacks and grays, planes and volumes moving in a slow dance choreographed to the rhythm of some alien heart. It wasn't at all like TV. I found it strange, but not nearly strange enough…

Then I was waking up, coming out of some malaise. Everything was dark. Even the TV was dead. The Pabst can by my foot was warm, but almost full. There was an odd sense of oppression.

I stumbled around. Lightswitches did nothing. We must have blown a fuse. Across the street, the neighbors' driveway light was still on, so it was just my house. *Excellent.* I had a flashlight somewhere, but I had forgotten where I stored it.

Given the funeral and the disturbing ride home, I was *not* going to fix this tonight. I was going straight to bed.

On my way to the stairwell, I stopped, thinking. I went down the half-stair to the back door and looked out at the darkness. A strange thought came to me: *Why don't you look outside?*

I unlocked the door and opened it. A faint breath of the night breeze hit me, rank with maggots.

I hadn't taken the trash to the curb.

Grumbling, I went outside. I found myself standing in the dark and blinking. I had meant to go get the trash cans, but now I was just staring out at the invisible yard. Maybe the trash could wait; I was awfully tired…

Bang.

The porch light came on with a buzz. A mountain of brown fur sat in stark relief beyond the bushes. It breathed like a drowning ox. It rose up and came for me.

I spun, fell, jumped up, ran for the door. Heart pounding. Right behind me, snuffling and thumping. I fell across the threshold. I leapt up and slammed the door. *Crash.* It hit the door. My weight against that of the monster, I don't know how I won; but I won. I fiddled the deadbolt and I got it locked. The beast slammed against the door again. It moaned like an organ devil-possessed. A huge white eye hit the window. The porch light popped. The eye stared in through the slobber, unseeing, uncomprehending. I just sat shaking. Then the creature left with a squelch.

I sat blinking. I sat grasping for thought. *All right.* I was imagining. I'd been reading too much Blake. Life wasn't myth; life was plain gray on gray. Today was no exception. A funeral, a troubling photo, a monster. Start with the funeral. That was true, and that must be where the rest had come from. But the rest was fake. I had made it up. My mind was broken with grief.

But the window was still covered in slobber.

I collected myself. I rose. Quiet and catlike, I crept up the half-flight of steps and stood in the kitchen under the naked light of the guttering bulb. My cookbooks, my dirty dishes, my mess was exactly as I had left it earlier that day. I blinked and rubbed my eyes. I felt myself sway, and I grabbed the edge of the stove and leaned against it. Even through the hall, I could hear the TV humming faintly again.

What a day…

Crash.

A long brown thing shattered the window above the sink and swept dishes onto the floor. It came for me, desire and matted fur. Its end was a sucker, a mouth searching for me. It knocked me down. It sealed over my face. I couldn't breathe. My feet found the stove, and I kicked. The sucker popped off my face. The pain, I swear it took my face off with it.

I kicked away. The brown thing came in through the window, longer and longer, snuffling, sucking up bits of broken glass and silverware like a Hoover. It came for my face again. This time I dodged. In the wreck on the floor, I saw my best vegetable knife. I grabbed the knife and jumped up. The sucker hit me in the back of the head and drove me down into the sink just as its girth rubbed the faucet handle and opened the water to full blast. Bubbling, drowning, I hacked and hacked at the window above my head. In the violence, the old wooden frame slammed shut on the flesh. The tentacle weakened, and I hacked harder, holding my breath underwater. Suddenly the knife went through. The tentacle popped with a rush of air. The sucker fell off the back of my head, and the muscles withered. I stood up, teetering. I had bathed in a water of dark alien blood like mud, like clay.

The severed stump withdrew, and the old window slammed shut all the way.

I stumbled through the house. *Just get out. Beat the beast.* I unlocked the front door and threw it open. But I heard paws pounding in the yard, on the sidewalk. The creature blotted out the neighbor's light. I slammed the front door. The whole house was eclipsed.

I stood in the living room, by the couch, equidistant from all doors. It had no reason to rush me now. It had me right where it wanted me. I had a space of, say, ten feet by ten in which I could stand without detection. I could breathe, but only so loudly. My very thoughts were compressed. It had mastered me in every way.

A solution came to me: get Austin. Get to the car. *Just get out. But how?* Just get out.

I went upstairs. I saw everything with razor focus now. In the bathroom, I rinsed myself and tore off my soiled shirt. In my room, I quietly put on another shirt so I wouldn't scare Austin. Then I crept into his room in the dark. He was fevered in sleep, his brow damp and furrowed. I picked him up and caressed him. If nothing more, I was his father—if not a husband, at least a father. *Forgive me, Molly, for that. I did love you then, and I'll save your son now. Lord.*

I glided down the stairs, through the living room, still perhaps undetected. I went into the TV room, to the window. My car was just beyond, just outside.

> *You see now that all those things you said about me were untrue, Molly. You see that you accused me falsely. If anyone has failed, it's you—and I'm not saying that out of—*

I unlatched the window—

> *Because whatever you think of those damn magazines, I never failed as a father. I was perfect. I rushed you to the hospital, and that was out of love. That was for him and you. I don't think you see that. I don't think you know my heart.*

"I don't think you know mine, Jim—as if those pictures don't do something to the way you see me—as if you don't compare me, don't compare my hips—"

I got the window up. I punched through the screen. It was tricky with Austin, but I started to emerge.

Thumping in the gravel. Ragged breathing. O, inescapable beast…

I backed out and slammed the window shut. Sobbing, I ran through the house and down the half-flight (the beast hit the back door again as I passed it) into the damp dark of the basement.

I found the chain and pulled it. I stood between rotting boxes and white mold-lined cinderblocks, the dreck of my uncollected past.

Austin shook and whimpered. I laid out a flattened box and laid him on it. He looked small and helpless under the light of that naked bulb. What *ever* had happened to this family?

We stayed there together for a long time, what was left of us. I must have slid down the cinderblock wall into some position of despondence, for that was how I found myself when it came.

Knock knock.

I knew that sound. It was the giant wrought-iron knocker on the front door, almost directly over my head. I knew what it meant, too.

Knock knock.

"Just come in, you devil!" That was my own deranged voice. "Just make quick work of us. Eat us or kill us or whatever you want."

The door creaked back on hinges. One gunshot of a footstep rang in the floorboards overhead. Now the house was not only eclipsed, but violated—

"Jim?"

—by a friend.

"Jim?"

Another explosive step—and silence. No beast. Nothing. Even through the floorboards, I knew that step, that voice.

I staggered to my feet and ran up the basement steps. The beast hit the back door again, detecting me. I ran into the living room. I stared.

Matt Gaddo, my best friend, my only friend, stood half-illumined in the open foyer door.

"Matt…" I stopped by the couch.

"Jim!" He smiled. Had he any idea of the beast—of the *time?*

Behind him, I saw the open front door. Behind him, I saw the neighbor's lamppost. I ran. Pounding, the beast obliterated the light and filled the door frame.

"Jim—what the hell—"

I slammed and locked the door and fell down against it. The beast crashed against the door, a hundred times heavier than me. The whole house shuddered.

Matt just stared at me.

Finally I got up and stumbled into the light of the living room. Matt's eyes were hard and young and probing. "What's going on?"

"Nothing," I said.

He laughed and looked back at the front door. Something was still hiding the lamppost that we should have seen through the diamond window.

"Nothing." He nodded. "Nothing." He began to smile, almost to laugh, as if it really were nothing. He could be such a fool sometimes.

"I don't know what it is," I said.

"Oh?"

"It followed me home from the hills. I got lost coming back from the funeral. It's been a horrible day."

"Where's Austin?"

Did he even hear my introduction to my misery? But I answered him. "Down the basement, sleeping."

"So this… *creature* has staked out the house?"

"Yes."

"Good heavens, Jim."

The basement steps creaked.

Matt looked at me. I couldn't move. I heard the deadbolt thrown. I heard the click of the knob, the cracking rush of the door opening. Then, in the silence, I heard the little boy's whimper.

"Daddy…go outside…"

"Austin," Matt murmured.

I glanced at the front door. The beast was still blocking the neighbor's porch light.

"I'll get him," said Matt.

"No! If you go to the door, it'll come for you."

He stepped past me and went down the half-flight of steps. But the beast didn't come. I heard Matt pick up Austin and murmur, "I got you, buddy." Then he must have stood in silence. "Jim."

"What?"

"Come down here."

I looked back at the front door. The light was still blocked. "It'll follow me," I said.

"Come down. We can get out."

"All right…" He said we could get out. He said we could do this. I could do this. I put one foot in front of the other. I walked down the hall. I went down the first step to the back door. I went down the whole half-flight.

It was already running up to the back door, snuffling like it couldn't breathe, pounding like a ten-legged elephant—

"Good lord!" Matt shut the door and locked it. He turned me by the shoulders and steered me up the steps. *Crash.* The house shook. Austin whimpered.

"This has been the worst day of my life!" My voice came out shrill and angular like squeezed animal. "This guy tried to touch my son—"

"So it definitely goes for *you*. It senses *you*. I came in through the front door not even knowing about it. It doesn't go for me. It doesn't go for Austin. Look, he just opened the door and stood down there. Lucky you left the front door unlocked, or I wouldn't have been able to get in."

"But I didn't! I locked it every time—"

"So here's what we do. We get something with your blood on it and use that as a decoy. We'll throw the bloody thing one way and you'll run the other way. You'll run for my van. You'll take Austin. I'll meet you after I distract the beast."

I just looked at him. We were standing now in the stark light of the one bulb that still burned in the living room. His eyes were glittering with purpose that could cut you if you weren't careful. I knew this guy. I knew that when he was right, he was right; and as gentle and understanding as he was in manner, he really didn't give a damn about your differing opinion or your feelings, your feelings.

"We need some of your blood." He touched my forehead and withdrew his hand to show the red. That was why my head was pounding. "We need a rag. Do you have any meat?"

"There's one uncooked pork chop in the fridge."

"I'll get that and a rag."

"Matt, that's the only food I have!"

"You won't be coming back here," he said. "We'll make up a nasty little meat package. The monster should go for that."

Like I said, I knew better than to argue.

In a moment he came out of the kitchen with the last of my food in stained white butcher's paper.

"Did it attack you?"

"Yes."

"Did you cut off that... *thing* in there?"

"Yes."

"Good lord..." He dabbed my forehead with a towel and tied the cloth around the meat. Then he lifted little Austin off the couch and handed him to me. The poor boy was still sleeping, but his brow was fevered.

"Carry him. That's it. I'm going to the back door. You stay here in the middle till I yell. Then run for the front door. Run for my van."

There was no disputing with him, so I said, "All right," and took his keys.

Then I stood in the middle of the house, listening. The deadbolt clicked back. The knob turned. I imagined Matt standing on the threshold of the back door, looking out into the night, looking for the beast. Then I heard a soft grunt—a gasp—"Now, Jim! *Run!*"

I ran. Through the diamond window of the front door, I saw the neighbor's light shining. One-handed, I threw the deadbolt. One-handed, I swung back the door. Matt's thudding footfalls were in the house. I went down the stoop, down the sidewalk. I saw that '35 Suburban, shadowy and salvific like the Lord God, waiting in the driveway to take us away to glory land.

Gravel crunched in the driveway: that hill of evil looming, swelling, breathing, coming from the backyard—

I got around the van. I tore the door open and fell into the driver's seat. I stomped on the clutch and cranked the engine. *Start, start. Come on.* Matt banged on the passenger door. It was locked! But Austin wriggled out of my arms—as if he'd been awake the whole time—and unlocked the door.

The beast hit the front end of the truck. We skidded back in the gravel. At last the engine cranked. Matt was in, holding Austin.

"Go, Jim!"

I put it in reverse. I revved. I dropped the clutch. In torque-spun gravel, we pulled a graceful little maneuver out into the street. Headlights showed something brown and shaggy and many-limbed—

I put it in first and we flew off into the night.

4

IT'S NOT AS IF I was sleeping in those days anyway, so I might as well run from a monster at this hour as sit on the couch, gumptionless towards all betterment. My mind had learned some sort of grasping elevated consciousness that leveled all times of day and all resulting emotions. I knew no cycles, only being and stimuli.

It was no different now. The jitter and tug of the wheel, the engine shuddering for a downshift, the half-lit bulbs bringing beacons to the quiet houses: there was nothing more.

"It isn't following us."

I looked over at Matt. Elbow jammed in the window frame, jaw held in splayed hand, he watched the mirror. His other arm held my boy. *Lord,* I would have died without him.

"Matt… why did you come to my house?"

The way his voice bounced off the window, he hadn't shifted. "I just felt I had to."

That was ridiculous. But I just nodded.

"You don't have to drive so fast," he said.

He was right. I let off the gas. Now the turns were softer.

"I know you're baffled, Jim. I know you don't want to tell me that."

I didn't say anything. After a while, he went on.

"For me, though, this has been a turning point. I began to feel new again from the moment I woke up in the middle of the night. This is the end of my depression. I've never experienced this kind of psychological phenomenon before, which makes me think it might be real. Or maybe it's just the old saying coming true: the best way to cheer yourself up is to cheer somebody else up."

Was he cheering me up? Maybe *he* thought so; but it was too soon to tell if he was right. He had saved my life, yes. Did that mean that he had saved his own as well by coming into that house and dying with me? The strangest thing was that he was not at all perplexed. It was almost as if he had expected this. Maybe he knew what was happening. To test him, I asked, "What should we do now?"

"Find somewhere safe," he said immediately. Then after a moment, "Let's try your uncle's house."

There was a certain resonance to the words. I knew without reason that it was a good idea.

"Mm," said Matt. "You know, it makes sense."

I glanced over at him again. He was almost looking at me this time. Austin curled in closer to his chest. Then we passed the streetlight, and it was all black.

"I met this woman on the bus, Jim. *On the bus.* Most beautiful woman I've ever seen—but I didn't *want* her, you understand; it was like running into the queen bee, the one you just fall down in front of. There's nothing else you can do. She changed my life, Jim."

"Changed your life?" I murmured.

"Do you know what she said to me? She said, *you look like one who wants to save the world.*"

"Interesting."

"It's beyond interesting."

"When was this?"

"Yesterday. That, and then the feeling tonight—the feeling that I should drop in on you." He laughed. I heard fear in the laugh, and yet eagerness at the same time. "Something is happening, but I don't understand. Or maybe I do. Maybe it's beginning to make sense."

"What?" I asked.

He shook his head. "I gotta think about it." He laughed again. "You probably think I'm crazy."

I snorted.

"But yeah, your uncle's house is a good place. We'll be safe there."

I drove for a long time.

Then my eyes were opening like dreams, like dawns. Matt was tugging

my arm and the wheel, straightening both. "Easy there. Pull over. Gosh,
I shouldn't have let you drive."

"I wasn't falling asleep."

He just laughed. "Pull over, before we crash."

I brought the van to a stop. We were on a vague and gravel road. It
was something like dawn, that time between death and living, between
gray and color. I got out and walked around the front of the van. The
engine banged and wrecked the stillness.

I lifted Austin out of the passenger seat and climbed in. My boy was
warm and limp in my arms, still sucking his thumb like a little baby.

"Matt, do you know the way?"

"Of course."

Then I was riding and holding my boy. He *was* my boy, damn it. It's
not like anybody had a hand in it, except her—and at this point she
didn't—but it was no use going there. She was gone, dead to me and to
him, and *dead* the memory of her half-cooked attempt at motherhood
that would have failed had he ever grown to see it. She knew full well
what she had done to him, and to me. But we weren't going there.
We weren't. Because it was a gray almost-dawn in the nowhere land
of almost-to-Phil's-house, and he was asleep, curled and warm and
sucking; and he was in my lap, my boy, my boy. Keep my boy safe. My
memories, my sleep.

He's down the basement, Matt. I put him there for safe keeping.

"Why? He isn't safe down there. You should bring him up into the
front room, where you can see him. Why do you want to leave him
down there with all your moldy boxes? They aren't his fault."

*Yeah, well they're not my fault either. Stuff just collects, you know. You
go out looking for a date, for something pretty to take to the ice cream
stand, and next moment you're a family and it turns out her sweet baboo
is a piece of garbage and she's going to say so every day. What do you do
then? Huh? You don't know a thing about it, Matt. You haven't got one
yourself. So take it from me.*

Oh wait. This was not last night, but that one time when I had run
into Matt at school. Or maybe I was sleeping in the van.

"But I can see that it shouldn't be like that," said Matt as he sauntered with me down the bleak corridors of some forgotten academic hall. "Can't I tell you that? Or are you too lost in your own head?"

You can tell me whatever you want, just don't get excited if I tell you where you're wrong.

"So what did you do?"

I didn't do a thing.

"She wouldn't have walked out if you hadn't given her a reason."

All right, sometimes I forgot to mow the grass.

"It had to be more than that, Jim."

She is dead to me.

He never said anything after that, but left me to the silence of that cold hallway of learning. Well, she *was* dead to me. So was Uncle Phil, but in reality, in truth.

My eyes opened for a moment. The colorless halls of memory were colorless halls of the woods; the floor, the road; and the forging ship of conversation, Matt's truck. Matt was still driving. Austin was still sleeping in my lap. I let my eyes close again.

Dead to me.

I told my aunt. I said into the phone, *Uncle Phil is dead. He's really dead.*

"Oh Jimmy—Oh Jimmy—did your parents make it?"

No. Of course not.

"I'm so sorry. To not have them here—"

Please, I said into the phone. *You don't understand. When these things come in waves, in layers, you gotta address one layer at a time. So the fact that they didn't come—I don't care. For now, it's just the funeral, the fact that Uncle Phil—as if they had any reason not to come—*

Molly gave herself a reason, I said. I walked alone with Matt down the hall. Somewhere, an open window admitted a colorless breeze which tossed some graded and abandoned failure of academic effort across the floor. *Molly found fault in me,* I said.

"Women don't give themselves reasons," said Matt. "I may not have a girlfriend myself, but I know enough about them to know they don't just make things up. Whatever she feels is real in her mind."

If she wanted perfection, she should have married the Lord Jesus Christ.

"Have a little more reverence, Jim. I know you're upset—"

How else can you explain this?

"Like I said: you gave her a reason."

We passed the open and sun-gorged door to room 220, where I had taken Lit I and Lit II and Rhetoric and Composition. The loose paper tossed and crumpled under our feet in white sun.

I did not give her a reason. I will swear to you standing upright in the sunlight with my hand on the book and the other hand up pledging allegiance that I did not give her a reason.

"You told me yourself that you've been looking at floozie stuff," said Matt. "Hell, I'm not comfortable with some of those pictures, and I'm a single man. It's like the stuff they painted on the planes. It's all fine for young bucks fresh out of high school, serving their country and missing their prom dates. We can make excuses for them, you know; in the absence of feminine company, the male mind turns to…"

None of this is relevant to the fact that Molly—

"Oh, but it is. Completely. Because you looking at those pictures told her that even in the same room with her, even in the same bed with her, you were absent from *her* company. And that must have ripped her—"

Austin sat bolt upright in my lap and woke me up for good. His head was revolving slowly to and fro, his vision fixed on some distant point. A gray bullet-rain was drumming the silly roof of the van, making washed-out and water-colored of the window views. It was not quite day.

Matt was laughing. "What's going on with him?"

"I don't know."

Then a mailbox popped up in the rain. Matt slammed on the brakes. "Can you read that?"

"I don't have to," I said. "That's Uncle Phil's driveway."

He turned into the river of a lane.

We swept through the woods. Austin was alert and quivering. I seemed to quiver with him. I don't know why, but I was not afraid. This Eden coming up ahead, of which the once-voluptuous Molly had been only an outplay and an echo—it was not that it was something like her; *she* was something like *it*—

Through the gray rain hanging like curtains on the windows, I got something like a flash of color not seen, not imagined, but sensed with a sense before unknown to me. My uncle's house had never before been the seat of all desire.

"Are you all right, Jim?"

"Mm…"

That is to say, yes, I am incredibly the most all right I've ever been. I don't understand, but I am not afraid. It's as if I'm moving towards consummation, and don't ask, because I don't know what I mean by that. But you see that through the rain, there is this sense of a scalpel cutting, and it's a most surgical operation, this cutting of the world, of the planet—though it isn't for the removal of a tumor, but rather for the triumphal presentation of what has been waiting-thumping-glowing-pulsing-warm beneath the surface all along. And Molly was never *it*, I see, but only an interpretation thereof. So what went wrong? But all that is wrong now is that a curtain hangs between us and *it*, and the fact that the scalpel has not finished the job. Once we get—

"Inside!" cried Austin, bouncing up and down in my lap and pointing through the trees, his arm turning with the turning road, as if an invisible thread tied his finger to a far-off but fixed goal. "Inside!"

"Are you excited to go back to your Uncle Phil's house?" asked Matt.

But the boy just stared at him, uncomprehending.

"He never knew Uncle Phil too much," I said. "Or did you, Austin? Do you remember—"

"Inside! Go inside! Go—"

Inside. Now. I imagined the warmth of a hearth beyond those curtains, but a hearth of accelerating heat, not of diminishing—a hearth that, once kindled, once uncurtained, once exposed, might consume the whole planet from the inside out. We must have dropped down on some alien world and found there, crawling up out of the crevice that its head had made, an insectoid and mechanical flame, a breath boundless and unquenchable of the first cause, of the source and ending of atoms, a sweet and voluptuous beast with the clout of atom bombs—

"Inside! Inside!"

The gray naked pillars of the woods rolled back and showed the white-trimmed brown sprawl that had once been the home of the greatest poet and novelist alive. In the rain it was all gray, even the uncut fields that should still be photosynthesizing despite the bleak come-down of October. Then the wipers swept and swept back and I saw the white frame of the door.

"Inside! Inside!"

"Getting there!" Matt laughed, pulling around the sweep of the driveway up to the grass-eaten stoop. "You sure got a lot of energy for being up all night."

I felt the gentle protestation of the rotors, their quiet grinding. Then we stopped, and the last pebble crunched under tire. Oh, that white-framed door spoke to me out of eternity…

"You have a key, right?"

"Right…"

I held Austin under the armpits, my hand poised on the handle of the car door. Cacophonous rain was not reaching my ears. This was a moment of I knew-not-what. The rain, my lack of sleep, my anguish, were inconsequential.

"We just have to go for it," said Matt.

"Right."

I opened the door. The cold steel rain came in. I bounded across the gravel, holding the happiest child who ever squealed for joy. Inexplicably, I felt in myself the same tremors of infinity. Then we were under the battered metal awning of the stoop and I could hear the Axis guns and the assault on freedom in the rain on the tin roof. I was just there under that roof; not a soldier, barely fit, found mentally incompetent, just fumbling for a key.

"Inside! Inside!" Austin was still jubilant and squirming.

Out of all the keys on that keyring, the first one I tried opened the door.

Austin dragged me into the house with locomotive force. He tugged with the joy of birthday and Christmas all in one. Was it strange that I felt like he did, felt like I hadn't felt since I was small? It *was* my birthday—it *was* that first remembered Christmas, mysterious and train-haunted both in gifts and dreams and the train, the wonder of infinite locomotive, was here in the house, prepared to go inexorably past and past.

But it wasn't here in the gray hall. There was nothing but the cube of light approaching, the spot where the doorless kitchen lit the dark hall with diffuse light. Still, my little steam engine charged ahead on piston legs, careless of dust and obscurity.

We must have approached the source of that wild exhalation. There was no other explanation for the hierarchical, the almost exponential increase. Diligent and primed, the logic of the atoms must be sitting in that kitchen, waiting, pounding, propounding.

Austin burst in, but it was gone. Only the silence of the spirit and the gray void coming down over the emptiness remained. But I hadn't imagined it, and neither had he. I remembered my emotions and I remembered his tug. We had focused on the same thing.

"Gone!" He stamped his foot and looked up at me, face puckered. "All gone, daddy! Where'd it go?"

I surveyed the kitchen. A cupboard door stood open. A black and red and yellow flannel sat draped over a chair. We breathed four years of sealed air and the disintegrating strands of cobwebs. I didn't know what we had imagined.

But then the squashing and the spiral tug resumed. In that infinite layering of dimensions, this place was incredibly small. To get to the source of all desire, we had to go across, not through. Austin knew the way.

"Over here, daddy! Come on!"—and we were off again, dashing through the gray halls. It hadn't departed; it had only moved—

Into the living room. We stood astounded. Here, in this very place, we met Spirit: alive, flaming, invisible, yet more true than truth—

It left. The cold ashes on the hearth stirred in the faintest memory of a breath, and it was gone. The colors of the couches and the carpet lay buried under years of gray dust. The light was stillness.

Austin pouted. "Where'd it go, daddy?"

"I don't know," I muttered.

The place fell. Fact swept over me. We were in a pedestrian moment in a most colorless space. It was nearly dawn after a night in which I had fled from a beast rather than slept. The previous moment, a dream of the roots of eros, had already washed away.

Crack. Matt's first footfall shook the house like a gunshot, like the step of one who didn't belong. And his voice—"Hello? Jim?"—broke the stillness.

We went back into the hall and met him in the gray cube of light from the kitchen.

"Jim?" He wore a serene frown. "What happened?"

"I don't know." I looked around vaguely. "Didn't you sense something?"

"No."

I nodded. Of course not. He was Matt Gaddo. He didn't have the sensitivity of the poet, of the prophet. He was an engineer. Everything was a mechanism for him to dissemble, analyze, and rebuild. That was why he smiled and nodded when I read Blake to him: he didn't get it. That was also why he was a stranger now.

"I guess this'll do," he said, looking around the hall. "We can stay here while we figure out..." He snapped his fingers. "Better build a fire."

But what would we poets do without engineers?

Later, we sat in the sunken couch in the living room, watching the blaze. Matt had brought in a stack of firewood to dry by the hearth, having gotten the fire going with what little wood had remained in the hamper nearby. Now, in that cold drizzly morning, I knew that I had been destroyed last night.

"Why don't you sleep, Jim. It's eight in the morning."

I shook my head. "Not if you're staying up." But I was dying. Adrenaline had given out with the coming calm. Now we were in an abandoned house in the middle of nowhere, for no reason. The beast must have been a nightmare, the nostalgic *whatever* in the kitchen a dream.

"Just rest, Jim." He got up and put his hands in his pockets and showed something indestructible in his face. "I'm going to have a look around."

"I don't know what you want to see. I can show you around the house. I can show you everything about it. This is my old haunt."

"I know. Don't trouble yourself. I've been here before."

Been here? When the hell had *he* been *here,* in the house where my uncle had showed me Blake and I had become my greatness and my ruin?

But he was already sauntering out of the room.

I DIDN'T MEAN TO sleep, but it was later when I woke up. The rain had stopped and the light had grown, though it hadn't broken out of a general gray diffusion. The fire was nothing but embers, and Austin lay half-buried in the couch, sleeping. Matt was gone. I got up and peered out the window. By the western inclination of the sun, I knew it to be some time in the afternoon.

I wandered around Uncle Phil's house, but it was obvious where Matt hadn't gone. Only the main hallway showed disruption of the dust, and that only as far as the entrance to the living room. On the kitchen table I found a note.

> Dear Jim,
> I went into town for supplies. Also, I went to talk to the friend I met on the bus. She may be able to help us. Don't go outside. I think this is a safehouse, but I want to be sure. I'll be back before noon.
> Matt

Back before noon. Oh. It's a good three o'clock now, and I've been sleeping. Anything could have happened. What were you thinking? *Safehouse?* Oh. If that beast could follow me home from the hills, there's no reason it shouldn't follow me anywhere in the world. You idiot.

I flung the note on the table and went stomping down the hall to the door. I gazed out the little diamond window. The driveway was empty. At least there was no sign of the beast.

I swayed. Lord, I was beyond hungry. I turned and sat down weakly against the door. I hadn't eaten since... since before the funeral? I couldn't even remember. I practically crawled into the kitchen and hunted in the cupboards. I found cans of beans, but a delirious onset of terror over trying to survive on them prevented me from finding the can-opener.

When my fear of starvation had subsided, I found that my hunger had as well. Now I was just lean and run down, my body flexing and gritting its teeth for a long ordeal.

I wandered the house as Matt had not, selfish fool. I disturbed the dust in the hallways where he hadn't gone for his look around. Even in my bitterness, I knew I had to stop. I knew he was just trying to help. So I reprimanded myself inside (hadn't done that in a while) and forgave him. All I could do was wait for him to come back with food, perhaps with answers.

Through the meandering and disheveled halls, through corridors spelled out in angles of tired light, I came at last to the door of doors, the portal into the study where I had become my greatness and my ruin. Ancient, oaken, transplanted from another world, that door could have held back the night and even the beast. I grasped the cold knob that had never warmed even in summer. Breathing, blinking away the tears that I don't cry, I turned the knob and went in.

"Read to me, James."

He leaned ravenously across the desk. Firelight flashed on his lenses, but it could not dim the hunger in his eyes.

Why do I always read? I asked. *Why don't you read?*

"I can't, dear James. I've lost the ability."

How? While you were gone? Where did you go?

"Just read to me, James. My soul is starved for words."

Chapter one. Lo, a shadow of horror is risen in eternity. Unknown, unprolific. Self-closed, all-repelling. Some said, it is Urizen. But the dark power hid. Is it Satan, Uncle?

"No, dear James." He leaned back in the creaking chair. "Read further. In chapter six, you'll see."

It sounds like Satan.

"It isn't."

Uncle Phil spun away from the bookshelf and glared at me with vicarious alarm. "It isn't her fault. To say that she's entirely responsible for this is quite foolish of you. Really, James, I expected more. Boys blame other people. Men examine themselves, even when they know—"

But I have examined—

"—even when they *know* damn well that the other party is in the wrong."

I have examined myself. I have found myself not-guilty.

"That's not what she thinks."

Since when do you take her side?

"James, as far as I'm concerned, there's only one side—the side of your m—"

Oh, I don't want to talk about that. I don't. If we ever had it, it's long gone. She started chipping away at marriage right from the first day. She—

"And how did she do that? You told me yourself that you've been—"

I pressed the receiver to my ear so hard that it hurt. *You say he's— he's—passed out? How? Why?*

"Just come down, son. Come now." My father's voice, metallic in the receiver.

But I just talked to him yesterday, I said into the phone. *I was over there yesterday, and he was as fresh as ever.*

"He aint fresh now, Jim. He's in bed wearin a heavy hell of a coat and under all the covers too. He's cold as ice but he aint dead. He breathes once every couple seconds."

All right. I'm coming. Just let me get Austin out of bed.

"What? Where's your wife, boy?" My father's voice.

She isn't here, goddamnit!

You know, the car didn't start that day either. And you would think that a mother with a baby only a month old would have been at home. But it was already so hard for her to be around me that she was off at her own mother's house, abandoning her role of mothering my son to be mothered herself, selfish whore. So I held the boy Austin wrapped tight like a little Jesus and I started the car by myself.

I blinked and hauled my consciousness back to the present. I had to leave that garbage behind. This was the here and now. The old study was dead, just like Uncle Phil. Four years of colorless dust lay over the rich brown mahogany desk and shelves that I remembered. Even the old leather chair, where he had sat on a godforsaken December day as snow had driven against the wrought-iron-framed window and he had said,

"Here, James. Take pen and paper. Take this on dictation, if you don't mind. Do you mind?"

Of course not, Uncle.

He looked out at the flowerbeds lost in snow. I knew that under them, I had not trimmed the weeds in late summer or fall, though he had asked me to do it several times.

"Do you ever think about how these are just words, just letterforms, just swept ink on the page?"

No. That's rather depressing.

"Ah, but it's true. These forms have only the meaning that we give them. The best way to protect the meaning of every word you know, or may have thought you knew upon a time, is to read. Read everything you can find. Make time for it. Don't go to ballgames; they're all the same anyway. This is the meat. This will feed your brain. Sure, run around the yard when your rear end falls asleep; but always do it to come back and read."

So what am I writing for you? Truth or fiction?

He always laughed right then. "Oh, James. Oh, James."

He paused and glared out at me with eyes of poetic vision. "Chapter one. Body text begin."

O, divine voice booming around that study…

"I have lived a long and strange life. Even now, I do not know whether the tale of my strangeness is complete. This writing may be premature. However, I will start at the beginning and tell as much of my story as I can. New paragraph, James. Continue. My life changed forever when I met Proton, who is called the Hiding Man, in that faded cornfield at the end of day."

You say it's the—I could not seem to say the words into the phone.

"Yes, James. It's the end. He's dead."

My God…

"I'm so sorry, James. I'm so sorry you have to hear it from me."

How did he go? I asked into the phone. *Did he know he was—*

"No. They said he never even flinched. They didn't realize he had passed until some time later."

I looked out the study window. All that remained of my flowerbeds, a responsibility only six feet by nine and, you'd think, quite manageable for a fourteen-year-old, were the broken bricks and shards of pottery that remembered the dead garden's delineations.

Enough. I turned back to the room. There on the mantelpiece sat a print of that same picture from the funeral. Uncle Phil's eyes glowed as they always did, but in that ancient image he was young and eternal and his hair was brown. The gas station attendant was in his fifties or so, just as he had been the other day.

It struck me. The blow was so heavy that I almost physically staggered. The stranger's face was the same that I had stared at throughout childhood and adolescence—the same face frozen in the same print that had sat for decades on the mantelpiece in the room where I had practically begun to live. How I hadn't recognized it when I put together the photo board for the funeral, I'll never know.

Hungry and sleep-deprived, robbed of my dear uncle and robbed of my wife, pursued by a monster, loved and abandoned by a strange glimpse of something *other* in the house, shocked at that picture setting me off with my nerves already rattled, I sat down heavily in the same springshot wreck of an armchair where I had read Blake to him and taken novels on dictation from him and waited in silence for him; and I, James Feckidee, man of steel, mentally incompetent, put my face in my hands and wept.

It was much later, after I had calmed down and been perusing my old friends on the bookshelves, when I heard a strange sound. At first it didn't stick in my mind. Then, when I listened more closely, I heard the familiar timbre of my son's voice, now strung and elevated to some higher energy.

I dashed into the hall, father instincts kicking in hard. Adrenaline does not need food for production. Pure emotion is enough. Thus it is possible to die by feeling things. Hence the slow march of my vitality towards disintegration. "Austin?" I listened, trying to catch the sound again. "Austin?"

"Ha! Ha! Ha!"

He was laughing, but I had never heard him laugh like that before. "Austin!"

His laugh echoed all around me as if trickling down out of the woodwork. I dashed through the halls. I couldn't find him. I tried the living room. I couldn't find him.

"Ha! Ha! Ha!"

I burst into the kitchen. He stood by the windows, telephone pressed to his ear so that the cord stretched through air across the whole room. He was jumping up and down and pointing out into the fields. Far away, the browning trees at the edge of the woods slept in afternoon sun.

"Ha! Ha! Ha!"

"Austin..."

But he didn't even turn to look at me. He stopped jumping up and down and stood still as if listening.

"Go outside?"

Now clutching the receiver in both hands, he turned to me and said, "They say we should go outside."

"Oh?"

I shouldn't have been alarmed, but I was having a hard time playing along. Something about my mood and the fact that he had already done this once before—

"Outside?" Now he was facing the window again, now pointing— "Over there?"

He dropped the phone. The stretched cord yanked it back across the whole kitchen. He ran to me and bounced up and down, yelling, "Outside! Outside!"

How could I refuse? He woke in me, as only he could, the eternal essence of *child* that I had learned to put away deep down beneath my responsibilities and my prestigiousness and my pomposity. He called to me out of the past and out of the future, younger than I and far more everlasting. So it was with unwanting unknowing surrender and joy that I dashed after him into the hall to the door and threw myself down and put my shoes on with him. Had I been truly free, I would have squealed from delight with him too.

Then he was shaking the doorknob back and forth with childhood determination and childhood strength until I threw the deadbolt for him. He flung the door open, nearly hitting me in the face, and dashed out into the afternoon.

"Outside! Outside! La la la…"

I wandered after him, remarking to myself at the flattened weeds and the tire tracks in the gravel.

He was running with airplane arms through the long spent grass, only his head and those arms sticking out. He wove a path as crazy as any fighter plane defending us from the Japs or the Huns. In the blissful rush of the wind at my back, I felt the same whisper of impetuous youth unchained. I ran after him.

We descended towards the woods. The woods mounted up in orange and red and brown, flaming in the brazen light of the afternoon sun, the first non-gray I had seen all day—or any day, for ages, for that matter. The wind grew fiercer and fiercer until we were not running but sailing, sailing with the dreck of the wind, these red and yellow leaves rushing past all around us as if towards something momentous, as if towards the world's birth or perhaps the end of days.

The wind gathered in a cyclone at the edge of the woods, and the leaves swirled in endless eddies. When we burst through, the wind stopped and the leaves fell everywhere; but the next moment, the wind reiterated with double force and propelled us, plunging and guided and powerless, into the woods.

We ran. I could hardly keep up with my boy now, though my feet punched perfect patterns between the crisscrossed fallen branches. He was the leader, leaping four-limbed through all the undergrowth like some great safari leader in the deeps of the jungle, bold and brave, a born hero. Was I his father, or was he mine? All around us, in confirmation of Austin's chosen course, the red and yellow leaves ripped off the branches and joined the wind that drove us.

The light was growing ahead, the ground rising. I couldn't catch Austin, even with the wind blowing me faster than I could run; but that was all right, because he knew where we were going.

Then all at once he was out and I was out and the wind burst all around us, showering us with October leaves. The air was still.

Before us, the grain mounted up in a blowing field, darklit by a sun lying lower than I had realized; and sunken into the hill lay the towering, teetering wreck of some great machine, some vast and dubious warhorse of the grainfields or of the rails. In its light, in its aura, there pulsed some dim refraction of that same Spirit which had dimly refracted upon our entrance into my uncle's house. I, overcome, sank to my knees in the grain. Austin stood before me, likewise transfixed. And no matter how many years have passed for me on that planet or on this, before or since, I live still in that moment, though now I write to you from the light of it, from the presence of *it itself*—

When at last my consciousness departed from that moment, the sun was just fading into a net of leaves and branches. Even as I blinked and watched, it sank lower, and the colors of the world retired. The crumbling machine and the hill of a field before us were black, looming now with the sinuous potential of the hill of fur behind my bushes back home.

"Daddy!" Austin scampered to me and fell in my lap, burrowing his head in under my arm. "I'm scared of monsters!"

And you know, the beast *was* a reality, wasn't it, and the light had gone out of the tired machine and the inexplicable was over—now the hulk was just a shadow, just a rusted memory of the industrious and devastating strivings of man. We were lost in the woods and it was dusk and we had lost track of time too. I swept him up and spun and went blundering into the brown woods, running now with no help and no wind at my back, without a chorus of red leaves telling me I was on course. And the barren twigs whipped me and drew blood, for there was no *back* in that place, only *forwards*. And I tripped in the crossed and layered branches where once my feet had found perfect patterns, for you couldn't reenter those woods, but could only exit.

Behind us came night, for the sun died with the fields. In that night came breath, came muscles, came the rush of something living.

"Daddy! Daddy!" He was wailing now, shuddering in my arms as I held him over my shoulder. I was wailing too, but I didn't show it. I was his father. If the father wails, what else is there?

At last we came blundering out of the ruinous woods. The black fields towered up before us, insurmountable. The brown house with the white trim tilted somewhere overhead. That trim was nearly the only thing visible in the fast-falling brown night. My legs moved in slow gyrations, nightmarishly hampered, stuck now in nettles, now in hidden burrows and undulations.

I knew the presence behind us.

At last I stumbled up to the door and threw it open and collapsed across the threshold. I spun and slammed the door and lay panting, clutching my boy. But there was no crash of beast against house. I rose, shaking, and looked out the little diamond window. There was nothing at all, just darkness over the trees and fields, and in the west, the faintest remembrance of a glow.

Then I saw it: a hill of shadow moving slowly across the dim boundary between field and wood, coming along, not toward.

I sank against the door and shook.

I DREAMT OF A dance between tires on country roads and a mountain of
fur in the fields, the two approaching my uncle's house in now-tightening,
now-widening spirals. When I awoke, the tires were crunching on gravel
and gray light was coming through the diamond window, but there was
no sound or sign of the beast. Then I heard a car door slam and steps
come tramping. Even through the walls, I heard Matt's exclamation:
Oh my…

I staggered to my feet. My boy was sleeping on his coat and my uncle's
dusty shoes. I had tossed and dozed on the doormat. It was almost day,
and even my accustomed sleeplessness was nothing compared to this
feeling. I was waking up, but it felt like dying. I was a piece of iron: stiff,
heavy, metallic.

Then Matt was opening the door of the house. That meant it had
stood unlocked all night—*again*, like the first time, because I had the
key and he did not.

"Jim." Matt stared at me.

I stared back. It was too early to say anything.

"Look at this." He turned and went back outside. I followed him.
Standing out in the gravel beside him, I looked around. The fields, the
thigh-high grasses and grains, were all flattened. Only those closest to
the house were still standing.

Matt turned to me. "It *is* a safehouse. That's what she told me—and
there's your proof."

"Do you mean that—"

"Yes." He turned and walked around the front of the van.

"Matt, I need to eat."

"I know that. I stopped at a diner for you."

"Where'd you go? You left me here alone with Austin."

"I know. I'm sorry. I went to talk to the woman I met on the bus." He opened the driver's door.

"Where are we going?"

"To her house. Get Austin, and let's go."

I could have laid Austin in the back seat, but instead I put Uncle Phil's long black coat there. I couldn't tell you why I took the coat, as the air wasn't that cold. But I did, and I held Austin in my lap up front. The smell of the greasiest and most glorious breakfast was coming out of a brown paper bag on the dashboard. A nod from Matt told me that the food was mine. Flabby eggs and bacon grease never tasted so good. I woke Austin and he had some too, poor boy.

"Oh." Matt lifted a thermos off the floor and balanced it next to me on the seat. "I thought you might need this, too." He cracked the seal. Oh glory, there was coffee in the car. I took it and drank deeply. He started the engine. We wound off down the driveway just as the sun glanced up through the distant tree line.

"We're going to meet your friend?" I couldn't hide the doubt in my voice.

"Right. Don't worry about it. I told them about the beast. They insisted that I bring you to them."

"They?"

"She and her husband."

"Will we be safe there?"

"Of course! They're fighting the beast, just as we are."

"I didn't know this was a battle."

"Of course, Jim." Then his mind turned to something else. Suddenly he said, "Oh! We're going to stop and pick up my sister first, if you don't mind. This is exactly her kind of thing."

"I didn't know you had a sister."

"Very funny, Jim."

In half an hour, I had figured out where we were going. It was a little town somewhere between here and there, the name of which I could never remember. Maybe that was where she lived. His sister? Of course he had a sister. I knew that. I tried to remember what she looked like, but I couldn't. I was a little nervous for some reason. Maybe, after Molly, the need to impress them was coming back. I did miss the way Molly had always squeezed my muscles when I flexed them, humoring me and pretending my biceps got her going, when they were the muscles of a writer, an academic, a man who preferred pure thought to athletic achievement. But it was a cold kind of missing now. It was just Molly.

At least today, I had autumn warmth and just-changing trees drenched in sun to caress my mind. For a while, I was content to watch the trees roll back like spokes of a wagon wheel as we careened up and down, straight and around the ruinous country roads.

Eventually, we came to a four-way stop straddling a steep hillside. Matt rolled through carelessly. The trees opened out to show a little white church with a red roof, and below it, a gravel parking lot running down the hill to the road.

I looked over at Matt. "She's *here?*"

He nodded and pulled in.

"But… there aren't any cars."

"She doesn't have a car."

We parked under the shade of the church. The van rocked back on the steep gravel hill. Matt got out and went up to the side door. I scrambled out, carrying Austin.

It was cool inside and smelled of mold. I didn't really understand the smell until our wanderings of the dim halls brought us past a corkboard on the wall. I was relieved to see photos of human presence tacked there. Then I realized that the pictures were all sepiatones of farm folk wearing ancient clothes. Moving on, we passed a half-open bathroom door. I saw the cobwebs stringing the door in place.

"What's that?" Matt murmured.

We stopped. The corridors murmured with a sound like the distant haunting of a low woodwind. As I listened, the sound grew and took on the sonorous cutting of a well-bowed cello.

Austin wriggled out of my arms, down to the ground. He lunged forwards, pulling me.

"She's upstairs," said Matt. But Austin was already pulling me towards the stairwell where white sunlight fell with silent grace.

We entered and climbed. The light on my skin had a strange vibration to it. So did the firm and buoyant melody echoing all around us. I wanted to climb from that stairwell into the autumn sky.

We came out into a brown and woolly narthex where many coats hung over dark faux paneling. Up here, the music was clear, supported yet fragile, a voice utterly human. It came from the right, where sets of doors opened to the sanctuary. We approached.

We stopped and peered into the sanctuary. A woman danced and sang near the front, before the altar. She leapt, she turned, she ran in the cutting sun. Her melody leapt with her and turned around her: she was a poem of light in her poem of sound. I adored her form, her voice, her echoing slapping footfalls on the cold stone.

I could have watched her forever. But Matt, after the perfunctory respect due to her, cleared his throat and stepped in. His footfall broke her song with a warning rapport. She spun, startled, looking. Then she laughed and came walking, trotting, running down the center aisle. The siblings met with an embrace.

"Ready?" he asked as he released her.

"Always ready." Her eyes fell on me.

"You know Jim, right?" said Matt.

"Of course!" she laughed. "How are you?"

"Good," I said. I looked at her. "Have we met?"

She laughed, then stopped, frowning at Matt. They blinked at each other. Then she got over it and turned back to me. "Yes. At your birthday—" She stopped and glanced at Matt again. "Right. At Matt's graduation. We met there. That was only the first time, though. Come on, Jim; you know me."

"Of course," I laughed. I hoped she would say her name. She didn't.

Matt's graduation, only the first time. Was this the second, or the twentieth, or the hundredth? I swear to you, I don't know. I told myself I didn't recognize her, but she was as familiar and elusive as a word you can't quite come up with.

I caught Matt shaking his head to her, like he was embarrassed, like he had to apologize for me. It was supposed to happen out of my range of vision, but they didn't understand the power of my eyes. Then he spoke to her in a public way, as if nothing secret was going on.

"Got everything?"

"This is all I have, dear brother." She lifted a dirty knapsack out of the nearest pew. Given that, I looked more closely at her clothes. God, she was a tramp.

In the hall, I held the side door for her despite the fact that she was a tramp. She passed through, nodding and blushing a little. Then I opened the passenger door of the suburban for her; but she must have thought I was opening it for myself, for she went to the back door.

"Oh!" I still couldn't remember my best friend's sister's name. In my defense, I had never really known her or thought about her much. I had already had a girl at the time. "That was… for you."

She blushed again and stood looking at me, a little frustrated. "Thank you, Jim." Didn't she know the dance of the sexes? My role, her role? I had done *my* part. Yet now she brushed past me and climbed into the front seat. She bent towards my boy and slapped her knees and said, "Austin! Sit in my lap!"

"Okay!" He clambered up.

So she knew my boy's name, but I didn't know hers. I really *was* losing it. But all I said was, "I don't know if that's safe, Austin. Maybe you should sit back here with me." I shoved Uncle Phil's coat over and climbed in.

"But I sat up front on the way here when I was sitting in *your* lap," Austin piped.

"Now, that isn't very fair, is it?" Her mischievous eye caught mine over the seat. Beguiled by her smile-curved cheeks and those blue eyes, I muttered nothing and even started to smile back.

"Well, Austin…" Her attention had left me already. "I guess you win!" She looked back at me with that infuriating superiority which wrecks your mind with eros.

How dare she try to charm her way into getting what she wanted? Our friendship or whatevership was going to go swimmingly.

"Were you waiting long?" Matt asked as he backed down the hill.

"I wasn't *waiting*," she said. "Or if that was waiting, then my whole life has been such—though I don't mind it."

"I saw you dancing for the birthday," said Austin.

"Ha!" She gave a wild, throaty laugh and ruffled the boy's hair. "I like that. *Birthday*. I never thought of calling it that."

Matt glanced at her. "Was that another one of those…"

"Yes." Her voice thrilled. "What can you do but dance? You're in the presence of—of—*birthday*, as Austin so eloquently put it."

"Eloquently?" My boy looked up at her. He never talked this much around me.

Again, that laugh like the strength of summer. "Beautifully. Fittingly. You know."

"Oh."

"Eloquently means with an elevated style," I put in.

"Exactly," she said, without looking at me. "You know, Matt, it really is a pity that you don't have the sensitivity. If you could only experience—"

"Excuse me." I wasn't rude, because *she* had started the rudeness, moving on like that. "What are you talking about?"

"The divine echo in the church," she said. "That's why I was dancing. You know, it's curious that Austin recognized it. At least, I'm assuming that's what he meant by *birthday*."

"It was," said Austin.

"That's interesting," said Matt. "Just yesterday, the two of you went bounding off the moment you got inside Phil's house. Austin tried to tell me about it after you fell asleep on the couch, Jim, but I can't say I understood."

"You'll all have to slow down a little," I said. *These idiots.* "My boy doesn't do things like that. He's just a normal boy. He's my boy."

Nobody spoke.

Exposing me like that, making me look like an imbecile, like someone with emotional difficulties. We're both quite normal. Not responding to my statement doesn't help the situation. Doesn't help reinforce what I'm saying about us. As if my boy—divine what?—your hogwash. I will *not* have his ears tainted. Fatherhood. Protect him. Protect him, James.

If you're going to do this to me, at least protect *him*. He is my son, James, and yours. But I'll give you custody, though I know you to be a megalomaniac and a psychotic and a narcissist and a drunk. *I am not those things. You shut your mouth. I am his father.* You may have begotten him, James Feckidee—and the shame of that union is all mine—but you will never know how to father him.

"Didn't he, Jim?" said Matt.

"What?"

"Didn't Austin drag you into the house?"

"Oh." I frowned.

"He kept calling it birthday and Christmas," said Matt.

"At Phil Feckidee's house?" said Matt's sister.

"Right."

"I wouldn't be surprised if it was a divine echo," she said. "Phil was communing with them all the time."

"You knew my Uncle Phil?"

"Of course!" She spun and looked at me, shocked, almost hurt. "I was at your infamous birthday party."

"Jim, please." Molly's voice was shrill and plaintive, her face strained, trying to hold together what was not there anyway. "Uncle Phil got it all ready for you. I made a cake for you. I spent the whole day decorating. We all helped. It's all for you, because we love you."

I know. I know. I want to be there, dear.

"Then why don't you stay, even if it's just for a little bit?"

I told Buck and Richard that I would go down to the Sotted Owl. We turned in our papers today, and it's only fitting, since it falls on my birthday.

"Oh, and drink yourself silly? I don't like it, Jim. You never used to do that when you first started taking me out. You always called yourself a straight shooter. You were proud of it, too."

I am. I am a straight shooter.

"How many rounds are you going to have?"

I don't have to tell you that.

"And you've talked of proposing to me? Oh, you *are* something to marvel at."

That has nothing to do with anything.

"I suppose you think *that's* a birthday barhop, too. I suppose you think I'm a term paper to write, or a beer to knock off. I'm not a job, Jim. If you—don't walk away from me!"

But I brushed past her and went down the basement where they really had strung up the low beams and girders with ribbons and balloons. Uncle Phil was bending over his shiny new walnut-encased wireless, fiddling the knobs and trying to find a station, any station.

"Ready to dance, Jim?"

Actually, Buck and Richard—

"So you were pursued by a monster?"

Matt's sister was looking at me again over the seat. Her smile shone against a canvas of flying October color. What could I say? She had no idea of my feelings, my memories. "Yes. I was pursued by a monster."

Her face fell. I recognized the genuine empathy, but I couldn't reach her to accept it.

"That's horrible. I'm so sorry." She pursed her lips. "I wonder what Proton will think of it."

"I already talked to him," said Matt. "Once he heard about the monster, he insisted I bring Jim right away."

"Excuse me, but who is Proton?" I said.

"Husband of Ihrel, the lady I met on the bus. They're the ones we're going to see."

"Oh really? And why didn't you tell me this before?"

"I did."

"You didn't tell me their names," I said.

"I didn't think you would know who they were."

The silence of my undeserved shame fell. He was always shaming me.

"So, Jim." Matt's sister turned and looked at me again. "Did you fight?"

I stared at her. "Fight?"

She blinked. "In the war, I mean."

"Oh, *that.* I was found mentally incompetent." I glared at her.

She blinked again. "I'm... sorry."

"It is what it is. Keep your distance from me." I laughed bitterly.

"You were doing a doctorate, right?"

As if she didn't care at all!

"I still am."

But she had this strange effect on my words, even my thoughts, like she could curve them back from apotheosis of ego or disastrous defeat, back to a middle ground that was better than either.

"Doctorate in what?"

"Literature." No, I would refuse her. Maybe my short answers would show her. Maybe she would stop interviewing me.

"What's your thesis about?"

"William Blake, the eighteenth-century English poet."

"Sure. So, you understand that stuff? I gotta say, I'm a little jealous. I can't make sense of it."

"The point is to stop trying to make sense of it. You just have to read it as color, as associations. That's the thrust of my thesis. For example, this week, before the funeral and—and the beast—I was working on a passage from the First Book of Urizen. He uses a phrase: *like the thunders of autumn, when the cloud blazes over the harvests*. Obviously, it's just a metaphor, a painting with words."

"Well I know *that*." She dared to laugh at me! She, a tramp, homeless, uneducated—"I'm a poet myself." Oh she was, was she?!—"Not a good one, of course, but I practice according to the measure of my craft."

"Really?" In spite of myself, I leaned forwards a little.

"Here, I'll show you something." She bent down for her knapsack, holding Austin off to the side but keeping him away from the gearshift. "Somewhere... my notebook..." She sat up and turned and handed me a tattered binder. "Careful, please. *Everything's* in there."

I couldn't help but hold it with some reverence as I leafed through it. She gazed over the seat and directed me. "No, not that. Not very good. Turn a few pages farther. Past the paperclip. Yes—there." She smacked the open page. "Read that."

I squinted and tried to make out her self-taught handwriting.

Us imagined the scattered rey misterioso,
telltale and only hobbled,
in a bulletproof replica.

Next to it there was a drawing of something like a steam locomotive.

I read it a few times. Beyond the obtuse construction (and I had yet to decide whether that was brilliance or idiocy on her part), I sensed in it something inexplicable: almost a memory of the memory of breath that had greeted us on the threshold of Uncle Phil's house…

"Offbeat, I know. Unclear subject and object in the first line, I know. But that's how it came to me. Do you write, Jim? Creatively, I mean?"

"Sometimes…" I shifted and straightened the page.

"Then you know the muse. It will come to you, this driving clarion of purpose, and you're just an oracle. You sit, breathe, and good heavens, don't dare think; you just listen and transcribe. And then sometimes you sit and wait and think hard about why nothing is coming, and nothing comes."

"Right. I've… read about that."

"I got this ready-made, just like it is. All I did was put it down on paper before it disappeared."

"Sadie is a spiritual being," said Matt.

"I… guessed that already," I muttered. That was her name: Sadie. Now I remembered. I filed it away.

"I don't think you guessed the strength of her spiritual nature," said Matt. "She still surprises *me*, and I've been digesting her visions my whole life."

Sadie laughed nervously. "Silly Brother Matthias likes to flatter. He has this way of popping out at just the right moment with a little ego boost. It's how he gets things done. That's why I keep telling him he should go into politics. What with his perspective, his personality, his connections with me and the rest of us and everything we're working on, he could do a lot of good in this country."

"I will never go into politics," said Matt. "This country isn't prepared for the kind of platform I would have to run on to be honest with myself. I'm living in the wrong time."

"She's right, though," I said. "You have a lot of practical insight. I'm sure you could weasel your way to the top."

He gave me an annoyed look in the mirror but drove on without saying anything.

"Oh, oh—" Sadie lunged forwards, pointing. "Turn there. Right there."

"Why?" Matt slowed a little, squinting.

"If we go to Blakely, I can show you one of the most lovely ones I've ever found," she said.

"How long ago were you there? I thought you said they usually decay."

"A month maybe, but this one is stable. Please, please, Matty? Please?"

"What are you talking about?" I demanded.

But Matt said, "All right," and turned down the road she pointed at.

In a few minutes we were meandering through another lazy and self-forgotten town. I watched the autumnal trees through the silent window. The trees were so cold, even in the sun.

"There." Sadie pointed. Matt slowed down. A rotting wooden sign in the midst of somber wintry oaks announced the remains of the Blakely Community Park. The drive was cracked and churned with tree roots, and acorns and fallen branches popped under our wheels. The slow work of the trees sought to destroy the pavement from above and below.

"This doesn't appear to be open," said Matt as we bounced over the broken asphalt.

"It doesn't matter," said Sadie.

We parked under a gigantic oak. My stomach thought it was mealtime. Sadie got some apples out of her knapsack, and Matt produced sandwiches from a cooler in the back of the Suburban. We sat at the rusty old picnic table and made a picnic of it. The table had been dragged to a place where it didn't belong: our feet played the broken bricks of what had once been a flowerbed. But the landscaping had long since eroded into brown weed, and before us, the meadow stretched brown and burnt down to the woods, where red and yellow and brown leapt off the black and gray trunks.

Sadie was a part of that sun-blasted autumn dream, autumnal herself in her threadbare clothes and her glowing shock of short blond hair—and O, how her eyes sparkled—

Guard yourself, Jim. They're all the same. They're all like her, even Matt's sister. Besides, what are you looking for? She doesn't have it. Not one of them does. It's your delusion. Whatever you want is not found in woman. Besides, she's a tramp, and she's Matt's sister. You would kill yourself after a month with her. She probably doesn't do dishes— hell, probably doesn't have a place where she could keep them. Bet that knapsack holds it all. How does someone end up like that? Good lord.

The grace, the grace of her lips. Her jaw, translucent at its edge where the skin was so delicate that the blown-out sun shone through it. Lashes, flicking down down, down down. Now up, now looking. She regarded me with eyes impassive and free and incapable of giving or receiving condescension.

"Do you like it here, Jim?"

"I would almost say I love it."

Her polite smile softened. A certain warmth came in under her eyes. My heart fluttered. I had not let anyone do that to me in a long time.

Austin smacked his lips with the last bite of sandwich and stood up. "Can we go now?"

"We haven't finished eating," I said.

"I wanna go now."

Sadie stood. "Just wait a moment while your dad finishes his sandwich."

"He's done," said Austin, watching me take the last bite.

"Just hold on," I said patiently, dusting off my hands and standing.

But Austin giggled, turned, and dashed out into the field.

"Hey! Austin—"

But Sadie ran after him, laughing, now looking over her shoulder. "Come on, fellas! Run with us!"

Matt stood and sauntered into the field. I was abandoned. *Idiots.* As if I didn't matter at all. Just an accessory, just along for the ride.

Sadie had caught Austin's hand. Now he was charging through the long dead grass, dragging her towards the woods. The sound of their laughter imbued the fields with languid euphoria.

"Austin," I called, "wait for your dad—"

But they were so far away, their laughter so infinite, that my voice surely didn't reach them. I trotted, then ran. They were already near the woods. I couldn't seem to run fast enough. I passed Matt. He was walking in the path they had cut through the grain, hands in pockets, casually disinterested. He gave me nothing but a nod.

"Austin knows the way!"

Sadie's jubilant voice rebounded across the fields as her bright face turned over her shoulder. Austin pulled her onwards, as inspired as any wound-up dog out for a walk. They were the movers, we the watchers. I wanted to be a mover, but Sadie, my inferior in all externalities, was somehow running ahead with my son, diving into the next great adventure. That ready-made pair had no need of me.

No need of me. As if I were nothing. As if this panting, this heaving of my lungs, were not given in the sincere pursuit of that which I trusted they knew. As if I didn't *mean* it, this pumping of my legs. As if I was just doing it to make them think I wanted to tag along—just acting on a false magnanimity—

But the funny thing was that there was nothing at all to see. Delusional, my son and this urchin of a woman who trusted his judgment—who trusted the judgment of a four-year-old, when I was back here ready to contribute and far more cognizant of the ways of the world than Austin was yet, or than she would ever be. What the hell did *she* know? She couldn't even buy a skirt. And I don't know how she didn't trip in that ratty old thing, leaping as she did through the long grass, now careening through the underbrush.

I wept.

No, I was a fool. She, *she,* held truth. I don't know what it is and I have never seen it before nor read about it nor written about it, but hers is truth. She never learned anything, and yet she knows far more than I ever will. I want her, I need her, I want her. She is mine! She is Matt's. She is mine. I will follow her. They're on to something. They're hitting a trail. She is leading me through my labyrinths to truth. That is why I am fighting her. She is leading me towards truth, and I do not want it.

I do not want your lies, Molly. *I don't want your lies.* I never once lied to you! You think that when I say one thing and your man's ears hear something else that I've lied to you. But I haven't. *Oh yes you have. Last night—*

She is leading me to truth. She does not know me. She does not know my struggles. She does not know how hard it is to choose whom to listen to. She does not know how many there are. But she does not care. She just sees the one true me, and she sees where it should go. I think she is calling to it, and I think the one true me should answer. But I do not know how to answer, and I think that I cannot do it on my own.

"Just up here!"

Sadie's face flashing like sun, like Christmas bulb, like lights. I think I am breaking. Broken-soled shoes flapping up under her skirt. Close enough now to see that. My hands and ankles are stinging, I think those were nettles, and where are we? The light is funny, silver not gold though it's nearly midday. They are charging through the dead leaves. I have never felt this way. I feel the lifting of a great burden, as if James Feckidee, this mess that I hate, has been lifted from the shoulders that I really am. Do you know? I don't think you do. And they are winding through the smooth trunks of trees. Austin always knew more than I did anyway. You could tell when you looked at him. And look at him now.

"Why are you stopping?" My ragged voice thrown and thrown back: the trees do not want it. The stillness does not want it. Standing, they absorb me and I stop and am breathing hard, I don't know why, I don't know what it is, but it is so beautiful that I weep, I weep for joy, I weep. I am standing there and I weep, I weep. You can't. You can't imagine. I see it now in the flesh, but even that old echo back then back there—oh, I remember it. You could never. If you were here with me now, you would understand. But that's why I write it out for you. I live there still, and *there* is the same as *here*, because he is the same wherever he always will be. I weep. You will not, until. This is beyond.

When at last my mind came up and out, and my spirit realized that the shimmering light over the creek was a dead echo and not the living thing, I saw the human form beyond the mirage. The form sat cross-legged in the brown and yellow leaves on the other side of the creek, under the boughs of the same boxelder that drooped near at hand over the water. The form sat as if studying the same manifestation of light that we had come to see.

And do you know, my boy was already climbing down the bank of the creek and splashing across, head nearly cutting through the shimmering thing that we had come to see, already climbing up the other side. Now the form stood to greet my son, and the face passed from the opacity of the vision suspended over the creek to the simplicity of real sight. I looked. I beheld the face of the ageless man in the photo, the face of the drunk at the gas station.

"Don't touch my boy!" I tripped, fell, floundered in the mud, but I got across and came up out of the creek. "I remember you. You were at the gas station. I saw you in that picture too. You can't fool me. Don't touch him."

The stranger looked at me with vague and unconcerned eyes. Then he looked down at my boy and picked him up, as carelessly as he might have cracked a twig.

"I said—I said—"

I lunged, but the bastard moved before I could get him, and I fell headlong. I dug something into my hand—wood—a stupid branch broken and left there for me to hurt myself on.

"Sorry," said Matt. "Don't mind him. He hasn't slept, and the breakfast I provided wasn't very good, and neither were the sandwiches."

Matt, talking about me as if explaining the idiocy of some child breaking things in a glass shop. Matt, making a fool of me. They'll never believe me now when I tell them that this vagrant tried to molest my boy at the gas station. That's two vagrants now, him and her. Well, maybe they'll make a fine couple. That would keep me from chasing her and getting my hopes up to get them dashed again. Besides, she's a vagrant. Don't chase a vagrant. Respect yourself. You've lost all credibility.

It was Sadie whose gentle touch on my shoulder turned me over in the leaves. I looked up into her sun-cut and glorious face.

"Oh, Jim—oh, your hand! What got into you?"

"Goddamnit, that's what," I burbled.

She stroked my hair. She did.

"Aunt Sadie said it was here." Austin's little voice cut through the woods. "We found it, together. She helped me. I mean, I helped her."

"Is he hurt?" said the stranger. I couldn't see him, but I knew he was talking about me.

"Not too bad," said Sadie. "He just stuck himself with this broken branch." She opened my curled fingers, which were hiding blood. I did not want her to see my blood, and yet I needed her to see my blood.

"What's wrong?" Matt bent over me, hands on knees, placid. I bled and bled. "Oh, that's just a splinter." He bent down and wrenched my hand. I screamed. "There," he said. "I got it."

"Did the beast touch him? Did it hit him or bite him?" asked the stranger.

"Yes," said Matt, standing up. "Really, Jim's had a hard time. He went to a funeral, and the beast came that same night. It attacked him. He cut off one of its tentacles. He didn't sleep at all because we were escaping, as I told you. He didn't eat anything the next day. He slept on the floor last night. I got him a pitiful breakfast today, and I provided pitiful sandwiches for lunch."

"Stop saying pitiful," said the stranger.

"I'm just explaining why he's acting that way."

"It isn't *your* fault," said the stranger. "Did the beast bite him?"

"No," said Matt.

As if he knew!

"Good," said the stranger. "It could have been far worse." He paused, thinking. "We'll do what we can. I wasn't expecting to meet you here. Ihrel is back at the house, getting things ready."

"Did you need more time?" asked Matt. "Did we interrupt you?"

"No, no. If anything, I want *less* time in this world."

"Come on, Jim." Sadie was rubbing my head. "Better get up."

I heard their feet crunching in leaves and I heard the splosh-slap of the stranger's feet down in the creek—*those,* the feet of the one who carried my boy while I lay still in the loam.

"Come on, Jim," said Sadie. She stood up and left me.

I teetered to my feet one-handed, clutching my maimed hand close to my chest. I lifted it, expecting to see a stain of blood on my jacket. But

I saw nothing. I looked at my hand: it was no longer bleeding. I guess it wasn't that serious.

The rest of them were already moving through the woods. Matt and the stranger and my boy were up front, far away. Sadie was following them. She may have led me to truth and she may have stroked my hair, but she had abandoned me now.

No, I had to stop. She had not abandoned me. She had only tried to get me to stand. Perhaps that was her intent in getting up and walking away.

Molly. Perhaps that was Molly's intent in getting up and walking away: trying to get me to stand up on my own. Perhaps it had felt like abandonment because my condition had prevented me from seeing it for what it was. I mean, she had demonstrated; she had begged. She had repeated and repeated. She was a saint and I was Satan. *Molly.* I don't know where you are but I would go back, back, and I would do it so differently now.

When I got to the Suburban, they were all standing around looking at me, waiting, even smiling.

"There he is!" cried Sadie.

The stranger had put my boy down. Now he reached a battered and grubby hand towards me. "I'm Proton," he said. "Don't tell me: you're Jim Feckidee."

"James Feckidee," I said, shaking his hand.

Proton looked at Matt. "Let's go. We can talk as we drive. It'll be a few hours."

Then I was in the back seat again. Proton slid in next to me and stretched his arm languidly across the seat, as if he might protect me from the night and even the beast. He stared placidly out the window as the acorns crunched under our wheels.

I woke up. We hadn't talked. I was slouched into Proton, but he didn't seem to mind. He hadn't moved, and he now bore my weight with a certain paternal stoicism. I sat up right away, embarrassed, but he didn't even notice. He just kept staring out the window at the serenity of sunstruck red and gold. I looked around. We were flying up and down jouncy hills in a wooded country that I did not know, and it was perhaps late afternoon. Sadie was asleep in the front seat.

"There's no question that the darkness assaulted you," said Proton.

I looked over at him. He was still looking out the window, still offering his arm across the whole top of the seat. Now, with senses cleared, I noticed his shabby dark clothes. When he turned to look at me, I saw the prominent scar down the length of his forehead, above his left eye.

"A beast came for you," he went on. "There's no doubt, by its actions, that it came for you specifically."

I looked away.

"The fact that you escaped, and that you know Matt, who chanced to meet my wife on the bus… you *do* realize that you would have died without help, right?"

"Right."

He smiled faintly at me, a smile that could have been a thousand years old and could have seen far more things to smile and frown about than I'd seen in my whole lifetime.

"Proton, I have to ask you…"

His smile grew somehow stranger.

"Did you know my uncle?"

"Your uncle…?"

"Phillip Feckidee."

He laughed and his eyes glittered. "Of course I know Phil!"

"How?"

Now he looked away. "I don't want to put it all on you at once, James. You're still recovering."

"I'd like to know everything right now."

But he just gazed out the window.

We flew down into a deep valley where the sun could not break the shadows. At the bottom, we shot straight back up. The engine roared. At this angle, the afternoon sun just broke the towering top of the ridge. We were driving into a false end of day.

"Remember to turn left," said Proton.

Matt slowed. At the last moment, a dark and tree-shrouded lane opened out on the left at the very top of the ridge. Crashing and bucking in the ruts, the Suburban left the roads of man and carved up the bramble-eaten gravel track. The ascent grew treacherous, and the truck skidded and wandered in the ruin of the woods. But the path went on clearly before us, an inward-opening shadow into shadows under October trees.

"Sorry about the ride," said Proton, still staring out the window. "We don't drive, you understand."

Sadie was awake now, and Austin was whining something inaudible. Sadie lifted him, straining. "Jim... here, take him." I leaned forwards. Somehow she got him over the seat. He fell into my arms, burbling, "Daddy, daddy." I held him, and he snuggled in close to me.

Now the trees thinned out on either side. I saw the tops of other trees at our level and below. Still we climbed with oblique daring into the woods, into a sky that was the woods; and still, we weren't there yet. I could not remember any mountain ranges, even any significant hills, within a few hours' drive of home. To this day, I don't know where we were going.

Then the woods thickened suddenly on either side and the light failed. We were driving between dense and towering pines. The gravel was lost under ages of needles.

"Almost there," said Proton.

"I know," said Matt. "I just drove here yesterday."

He hadn't told me that. But maybe it did not matter. Maybe I had been wrong not to trust him.

With a bounce and a crash, we got over the top. The path leveled out, and we hit a rotting and irregular smear of asphalt that wandered through the pines. The autumn light on the gray bark all around was diffuse and pale.

"Slow down," said Proton.

We swung around a bend and down a long shallow slope. The asphalt died with a little undulation of the ground. The pines stood thick and sentinel all around, so tall that the roof of the van hid their tops.

"We'll have to go on foot from here," said Proton.

"Is it far?" I asked.

"No."

Matt stopped the van at the edge of the pavement and we sat for a moment, listening to the stillness. Then Proton got out and Matt got out. I opened my door. It hit me: I was thirsty. I was hungry. My head was foggy. I could hardly move my limbs.

"Follow me," said Proton as he struck off between the faceless pines. We loped along after him, stretching and yawning. In five minutes the van was out of sight. The strange shifting of the pines was identical in all directions. Soon the ground fell in an endless shallow descent and the trees began to thin. In place of the trees, weather-worn stone in tilted strata stood half-blossomed in the mould.

The trees failed completely ahead. A few more moments, and we stepped out of the woods. The bare ground fell away to a precipice of impenetrable mist. I saw warm windows like home and battered white siding glowing there—a little wreck of a house perched on the edge of nothingness, puffing smoke into the obscurity of vapors. Even at this distance, in the cool damp and fast-coming dusk, I could smell food.

We passed through unkempt gardens around the house where wildflowers had grown with abandon that summer. Proton walked up the buried garden stones to the door of the screened-in porch. The door opened with a squeak and admitted us into the veranda, where scads of things lay juxtaposed in apathetic collection. I heard the muffled warblings of some musical instrument. Proton mounted the three concrete steps and opened the unlocked solid door. The warm light of a home came out. With it came the smell of onion and garlic and tomato sauce and ricotta cheese, and the affectionate jangling of an old piano.

"Threl," Proton called, "I'm back."

The music stopped.

"They found me in the woods, so I just rode with them."

"Glad you made it back, dear!" A voice as musical as the piano drifted through the halls. "The mists are getting thick. I was a little worried."

One by one, we stepped in after him.

I came into the kitchen. A woman in an apron was just entering from another room. She had the blackest hair I have ever seen. When she turned and smiled at us, I saw that her face was neither young nor old. I remembered that Matt had used the word *queen bee* to describe her.

"You know Matt," said Proton to his wife. "This is Matt's sister, Sadie. This is James. The boy is James's son, Austin." He pointed at each of us in turn. "Everyone, this is my wife, Ihrel."

She smiled, and candlelight glittered in her eyes. She pointed at the table, which was set for six. "You can all sit down. Dinner will be ready in a few minutes. In the meantime, I'm making a salad—or I was, before I started playing the piano!" She laughed. "Proton, be a dear and get a few bottles of wine from the cellar." He nodded dutifully and left the room.

The glow of their hospitality faded a little in me. I felt terribly inadequate, terribly conscious of my gratefulness, even terribly proud.

"So, James." Ihrel looked over at me but kept tossing the salad, perhaps by feel. "You've been attacked by a beast."

"Yes. Right." I looked away from her beautiful, caring gaze. I felt too warm. I wanted to be at peace here—wanted to eat and drink and be friends and be human—but I had nothing to contribute and I would owe them all forever for their generosity and I didn't deserve it anyway given Molly and the magazines that had started it all and—

"I'm sorry, James." Ihrel stood looking at me. She was on the verge of weeping. I sat down. Sadie sat down next to me—*next* to me!—and touched my hand. Austin in my lap clung to me, and even Matt's vacant stare into the candle flame spoke to me of love. I was among family. Why was I trying to measure up? Wasn't that an imaginary obstacle?

But I had just met these people—

No. I was among family.

"It followed me home from the hills," I said. "You know my uncle, Phil Feckidee, right?"

"Of course." Ihrel brought the salad over and got out the dressing.

"I went to his funeral—"

"Funeral?!" She dropped the bottle of dressing onto the table. Everyone jumped. Somehow, she righted the bottle before anything spilled. She was giving me the strangest look. But even as she stared, her face changed to a slow smile. "Funeral, eh?"

I nodded slowly.

She shook her head, still smiling.

"I'm sorry," I said. "If you knew Uncle Phil, I assumed that you knew."

She stood tapping the salad dressing bottle. "That is *very* strange. I'll have to talk to Proton about that. I'm not sure what that means."

"It means… he's… passed away, I'm afraid."

"Oh, no, no. He hasn't." She sat down across from me.

I blinked at her. "What?"

"I'll have to discuss it with Proton."

I saw a look pass between Matt and Ihrel, but no one said anything. We began to eat our salads. Proton came back with two nameless bottles of wine. He opened them with satisfying pops and began pouring them out methodically until all the glasses were full to the same height. Then he sat down in silence and cut into his salad.

"Are you going to discuss it?" I asked.

"What?" said Proton.

"My uncle. Ihrel said—"

"We'll discuss it in private," said Ihrel. She gave her husband a look that excluded everyone else. "We don't want to tangle you up in something before it's time."

"You'll have to be clearer."

"That's what I'm saying: we can't be clearer. Not yet." She smiled, but I wasn't really taking that with a smile. Going to tell me that my uncle *isn't* dead when I've seen him in the casket myself, seen the huge white hair and the jaw so masculine and strident and the mouth once accustomed to quick laughter, and going to tell me you can't tangle me up in it? Excuse me, I'm already in up to my neck. I'm drowning in these feelings. He was my great-uncle, and damned if he wasn't my father, even my brother. He's the one who taught me Blake and he's the one who taught me poetry that could change a life could save a life, and everything else. If you had been there, if you had grown up like that, you wouldn't keep it from someone. You would tell it all, the whole thing. He wasn't your uncle. He was mine.

Oh my memories, like drunkenness, like head spinning falling down…

"Just stay a moment, Jim," said Uncle Phil. I had never heard him plead with me before. He had always just told me what to do. But maybe I was an adult now. "Just give me five moments, if you will. This thing is brand new, and I just can't get it to work. Ah, radio will never last anyway. It doesn't stimulate the mind like reading does. If we listen to this thing too much, we'll become a nation of idiots, and those Nazis will get us. Believe me."

I just need to go, I said. *Buck and Richard invited—*

"Richard is a dunce. His glosses of Chaucer are all wrong. You'll learn nothing from that boy."

Please, Uncle Phil.

"I wish you would listen to your better sense sometimes. Molly put this thing together. She expected you to—"

Well, they made plans with me. It's my last night.

I do remember how he turned away and went back to fiddling with the wireless. And even as I turned and went back up the basement steps, through the hall, out the door, I never once heard it come into tune.

Fellas.

"If it ain't Jim Feckidee."

"Did you call ahead? Tell em we need an extra shipment."

"I don't think the Sotted Owl will ever have enough Pabst on hand for you, Dick."

"Ha! Ha! Buck, you bastard."

"No, Jim's the real one. You getting sloshed tonight, Jim? Your birthday, right? With that and finals—"

I don't know.

"Come on, ya girl. What's got into you?"

"Aw, look. He's pining for her. That Molly. I'm not gonna lie, Jim, I'm a little jealous. I'm still missing those lips. How are they, buddy?"

Shut up. You never touched her.

"Ah, that's what she'll tell you—"

"He's just pulling your leg, Jim. You gotta lighten up."

No I don't, I said. *I take her very seriously. I don't appreciate that.*

"Well now, Mr. Scholar! Excuse me, he takes that *very* seriously. Take notes, class, because there *will* be a qu—"

That was the moment when I punched his sick leering face and felt his breaking teeth cut into my hand. I relished that feeling, and I still bear the scars with pride.

Control. These are only memories. They can't touch you unless you let them. Then why am I weeping? Why am I so fixated on these things if they aren't still reverberant inside me? Economy of soul necessitates the dropping of all that's irrelevant. So perhaps I still need this. Perhaps I am still bleeding.

"Jim."

Sadie was touching my hand. When I turned my head, I saw through the blur that she was bent and gazing into my face. Why did she care? She shouldn't have. I was nothing but the idiot friend of her brother. Our interactions should have been cordial but respectfully distant. And now, this: her arm resting upon my shoulder with a certain gentleness long missing from my life…

"I don't know," I said. "I don't know." But I couldn't hold them in and I was so broken that shame itself was a kind of relief to me, or perhaps it was the admittance of shame, the end of the fight. Austin was staring at me with his mouth open so I said, "Sometimes even daddies… have to… cry." But I don't think he understood.

When I calmed down, it was still dinnertime, and I was still hungry. Everyone was eating peacefully, as if my behavior were not alarming at all. Perhaps they *were* family.

I felt the great empty peace that drains out of your head after tears. I ate the incredible lasagna and I watched the warm gentle eyes around me flickering in the candlelight.

Long since sated and basking in the peace of digestion, I sat with them at the table, listening to the quiet conversation. Finally Ihrel said, "Why don't we move to the sitting room? I'll brew some coffee and get out the cookies." So I stood with them, teetering in the haze of pasta. Austin ran into me, looking up, grinning, wanting to be held. I heaved him into my arms.

We passed through the dark doorway. Proton threw the light switch, and the room came to life. In the close cozy illumination, a mural in dense graphite leapt from the yellowed walls: machine, infinite and incomprehensible, reaching all around in circumference without discernible function. The room was too small for it. I was too small for it. I must have gasped audibly.

"Your uncle drew it," said Proton. "I haven't seen Vaulan in the flesh, you understand, not having the ability of travel that he does; but he is a poet and a dreamer, a pilgrim, and I take his visions on faith. According to him, he saw the machine in the flesh."

"What *is* it?" I murmured, gazing around at the wild gray mechanisms on the faded walls. I didn't know why I had thought immediately of the rusted thing in the field behind Uncle Phil's house.

"It's the logic of the atoms," he muttered, sitting on one of the sunken threadbare couches. "It's the dance. It's the self-instrumentation that is the purest fusion of form and function."

I raised an eyebrow at him, but he just grinned.

Ihrel came in with a plate of cookies. We were all standing around, still puzzling over Proton's remark.

"Sit down!" she laughed. Then she saw our faces and the way our eyes crawled in fearful adoration over the fierce graphite angles of pulley and wheel, arm and axle. "Oh! That's our mural. Don't be alarmed. You don't have to understand it to be part of us. We don't understand it ourselves."

I sat down with the others. Ihrel put the cookies on the low table between the couches and went back into the kitchen.

"Vaulan used to live here," Proton murmured, as if out of the haze of years. "Our planet was his home. Those were brighter times. I bet you didn't know you were living in the twilight of our world, of our very species."

"Who lived here?" said Sadie.

"Vaulan. Sonapétpik. He had many names. Actually, you know, those weren't even his names originally; they were just the beginnings of the salutation by which we used to address him, in the language that he is. I have almost forgotten that language."

In the dim lamplight, his tired eyes had sunk into caverns, and his left eye especially hid in the doubtful shadow of that ponderous and world-weary scar.

"You know," he went on, "there was a time when you could walk in the woods and find him dancing in the loam. A flash of sunlight, a swirl of leaves without breath, and you had come upon his finger. But he was not a machine then. He became that, to adapt to *us*, I suppose; but then…"

"That's what we found!" cried Sadie, leaning forwards, face charged with impossible yearning.

"What?" Proton looked over at her as if she had woken him up from a nap.

"A flash of sunlight—in the woods, by the creek—when we found you today."

"Oh." He shifted. His face showed the grinding of great gears in his head getting him from one region of thought to something entirely other. "No, that wasn't him. Not in the flesh, anyway. But I suppose… you could say that was his *echo*."

"So it was like that?" Sadie whispered.

"Like that in quality, yes. In degree… but I can't even describe to you what it was like in degree."

"Let me see if I understand," said Matt. "There was a being who—"

"Vaulan left." Proton's eyes had sunk again. "Vaulan had always wept for our disgusting habits; but at some point, he rejected the sum of them and abandoned this planet." Proton's eyes closed at last, and the lamplight showed the creases of long wrestling and spiritual agony in his face. "If I could find him again, I would go. I would ask him to return and cleanse this planet, even if it would mean apocalypse. That's why your uncle…"

I waited. "My uncle?"

"We'll see." He didn't open his eyes.

In a few minutes Ihrel came in with the coffee. "Have some cookies!" she cried, seeing that her arrangement on the plate was undisturbed. "Doesn't anyone like cookies?"

Sadie grabbed one, bit it in half, and leaned towards Ihrel eagerly. "Proton was just telling us about… Vow? Vow-something. You know, the one who left the echoes."

Ihrel nodded. "Our lover, Vaulan." She sat back and sighed. "I miss him dearly."

I had a cookie but no coffee. In the struggling lamplight, the harsh graphite on the faded wallpaper seemed almost to throb with universal intervallic reciprocations. Proton could hide it now, but the truth was going to come out. I was going to know.

"So you've seen him?" Sadie hugged her coffee in both hands, and the light of her face and that of Ihrel's face fought forwards with the sum engagement that only women can create together. "You've seen Vaulan in the flesh?"

"Yes, but not in this form." Ihrel indicated the mural all around.

"I seem to sense him everywhere," Sadie mused. "I guess they're just his echoes, as Proton says. But I can taste them, you know? They... *resonate*, if you get close enough."

"You're lucky to be able to feel them," said Ihrel. "Most people have lost the ability."

Matt stirred uncomfortably.

Suddenly, the light of Sadie's face fell on me. Her syllables came short and quick, eager to assemble. "Jim. You know what? Austin sensed the echo in the park." She tapped her mug, *ping ping ping*. "He practically pulled my arm out of socket getting us here. He knew the way."

I looked down at Austin. My boy looked up at me with an odd grin. I saw there the embarrassed child, yes, but something of the fearless and self-assured adult too...

"What are you talking about?" I muttered.

"I knew the way across the fields and into the woods, but *he* knew it too," said Sadie. "You've never taken him there, have you?"

"No."

"Exactly."

"So the boy knew the way?" Now it was Ihrel who leaned in with strange eagerness—leaned in as if they all knew something I didn't. Probably did. How dare they. Conspiring without me, and expecting me to offer up my boy, a sacrifice to their monolith condescension.

Ihrel dared to address my boy. "What was it like in the woods?"

"I don't know." He shrugged, looking up at me with a sheepish grin, as if he needed my approval to say that. My approval? I love you, boy, but you don't need my approval. *They*, on the other hand—*they*. And the assumption that I would even be willing to *let* you speak. As if I am nothing and there is some purpose at play that gives me one chance and then in its arrogance, its narcissism, passes me by when I dare to question it. There is more than one answer to everything, and do they know that? As if you felt anything in the woods other than the young springing bravado you have always displayed, have displayed, what you displayed at Uncle Phil's house when we first entered and when we… ran into the woods there…

My grip, my grip.

"But you felt it," said Ihrel.

My boy nodded.

"Now hold on." My voice was too loud and they all jumped and sat back, a little stunned. Proton woke up from a doze. "He didn't feel a damn thing," I shouted. "He was out in the woods and he felt like running." My voice was too loud, but I *would* anyway. "He didn't know."

Austin got very quiet in my lap. The faces everywhere were blank and shadowed in the candlelight.

I made it clear. "This has been a nice vacation, but…"

Proton laughed to my face. "Vacation?" He looked at Ihrel and laughed again. "Ha! I mean, you *are* vacating, yes; you aren't going back. I suppose it *is* a vacation."

8

When at last they had all left me one by one, I sat throbbing under the stark shadows of my uncle's drawing. From a distant room, the indistinct murmurings of piano and voice, some negro song of old Americana, came spilling down the halls. Rising, falling, a tremulous voice wandered across the mountainside of the old melody.

Wheel, oh wheel... wheel in the middle of a wheel...

It must be Ihrel again. But there was nothing for me to do or say, for they had all abandoned me.

Zekiel saw the wheel of time... my Lord and the chariot stop... way in the middle of a wheel...

It was strangely like Uncle Phil's house as it had been a few days ago—or this morning, I mean—when Matt had abandoned me but had finally come back only to abandon me again in a far deeper and emptier way, a more insidious way, by bringing me here where idiots laughed to my face when I said *vacation*. I'll vacate *you*. I will.

The note said to vacate within ten days, I said. *Can they do that?*

"Of course they can, Jim," said Matt. The white sun through the doorway gave him a sort of heartless authoritarian shine. "It's their place. They can do whatever they damn well—"

Damn them. I'll vacate them. I'll put a brick through that window. I will.

"Jim, don't be silly."

I will.

"Did she already take her—"

Of course she did. I told you that. Gone two days ago. Don't ask me where.

I breathed and waited, but Matt never said anything just then. He always left me up to silence, refusing to rescue me from my words that came next, always, again and again forever.

I don't give a damn where she is.

Molly, where are you? You must be happier than here, happier than the inside of this head. I never knew there were cords between us, and now that they're broken, they've broken the moorings that held my head to my head. The whole thing of my head is broken without you.

"I saw her at the train station," said Matt as we turned away from the sun-gorged door to room 220. "She was getting on the westbound for Chicago."

Don't tell me that!

"You need to face the truth, Jim." The paper crunched under his feet as he set off down the hall again. "I'm your friend, and it's my business to show you the truth."

No it isn't.

Uncle Phil straightened the paper in front of him. "It isn't my business, as you're an adult now; but I couldn't help noticing your grade sheet from last semester. You left it on the kitchen table."

Do you think I can't manage my own life?

"Just hold on, Jim." The raised hand quivered, and I saw the sword of truth in his eyes. "I pulled a lot of strings for you to get those scholarships. It's too much to say that I expect something of you—that would be unfair, since you are largely unproven; but I *do* want to see you try. Thus it concerns me greatly to hear how things are going between you and her. Literature may be a dry and bookish field, but it will require your full attention to make a great scholar of you; and if your relationship with her reaches a point of such explosive negativity that—"

I put the brick through the window.

"Jim, this is my friend Sadie—the one I was telling you about from Poetry Club—you know, Matt's sister."

Molly turned me around and I saw the alarming ragtag beauty of Ms. Gaddo.

Pleased to meet you, I said.

"Hi, Jim," said the lovely Ms. Gaddo. "I've heard so much about you. Oh, and happy birthday!"

It's James, I said. *James Feckidee.*

A floorboard creaked. Sadie stood glimmering in the wide doorway, cutting through the intricate mural of machine.

"Still here?" She came in and sat down across from me and took another cookie from the plate. She felt the carafe of coffee, but must have found it too cold.

"Still here," I muttered, with all the shame of the hometown hero and the eternal student and the clueless father.

She munched the cookie. Her very reciprocations of jaw were perfect, silent but for the pleasant muffled crunch of nuts.

"I *do* feel for you, Jim." Her large eyes shuddered across the candle flames as they drank in my form.

"Why?" For once I was able to return her gaze as a normal human being might have.

She laughed. The little corners of her mouth turned, pleated universes warmed in the tired light. "Why not?"

"Because…" I shifted clumsily, too heavy to sit up. "Because I'm an awful man. A terrible father. No longer a husband. Just the idiot friend, the drinking buddy of your brother."

"I've been drinking with you before," she said carelessly. Her eyes glittered.

I couldn't remember ever going drinking with her or any other woman. The very idea was stupid. We had always drunk beer anyway, and it had always been the guys anyway.

"I begin to think you don't even remember me."

I looked at her again. "Gosh. I'm sorry. It's been a… a hell of a time, these last few years."

"I know."

Oh, her smile…

"So is it Jim or James? You always used to correct people who called you Jim, but you're not doing it anymore."

My glance must have fallen more harshly than I realized, for her eyes gave a flicker of a start. But then she put the fear away and stared me down with an even wider, even more joyful gaze.

"At your birthday party, Molly introduced you as Jim. But you corrected it to James. James Feckidee."

She remembered the very conversation I had just heard in my head. "I guess Jim stuck," I muttered. "I certainly didn't want it to stick." I looked away.

"So why did you prefer James?" She had picked up her cold coffee mug, perhaps needing something to stroke. She was staring at me now, but I just raised an eyebrow. "You prefer pomposity," she went on—how did she know that word?—"Academic and whatnot. Can't have a Dr. *Jim* Feckidee, after all." She dropped her voice by an octave and stuck her shoulders out in idiotic parody of a professorial gait—"The test is this Friday; you *will* prepare"—but even in that she was elegant, glorious.

"That doesn't even…"

"Or at the root, perhaps it's some sort of self-hatred," she went on, now her simple self again. "The real you is Jim, but James keeps coming back and beating you up."

"I don't know what you're talking about."

"Jim," she murmured, "I'm only trying to heal you…"

"Oh, is *that* it?"

Her tender smile, like a mother's smile. "…if you want it."

Did I want it? Did I want to be healed by this bohemian child of the brothels and bars, this moonstruck woman, composer of incoherent rhapsodies? I had never known the meaning of *want.* I had never known the meaning of *healing.* I had never known the meaning of *child.*

"You're a beautiful man, James Feckidee."

I sat up, feeling a little warmer, or maybe just warm. I blinked at her. "Beautiful… man?"

"If you would just get over yourself, you would go far."

"I…"

"Or, you might just settle down and go nowhere at all and be happy as a dandelion doing it. Maybe *that's* who you are. Maybe it's running around doing other people's work that's killing you."

How she shimmered through those flames.

"Enough about you." She giggled, then just as fast turned serious again. "Ask me about me."

"Ask you about…?"

Her eyes smiled gently. "Don't you remember how to talk to a girl?"

I didn't. Why would I ask her about her? She was Matt's sister. She did drugs and wrote poems. I knew that. I didn't need to know anything else. I could already see her, could already see her beauty. But maybe she needed…

"Go on," she whispered.

Never mind. I shifted, surveying the mural. "What do you think of this?" I pointed all around.

She sighed and sat back, looking in all directions, clutching the mug two-handed.

"It might sound crazy," I said, "but I'm seeing this thing everywhere."

"Oh, I know." She grinned at me with a strange potential, as if we were both on the same hunt. "So am I."

She waited, but I sank lower into my own reflections. Glancing up, I saw patterns of frustration pass over her face. But she put them aside again, and her eyes calmed and brightened. "I can tell you exactly when it started." She nodded at me, tapping her mug. "I had a dream when was a child. Now, see, I don't usually remember my dreams; when I do, they're just colors and shapes, things I can't explain to other people. But this dream was different. I was down by the shores of Lake Erie. Me and Matt grew up there—but you already knew that. There was a carnival on the beach, and throngs of people were bustling around under a bleached red sun like memory. In the midst of the booths and crowds, ferris wheels and hotdog stands, a gigantic contraption sat half in the water and half on the sand." She looked around the room at the mural. "It wasn't like this, though. It was all red and yellow and tired gold."

"Tired gold?"

She blushed. "You'll have to bear with me. Sometimes I think in metaphors and such."

"I don't mind that at all." I bit my tongue, but said the rest anyway. "It's quite beautiful, actually."

Her downcast lashes brushed soft cheeks. "Thank you," she murmured.

When she had said *tired gold,* the first thing to come to mind had been the wild experience in the woods at Uncle Phil's house, that chase which I denied to be the same as the chase in the woods with Sadie. I should have told her about the connection, but suddenly I felt as bashful as she did. My mind scrambled for something, anything, that would change the subject.

"Could I... see more of your poetry?" I stammered. *Good lord. Flirting with her? Lost your mind? Being a magnanimous ass?*

"Yes!" She beamed at me. "Be right back."

She emerged again from the dark kitchen and threw that knapsack, the sum of her worldly existence, on the low table. She rifled through her shabby ruinous notebooks, muttering and humming to herself. "Here. That's a good one." She passed the twofold mess of papers to me. I took it carefully into my lap.

"Where the red ink starts," she said. "Read that."

> Crosswise and overborne in the brown blowing.
> Gloaming can't hide it, reiterant and pliant.
> It will come to you.
> Ask yourself, under breath and silver sheening,
> Will you deny it?

For a while we didn't look at each other or say anything. She, the artist trying to convince herself that she could take rejection because it was about the work, not about herself, sat with hands folded over one knee, gazing around at the mural. I digested, felt, and thought, as yet incapable of telling her what the poem caused inside of me.

"It's kind of stupid," she muttered at last. "I know it doesn't make any sense—"

"You know it doesn't have to make sense." I couldn't stop my smile. She looked suddenly at me, perhaps for validation. Warmth swept across her face.

"Do you like it?"

"Your poem doesn't give me space to like or dislike it," I said. "It's beautiful."

Her eyes grew red and she murmured, "Thank you, James."

I looked away.

When she spoke after a while, her voice had grown strong again. "So you've been seeing this thing everywhere?" She pointed again at the mural.

Had I? What could I tell her? Nothing, really. I didn't know what I had seen. I had been delirious. The loss of my uncle, the supernatural attack—you know.

"Tell me, James."

"There's nothing to say." I stared at the cookie plate.

"Come on." Her voice was so plaintive that I couldn't help but glance at her. She looked like she was going to cry.

"Well… I…"

She raised her eyebrows and nodded desperately. "Go on!"

"I was with my boy, Austin." Her face softened under a smile at his name. She'd be good with kids if she could just clean up her act. "We were at my uncle's house—the one you've heard us talk about. That's where we were before Matt came and got us and we met you at the church."

"Jim." She laughed at me. "I've been to your uncle's house before."

I was an idiot.

But a strange glow had come into her eye. "So you saw the machine at your uncle's house? That doesn't surprise me at all."

"Not really at the house." What about when Austin and I had dashed inside—but I put *that* away. *That* scared me even more than when we had dashed out into the woods after my boy's second incident with a dead phone. "We saw it out in the woods," I muttered. "Austin led me there. We came to a field, and we saw it."

She was nodding slowly.

"I don't know what happened."

"So *Austin* led you there?"

"Yes. He pulled me—like a little steam locomotive." I laughed.

"And he found the echo in the woods, just today." She was whispering. "He pulled *me* like a little steam locomotive, too. Good heavens, Jim. He senses them."

"I don't think he…" But I knew he; I *knew* he.

She hugged her knees and rocked back and forth, her face ponderous and precocious. "Austin senses the echoes."

And I hadn't even told her about that business when we had first arrived at Uncle Phil's house.

9

I AWOKE IN THE same room, on the same couch, from a sleep unlike any other. Dimly I remembered my conversation with Sadie trailing off last night, but I could not remember anyone building the fire that now lingered in the grate as trembling coals. The diffuse morning sun rendered the mural on the walls all around dense, artistic, but domestic. I could hear dishes clinking in the kitchen over the murmuring hum of a slave song. That was Ihrel's gentle cadence: *Babylon's falling to rise no more… Oh, Jesus, tell you once before… Babylon's falling to rise no more.*

I found Ihrel in the kitchen. She was all smile and warmth. "Morning, Jim!"

"Morning."

"How'd you sleep?"

I actually laughed. "So well, I can't even remember."

"I'm so happy for you! I was going to show you to a bedroom, but you looked so peaceful on the couch that I couldn't bring myself to disturb you."

"Oh, I was quite comfortable."

"And did that fire keep you warm enough?"

"Well… I don't remember feeling cold. In fact, I don't remember anything at all."

"Good!" she laughed. "I'm sure you want breakfast. I'll prepare that in a bit. The coffee is already brewed, though." She dried her hands and took a mug off the rack and took the carafe off the burner. "Black?"

"Black, please." I had not had coffee in several days. Well, perhaps not since yesterday. I think. But in the aura, the very smell, I detected the rush of caffeine.

She poured. "Black it shall be, and this is some of the blackest." She carried the brimming mug to me. I had never seen a head on a cup of coffee before. I had never seen that kind of brewing apparatus either.

I sipped. *Oh, lord.*

"Do you think you can wait for breakfast?" asked Ihrel.

I nodded, still savoring.

"All right. Feel free to go exploring. I won't keep you."

"Where's Austin?"

"In the bedroom at the end of the hall. Just go back into the living room and out the doorway on your right. The hall goes toward the back of the house."

"Thank you."

I wandered. The old floorboards and the lacquerless path worn into them spoke of a building so long ago made home, made refuge, that it had begun to suffer neglect. I did not understand the architecture or the décor. There was something in it of old familiarity, but here it came out skewed, as if some other pull, something alien and far more ancient, had taken that cozy old Americana and spread it like clay.

The strangely carved door to Austin's room opened with a tired creak. I looked in. My son slept on billows of faded homespun. Even the door could not disturb his oblivion.

Past his door, the floor of the hallway rose one step to an even stranger door. Certain of its being locked, I reached in among the carvings and turned the knob. But it was not locked. It swung silently out, and I saw the diffuse and real morning.

I stepped out into the frigid gray. The weathered boards of the deck creaked beneath my feet. I was walking out over a bottomless world of mist. Behind me, the house straddled the edge of the valley; before me, the cliff dropped into obscurity. I could not even see a distinction between land and sky.

Yet even as I stared, the low angle of what must be the sun increased, and a warmer light without direction began to dissolve the mists. As it did, a dark and indistinct hill began to emerge in the clouds perhaps a mile and a half away. I waited, thinking the thinning of the vapors might show me more details of whatever it was. But the mists did not clear any more in the growing light.

Looking down, I saw that the dawn *had* cleared the view closer at hand: several hundred feet below, on the valley floor, I could see the vague forms of trees and gray grass and dark pools of water. The land looked strange and sunken from here, the world of a dream.

I saw a figure down there: a body striding fiercely over the rolling grass between the pools—a tall, determined, and angular form in a brown waistcoat and red tie (the colors cut upwards out of the gray mist)—a heavy head with an oversized brain in a huge shock of white hair—a walk like vision, like derisive know-how—

My god.

"Uncle Phil?"

But he couldn't hear me, so I shouted it. I threw my voice into the valley.

"Uncle Phil! Hey!"

Oblivious and unswayed, the figure battled up a grassy hill.

"Phillip Feckidee! Can you hear me?"

The sun faded and the mists rolled down, gloating, grinning at me. But I caught another glimpse. I memorized him. He was still striding. He was still Phil.

I dashed across the deck. A set of rickety stairs began the long descent to the valley floor. I took the towering steps. I flew down and down, grasping the railing where it was not a splintering disaster. I glanced at the steps and glanced at the valley. I glanced at the steps and glanced at Phil. He was still striding.

I dropped into the cold thick mist where the sun would never come. The dense vapors cut off my view of Phil and everything else. I saw only the rotting steps passing upward beneath me.

How could you have seen him? You can't get a driver's license without glasses, and you don't have them with you. You wore them every day in school so you could read the board from the front row. If that's a few hundred feet down, it's a thousand. How could you have seen a brown waistcoat, much less a red tie?

Uncle Phil. Uncle Phil. I'll find you. Ihrel said you aren't dead. I don't know what I saw in that casket, but I've seen you now.

You *did* see the casket. You saw the brown waistcoat and the red tie there, the things he always wore in life and which, to honor him, they draped on him in death. *In death?*

Dark mists rolled, curled, like billows sweating cold on me.

He was a strong man, an energetic man. Did you attend the burial? No. You left, upset about the picture. Wouldn't it have been in the paper if there had been some sort of mistake, if he had just up and walked? But the attack—the next morning you were rolling up to his abandoned house at dawn, so you never even saw the paper. Ihrel dropped the salad dressing, and you haven't seen her or her husband this morning other than the coffee, and last night it was just you and Sadie, meaning they had plenty of time to discuss it in private and decide how much they would draw you in. And Matt was with them too, wasn't he, if he didn't show with you and Sadie. So it's quite possible that Uncle Phil never…

The hoarse and ragged thrill of my voice fell dead in the density of vapors. "Phil—Phil—Uncle Phil—"

Green grass rose up like just another step. I braked my mad career and came stumbling off the last step into wet, dark weeds. Panting, up again, I could not breathe. This wild phantasmagoric mutation of a lightless day, this stuffed and rendered imitation of a wood. I could not walk between the widespread trees and the lurking pools if I could not see my arm in front of me. It was all goddamnit. "Phil! Phil!" The shouting like sweeping your arm back and forth through deep water—it wasn't so much that the sound didn't go anywhere, but that the heavy solid air wouldn't allow the production of a sound, even the filling of a diaphragm. "Uncle Phil—"

Seeing or blind, I don't know which, I was bounding off through grass the color of pines between pools of still slate. Dripping, dripping. My clothes were already wet. The air itself was a pool. The black, twisted, dripping trunks showed themselves at the last moment. I must have carved out the idiot path of a fly.

"Uncle Phil—"

You never saw him. This heavy mist waits to show you the running trees, so how could it have ever cleared to show you *him* from worlds above? Again, you have followed fantasy. Again, you have taken a glimmer of sight and rammed it through the infantile curves of your desire and you have claimed a reality—only that isn't what you have, and you know it.

But I know I saw him. I saw the brown waistcoat and the red tie and the huge white hair.

Why would he wear the same things he wore in the casket? You've projected your last glimpse of him onto a trick of the mist.

I want to see my uncle.

Then revisit your memory of him at the funeral. That's what you did from the deck.

I stumbled around a tree. The vapors opened out. Phillip Feckidee sat on a black rock, on the broken molar of the earth. He wore his brown waistcoat and his red tie. His stiff white hair defied the dripping mist. His stunningly tall head turned and his dark eyes surveyed me with an interface to unreadable worlds. His foot, pulled up over his knee, twitched and batted fitfully. A slow smile spread in the leather, filling out the lines it had branded into the skin.

"Jim!"

"Uncle Phil!"

He bent and creaked to his feet and opened his arms. I came in. He crushed me in his wiry, tweedy limbs. His smell...

"Just a moment, Jim. If you can't spare me a moment on your own birthday, so that I can bless you with my affection, then I don't know what you can do. You don't understand that Molly prepared all of this for you."

She's too young to love me. We haven't been together long enough.

"Tell that to her. She's been here all day, preparing things while you were in classes."

I just can't stay. Buck and Richard invited me out. It's finals week and everything.

"All right, Jim. I won't badger you any more. Just go. Just get out of here. I don't know when you'll learn."

I do remember how he turned away and went back to fiddling with the wireless. And even as I turned and went back up the basement steps and out the door, I never once heard it come into tune.

"It's good to see you, Jim." His arms were skinny but strong around me: he, my father, my uncle, my all, my adoration and my adoring, who dared to tell me. Dared to tell me I ought to love her better. Dared to tell me to go to school, to study Blake because I loved it not because there was money in it because there wasn't. Dared to tell me. Dared to sit on a black rock in the valley at the bottom of the world in the mountains that didn't exist in the time after the beast, in the time when my time was no more and I was a prisoner to this slow healing, this slow discovery. Dared to tell me by brown waistcoat, by red tie. Dared to tell me by white hair, by incomprehensible indomitable eyes welling with the majesty of the poet's vision. Dared to tell me by Phil himself, by all the means therein and in that grandiose person, that he was Phil, no other, nothing less, nothing more.

His flash grin too white, coming into my eyes, into. I am not ready. Thinking dead, had lost contact with the old honesty, I guess. Not at all ready to touch down again. Floating? Where *have* I gone anyway? Such dependence never shown until the base of it was blown to bits in a dream. It must have been a dream, because he is standing in front of me now, arms around me, and I am sobbing into his shoulder into the scratchy white into the sanctuary white. It hurts me, and his bone hurts me, and I am not, am not, am not dreaming now.

"Oh, Jim. There, there."

There there where he used to throw parties for people who went out to get drunk with false friends instead, where he used to make me read aloud, where I took novels on dictation with no understanding of my instrumentation, where now the cobwebs stretch thick and the dust makes it all gray as if color will never return there except for that flannel shirt—and even that seems faded under years. *There there* is dead now, an empty house not even echoing with the foreign memory of a home, except perhaps in the whisper on the threshold and the breath on the hearth, relics of a far truer home that in effervescent insolence defies the slow mouldering of wood. *There there.* Take me back there, my uncle, my adoring. I am tired and cold and my heart hurts.

"Goddamn." He stood back, still patting my arm with the gigantic gnarled hand that would have written the paeans itself were the mind not damaged beyond repair. "You're here… with *them*… and that means I've already failed." He passed the other hand over his laden brow. I saw the glimmering of tears on his eyelids—lit perhaps from within, for there was no other light source in that close dark land, and his eyes glittered with diamond radiance. "Come on, Jim." He patted me again and turned and began striding into the mist.

Uncle Phil mounted the last step to the deck without fear. The back door opened, and Proton and Sadie came out. It was not shock on Proton's face, but a placid smile, the kind that leads to a handshake. He said, "Glad you're back safely." My Uncle Phil was back and he was safe and they already knew each other as they had long ago in a strange photograph, but I was not afraid of that now; had positively *never* been afraid of that.

"I see I've already failed," said Uncle Phil.

My uncle and Proton moved over to the railing of the deck.

"If he is *here*," said Uncle Phil, "that can only mean that he was attacked. Where's the boy?"

"Inside, asleep," said Proton.

"What are you talking about?" I came over and stood behind them. They waited too long to turn around.

"Jim…" Uncle Phil spoke to me with pain as he had at the birthday party, but now with something like pity, not with the anger of the invested teacher. "Why are you here?"

"A beast attacked me at home, on the night of your funeral. Matt came for some reason, and we drove. We stayed at your house, but it was empty and nasty. We came here. I don't know when that was."

"Any aberrant behavior?" asked Uncle Phil, but to Proton, not to me, as if I wasn't even standing there!

"Some," said Proton. "He and Gaddo maintain that the beast never bit him, though it touched him."

"Good." Strain broke like sweat on Phil's brow. "It could have been far worse."

"You know, I'm right here," I growled. "You can talk to me directly."

"How are you feeling, Jim?" asked Uncle Phil, stepping closer and putting a hand on my forehead. "Heavens, you *are* a bit warm."

"I just ran up thousands of steps after you. Of course I'm warm."

"Your eyes are bloodshot."

That was because I had cried on his shoulder in the valley, but I couldn't say that in front of Proton, in front of Sadie. I don't cry.

"Uncle Phil, I saw you in that casket. You were wearing the same stuff exactly. It was you, I swear. It was your funeral."

"Funeral?" Uncle Phil looked at me strangely, great waves and equations of cognition passing behind his dark eyes. "There wasn't a funeral. I never died." Then his eyes flickered and his jaw dropped a little. "Oh wait." He turned to Proton. "My funeral, and the beast attack the same night? When was that exactly?"

"Three days ago."

"Three days in diurnal rhythm... I've been so long removed from that cycle that I can't... oh, good heavens."

"What?" I shouted, but Uncle Phil brushed past me and strode towards the door.

"Every second is precious, if the beast has been loose for three days."

"The beast can't find them here," said Proton calmly. "You know that."

"Are we going to resolve this thing or not?" Uncle Phil stared at him, not at me, never at me. "They don't want to go on living in hiding here for the rest of their lives." He turned and flung the door open and went inside.

"What is this?" I went after him. I would ply him for everything. "Tell me. I don't understand."

"You wouldn't."

"You never told me!"

His voice echoed through the hall in there. "I couldn't tell you before. I was in the heat of it."

I stomped down the hall. Returning, my precious uncle, and now already talking around me. I'm the foreigner here and I deserve to be filled in, don't I? Am I not a son to you, a confidant, a brother? This is not all over my head, and how dare you do things that I know nothing of?

"Ihrel!" The stepping form of his back and head ducked into the kitchen. I heard the sound of a hug.

"...back safely." She smiled and released him as I came in. She kissed him on the cheek. I *would* possess him.

"It is all falling." Phil helped himself to coffee. "Gods, I need this." He sipped, and a tremor ran through him.

"James said you died," said Ihrel, but she didn't look at me in speaking my real name, even though I was just on the other side of the table.

"Right. And that seems to have lined up with the breaking I experienced. I had the dark servant in a stranglehold—for years, perhaps. Then he broke out, and others pursued me. It all coincides, but I need to know more. There are still questions."

Proton and Sadie spilled in around me. Sadie touched my hand, then touched it again and held it. "What's happening?" she said in a quiet voice.

"A lot," said Phil, turning and looking at us at last.

A lot that you never told me. All these years, I thought I had you. I thought you were dedicated to me, but you were working in secrecy behind my back on things you never meant to tell me. *Never meant to tell me!* I can't believe you. Who are you anyways?

Phil swayed like he might fall. Ihrel gasped and caught him. Proton bounded around the table and caught him. Together, they lowered him into a chair.

"Nothing at all," he bellowed, eyes wide and roaming, a look of old fighting on his face. "I'm just dreadfully hungry. I haven't eaten in years."

"I'll make breakfast right away," said Ihrel.

Good lord, it *had* been years. He had taken sick upon Austin's birth.

"Did they hurt you?" asked Proton.

The white head fell heavy on the table and the voice rang in the wood. "They tortured me."

After he got some food into him, Uncle Phil went straight to bed. Proton helped him up and out into the hall. I should have helped, but there were so many in me, and all at war. I forgot my allegiances in that time.

"Who is my uncle?" I said weakly, without looking at anyone.

"The greatest fold-traveler alive," said Ihrel from across the table.

"I thought he was a writer."

"Of course. But what did he write? Stories of other worlds. And the best writers write what they know."

"You mean… those novels…"

She nodded.

10

MATT FOUND ME kicking around the gardens outside the house. The gray day had grown no brighter and no more colorized. It was the bleak cold dawn of a strange new history, a narrative in which my uncle was not the man I had always known. So there was no point, and I don't know what Matt was looking for.

He had followed me outside and stood now, hands in pockets, on the other side of a ruinous and vine-encumbered azalea. Without looking at me, he said, "I've been silent for too long."

"What?"

He shot me a quick glance. "Want to go for a walk?"

I didn't say *not really*. This guy had saved me, and I had lost touch with him, if I had ever been in touch with him at all. So I owed it to him.

"Come on." Matt turned and stepped over the dense fallen wildflowers and struck off up the slope into the towering pines. Feeling strangely nothing at all but loyalty, I went after him. We moved in a slow world of mist, and we did not stop when the house disappeared behind us.

"This has changed everything," said Matt, striding with a quiet *swish-swish* through the pine needles, leaving me to trot along two steps behind. "I'm finding my calling, Jim. From the moment I woke up on the night of the beast, the sense of purpose was present and complete. It hasn't let up."

"It's only been a few days," I muttered.

"Look at me," said Matt, without turning to offer the view. "You know me. You know my depression."

"Maybe you're just..." I was going to say *having a good day,* but the words had a vicious ring in my head. "Maybe you're... growing. Stumbling towards something."

"Aren't you, too?"

We stepped fast and fearless over the mouldering trunks of fallen pines. *Growing.* I remembered that feeling. I remembered the sense of potential, of good things developing. I had almost smelled it a few years ago. I had sensed it when I met Molly. I had sensed it when I started school. Good god, I had changed.

"I don't know," I muttered. "If I'm stumbling towards anything, it may just be my death. Sometimes that's all I have to look forwards to."

Matt said nothing but veered off suddenly towards mounting higher ground. The sun was lost, and the new elevation brought no clarity to the gray armies of the woods. If anything, the day was getting darker and drippier with the heights we climbed.

"So you want to die?" said Matt.

The words welled up. "The sum of what's gone into me is so great that I can't bear it alone and no one will help me because no one *can* help me."

"The sum of what's gone into you, huh?" He walked on with no hesitation. I looked back. I did not know the land. The house was already out of sight. I was cold. I wanted to go back and talk to Uncle Phil. But Matt went on. "The sum of what's gone into you. What about the sum of what's gone *out* of you?"

"I don't know what you mean."

"Sure, you need saving, Jim; but so does everybody else."

"I can't save anyone. I'm too crushed inside."

"So is everyone else."

"Goddamnit, Matt."

"Do you expect *me* to save you? Do you expect Sadie to save you? Do you expect Uncle Phil?"

"Goddamnit!"

To tell me that I am *that* fundamentally alone and lost—on a day like this, when my uncle is miraculously back but not really, when he turns out to be something I never knew and still don't—did Matt have any concept of what an agony it is for me to think and feel? Had he dwelt in my soul with me on the dark nights, in the waste places, in the deserts without water?

As I stormed off to the right over falling open ground and long dead gray grass, something like a voice said to me, *have you ever dwelt in his soul with him?*

"No!" I shouted. And glancing over my shoulder to the left, I saw Matt still toiling up the ramp of the land. The growing wind with its scent of a cold rain whipped at his jacket and his bowed and determined black hair.

"I will die," I heard myself mutter. "I will die. I will kill it all."

If you die, said the woods, *we will never acknowledge you. We will never take your atoms unto our roots, for we can draw no sustenance from you, O abomination of your race.*

The wind broke the mist at last, but the rain swept down in its place. I tripped in the holes and careened through the nettles. Ahead, in the breaking trees, I saw the broken sky.

He had left me. Last refuge, he had spoken like nettles. You are this, you are that. It's all your fault that you want to die. You haven't given enough. Given? What is there to give? When I give away my void, it kills other people too. So don't tell me I haven't given. I've given exactly and precisely what I am.

Then why do you need something more?

"Shut up!"

My shriek did not sound like me as it rebounded off the trees and the coming curtains of rain. I blundered through the briars and fell forward with the falling ground. The rain lashed me and the prickers came out to find me.

If there is no Uncle Phil, if there is no Matt Gaddo, then what is there? I am lost. I am alone. I am without foundation, and so are they; and thus we are all so dreadfully lost and alone. *Goddamnit.* Where are you going, you idiot. *Goddamnit.* Even Sadie can't save me? She should. What is she there for? And they both start with *say.* That ought to count for something. Where are you going. Go back. Talk to Phil. You're overreacting.

The trees broke and I stood in a bleak and tilted corridor of the land.

Under the beaten grass, under the beating rain and amongst the hesitant saplings, twin sets of rusted rails carved off straight to left and right. The open sky was a blasted and hopeless brow. There was nothing but a glimmer of red down on the tracks. In the blear of my weeping and the sobbing skies, I could not make it out from here. So I pitched down through the grasping weeds, down the embankment, to the tracks.

A rotting chair sat squarely between the rails, twined with nettles and the red of autumnal poison ivy. Sure, the tracks were overgrown, but wasn't there always a possibility?

I stood staring at that chair. Oh angel of death, work swiftly. Take me out of this gargantuan shifting, this endless recombination. If there is no stillness in life, I choose *other*—or, if it must be, nothingness. Oh, give me a train.

Crosswise and overborne in the brown blowing. I forget the rest. *Gloaming can't hide it, reiterant and pliant. It will come to you.* I can't remember the rest. Oh, yes you can. *Ask yourself, under breath and silver sheening, will you deny it?*

The twist and crunch of broken saplings. I spun left, but it was not a train. Matt was stepping slowly down out of the woods, looking at me, then away, then back at me. When at last he stood beside me, hands still hidden in pockets, we said nothing to each other. We just stood together and felt the rain.

"You know," he muttered, "the longing for death is not unholy."

I looked at the chair between the rails. It would make no difference if I got poison ivy from it.

"We've come to the right place, Jim."

I looked at him, surprised. "You want to die, too?"

"No." He frowned. "I meant this place, with Proton and everyone else."

I turned back to the chair. For a moment, I had thought he was with me.

"Proton was talking about renewal," he went on, as if to himself, "cleansing the planet. I'm not quite sure what he meant."

"Nothing can be cleansed," I muttered.

"Can't you tell that something's missing? Our life is like a sentence without a subject."

"I write those all the time," I growled, though I had never done that, and it was just for show.

"I feel it," he went on, oblivious of me, always oblivious. "The first hint of a subject came when I woke up on the night of the beast."

"Good for you," I muttered.

"No, Jim." He turned and, for the first time I can ever remember, looked me full in the face without immediately looking away. "Good for all of us."

We locked eyes. I didn't know why I was wrestling with his spirit—probably just for show. But then I quit. "I'm going back." I turned away, but he caught my arm in a vicegrip of love.

"No. Come with me further into the woods." Again he looked me plainly in the face. I turned back and crossed the tracks with him and we tore down through the underbrush on the other side.

"That's why you need to be here," Matt grunted, hands in pockets again, looking straight ahead again. Up there, the pines were opening out. On the left lay the void of the mist. Somewhere in front of us, the lights of Proton and Ihrel's house winked through the trees. The sound of a child's laughter rang there too—the sound of a child—the sound of my son, my son.

I walked faster and passed Matt. I was so hungry. I carved through the red and yellow poison ivy in the straggling thickets under pines. The trees failed. I saw Austin and Sadie on the gray slant of the land, in the weed-eaten gardens of the house, bouncing a red rubber ball. I walked and ran and wept. I could see nothing through the gray rain of my eyes but that red ball, moving, moving.

Never mind the failures, the way I had ignored my boy of late, the way I had been stuck on myself. Oh, he was in my arms and he was laughing; he was joy. I would begin fathering, and I would begin now. I held him tight. I knew my impossibility. I knew my internal lies. I knew my staggering disconnect from the world around me. I saw no remedy, no true and lasting remedy, but I saw the need of it at last. And I would start, empowered by something I did not know, by making myself lowly and smiling about it.

"Austin! Buddy!"

"Ha! Ha!" He giggled, twisted, wormed. Then he saw my face. "Why are you crying, daddy?"

"Even daddies have to cry sometimes," said Sadie. Her blue eyes were glowing.

"She's... right," I burbled.

Sadie touched my arm. "Your uncle was asking for you."

"Really?" The way he'd been talking, I thought he had found more interesting things to ask about. But I should have known he would never change *that* much.

"Oh!" she laughed. "Silly man. You missed lunch."

"I thought so." My stomach had given up on growling a while ago. "Is Uncle Phil all right?"

"He just had to rest a little," said Sadie. "Come on." She took my arm and led me through the dying flowerbeds.

From the first opening of the door, I heard him shouting. When we came into the living room, his voice rang with an immensity that almost caused his graphite delineations to dance from the walls.

"You know that when I first saw it, it was larval, a black and white skeleton, even as I drew it here." My uncle sat spread across an easy chair, pointing around the room. "I was shown a glimpse of its becoming, when in the fullness of its maturation it would colorize itself in red and yellow, brown and gold. But it wasn't *that* when I first came to its fold some sixty years ago." He looked up at me, dark eyes darting with purpose under lenses. "Jim. Welcome." He nodded at the Gaddos, too preoccupied to pull up their names—these, the youngest generation of his children, these who had *not* been there on the winter days in his study and had *not* taken books on dictation through long hours of a cramped hand and eyes stinging with ink, white, ink, white...

"But I swear to you, I stumbled across its fold again as I fought," he went on. "I know the way back now. The machine is no longer larval; it is full, but dark and gray, a printing press of vast proportion. It is the words coming out of it that are fire and pounding gold."

"Has Vaulan changed form *again?*" Ihrel whispered.

"It looks that way," said Uncle Phil. "However, this is just another way in which he is still machine; so in a sense, he hasn't changed at all. Anyway, while I was in that fold, I saw the work of the printing press that Vaulan now is. The writings coming off the press bear a strange and startling resemblance to my work: in fact, Jim, to work that you took on dictation…"

I frowned.

"…which leads me to believe that the answer to our question may lie in one of my books. There's nothing else it could have meant."

"If you saw Vaulan, why didn't you ask him to return to earth?" said Proton.

Uncle Phil blinked at him. "What are you talking about?"

"I think you're answering the wrong question."

"Well then, what's the question?" growled Phil.

"The question is, can we persuade Vaulan to return and cleanse this planet?" said Proton.

"Oh." Uncle Phil shifted and blinked, big lids covering and showing big brown eyes. "My running into Vaulan was just incidental. I thought the question was how best to protect Austin."

The boy looked up at me, grinning.

"That may be incidental," said Proton.

"Or it may not be," said Sadie. She was joining in, as if she knew. "Austin led me to the echo in the park."

Phil flung one leg over the other, pleats all over his body splaying like genius, crooked finger jabbing at her. "And *that* is our strongest clue. We have *never* seen this kind of targeting before."

"Targeting?" I mumbled.

Phil nodded. "Yes sir."

My knees were getting a little weak. It must have shown, for Ihrel jumped up from the couch and said, "Sit down, Jim. I'll get some chairs from the kitchen." Bustling out of the room, she muttered something like, "Oh, and you weren't here for lunch."

I stepped over legs and the coffee table and flopped into the cushions.

"It doesn't target Austin," said Matt, as if he knew things too. "It targets Jim alone."

"Explain." Phil gazed at him ravenously.

"When I came to Jim's house, the beast was chasing him from door to door, as I said. Jim had moved Austin down the basement, probably in an attempt to protect him."

How dare he. I was in the room, you know.

"Austin was sleepwalking," Matt went on. "He went up the basement steps and opened the back door. But the beast didn't come for him; it only came when Jim went to the door to get him."

"Now see, that doesn't work." Phil shook his head, but his white frizz refused to move independently. "The boy's birth coincided with the first movement of the dark servant. When Austin was born, we realized that we had to take action at once or else consign him to certain and immediate death. That was why I left."

"What are you talking about?" I said.

Phil regarded me coolly. "Jim. They told me that I was sick for four years on this earth."

I nodded. "I moved you into hospice. Your house is still sitting empty…"

"I wasn't sick. I was in another dimension, if you will; another reality—another fold, to use the technical term. I was protecting your boy from the beast."

With the jitter and yet the self-assurance of an old man, he began unbuttoning his waistcoat, then his shirt. He tore his clothing open. His old and failing torso bore the crossed, scarred lacerations of claws. I felt my breath fail me and my eyes roll into the back of my head.

"Just needs to eat."

They were touching me. Cold, wet. They were touching me. The women's faces, twofold salvific beauty. The smell of something hot and edible.

"Just get him something to eat."

Sadie was holding Austin now, on the other end of the couch. Austin was looking at me with fear. At his own father, and fear. They were touching me. Phil was gone. Proton was gone. I could hear Phil's voice in the kitchen. He was shouting.

Then which question is it? I had no intention of messing up your plan. We must have miscommunicated.

"There, there." Ihrel was feeding me, but I was not a child.

"I got this." I scrambled to sit up. I was very weak, but I scrambled to sit up.

"Easy there, Jim."

"It's James."

"Let him feed himself," said Sadie.

"I got this." I took the bowl and spoon and fed myself. I was *not* a child. But I did make a mess.

That's pure arrogance, my friend. I understand your mission, and yes, we agreed on it—

I felt Sadie's gaze like calm but probing points. When I turned my head, chewing fitfully, I saw that her eyes were bent on me with a care that must have slumbered till she met me. She said, "You're really having a rough time, aren't you?"

"I got this." I fed myself.

My goal was never to ask Vaulan to return. My goal was to protect the boy.

I understand that, Phil. I'm asking you to go back to that fold and try. That's all.

No one said anything. Uncle Phil and Proton came back in from the kitchen. Uncle Phil glanced at me. "You don't look too good, Jim." Then he addressed Matt. "You're certain the beast never bit him—never broke skin?"

"As far as I know," said Matt.

"And I caution you to sift ego from truth," Proton went on, towards Phil, always towards Phil. "That business about a printing press and *your* words smacks of ego."

"Got it," said Phil, swatting as if at a fly.

11

THE DISCUSSION BROKE up. Proton and Phil seemed to have come to some impasse that was beyond my comprehension. Proton went into the kitchen, saying it was his turn to make dinner. Sadie and Ihrel took Austin outside. I don't know where Matt went. Soon it was just Uncle Phil and I sitting under the brooding lines of the mural. It was strangely like old times, yet strangely unfamiliar.

"You're probably confused," said Uncle Phil.

I nodded. I didn't even know what to say to him.

"I don't blame you," he went on. "It's a strange reality."

"You never told me," I said quietly.

He glanced at me, and I saw strain in his face. "I *couldn't* tell you. Had I given you any notion of the fact that a beast was seeking your son, the beast would have preyed upon those inklings of fears in your mind. You can't imagine the metaphysical structures involved. I had to protect you. That's why I appeared to be sick in the body, while in reality, I was endlessly battling the enemy."

I just blinked at him.

"Had I told you, the beast would have sensed your knowledge. I would have been even less capable of containing it."

"But you *couldn't* contain it."

"Right. But in the long run, it turns out not to matter, because you made it here. You do realize, though, that you were in real danger."

"Of course."

He looked away, still nodding. "I confess, I don't know how we're going to make this right. Proton is fixated on the notion of me asking the machine—Vaulan, I mean—to return to earth and cleanse the planet." He shook his head. "Proton's brushstrokes are too broad. There is a boy to save, the son of my great-nephew. To be honest, I don't give a…" He stopped himself, tapping his chin. "Although I suppose his goal is plenty noble as well. Maybe I just don't feel up to it." He looked sharply at me. "Anyway, I'm returning to the portal tree tonight. I'm going back to that fold, if I can find it again, and asking Vaulan to return to earth. You see, Jim, I'm the only one who can enter and use the portal. It's some Feckidee strangeness. I wouldn't be surprised if you had it too, or Austin—probably Austin." He sank lower into the chair. "Anyway, I *have* to go. It's for the common good. I'm not too proud to do it, though Proton *is* being a bit of an ass about it." Suddenly he looked at me again with glimmers of the old tenderness around his eyes. "How are you, Jim? How are you holding up?"

"I'm not," I muttered. I did not fear him in my deepest heart, so I said, "Earlier, when I went on a walk with Matt, I wanted to die. Really wanted to die."

"Jim, that won't do."

"I don't feel that way any more."

"Why did you want to die?"

"You see…" I stumbled towards expression. "Something is missing."

He stared at me, waiting.

"The point, the good part, is missing."

He began to nod.

"Matt said our life is like a sentence without a subject…"

Now he nodded gravely. "Ah, I wish you could fold-travel, Jim. I wish you could see Vaulan in the flesh."

Again I looked around the room at the terrifying machinations of the mural. "What *is* Vaulan, Uncle Phil?"

"Oh, Vaulan." He shook his head, seeming to brood over many thoughts. At last he chose one to articulate. "Vaulan is a manifestation, but not the source. An instrumentation, if you will—the latest iteration; yet at the quick, non-iterating." He glanced at me, as if to check for comprehension.

"I don't know what that means."

"Vaulan… is… a structure self-built for us." He looked away, frowning, scrambling for frameworks I might understand. "It isn't the source or the ending, but rather the form of the tool into which it has put itself for our better use."

"Is it… some sort of God?"

"No. Your *God* is some sort of *it*."

"I don't believe in God."

"Irrelevant. Your projections of deity are a dim sloughing-off, like throwing mud on an infinite wall in an attempt to strengthen it against the storm. Vaulan does not need your belief for himself to go on existing."

"I'll believe in the existence of this *Vaulan* when I see it," I muttered.

"You *have* seen it, and you will see it again. Furthermore, you've had it on good faith from a trustworthy source." He pointed around at the mural. "*I* have seen this thing in the flesh."

"Why does it matter what I think of it?" I asked.

"Cosmically, it doesn't. That's what I was saying. If you want to go on complaining about sentences without subjects, do it. Vaulan goes on without you, though he *will* grieve for you."

"Is Vaulan the *subject*, then?"

He beamed at me. We had always spoken the same language of interconnected allusion that no one else understood. "If I could say yes with certainty, he would no longer be the subject, would he?"

I frowned, grasping for our old way of thinking, our old understanding.

"Certainty is the end of investigation," Uncle Phil went on. "Investigation is the whole motivation of a sentence—even of a declarative, because a declarative seeks relationship in asking to know the response to its declaration. The end of the declaration is the end of the investigation is the end of the sentence is the end of the purposiveness of the subject."

I stared. To think we had once had this kind of conversation all the time! It was a foreign language to me now.

"That's why he is always changing, which is why I said that the machine, Vaulan, is just an instrumentation and not the indivisible essence of the source."

"I don't understand."

"Right now, Vaulan is a mechanism. Decipher him." Uncle Phil settled down into the chair and began immediately to doze off.

I tried to connect this man to the Uncle Phil I had known, but it was hard. Ihrel had said something about those books being *true*, as if he had really seen the madness he had dictated to me; but somehow, I just couldn't accept it. Most puzzling was his fixation on this god or being, this creature or machine, called Vaulan. Uncle Phil had said that Vaulan was the instrumentation, but not the source—perhaps a form, but not a function. All right, but why a machine? I saw no need for that.

At Uncle Phil's house, on the first dawn after the beast, I had met something deeper in the hallway, and again in the empty grate among the gray ashes. But I didn't know what to think of it now. Oh, and in the woods, I had found a farm machine or something. Was that what Uncle Phil meant by "you *have* seen it"? Really, I hadn't seen a thing. He was wrong. But... had Austin seen? There was no denying the way he had led Sadie through the woods.

I studied my uncle. His lungs raised and lowered his folded hands in a peaceful cadence. He looked old, even tired, but not ungrateful. How was it that he continued to ooze purpose and direction, even after a false death? And how was it that he was alive at all? I remembered how it had all started.

"Jim. He's taken sick." The voice of my father, metallic in the phone.

What do you mean? I asked.

"We need an ambulance, boy, or we gonna hafta drive him ourselves."

Now, after my wife has just given birth to a son. Now, when I am already in over my head. Can't you take him? I'm caring for a newborn here.

"Jim, I can't carry him to the car all by myself."

Carry him?!

"He aint movin. He's in bed, wearin a heavy hell of a coat, and under all the covers too."

But I just talked to him yesterday. I was over there yesterday, and he was just as fresh as ever.

"Well, he's cold as ice now, but he aint dead. He breathes once every couple seconds."

All right. I'm coming. Just let me get Austin out of bed.

"What? Where's your wife, boy?"

She isn't here!

You know, the car didn't start that day either. And you would think that a mother with a baby only a month old would have been at home, doing baby things. But it was already so hard for her to be around me that she was off at her own mother's house, abandoning her role of mothering my son to be mothered herself, selfish whore. And I had *chosen* her! But I held the boy Austin wrapped tight like a little Jesus, and I started the car by myself.

"Mr. Feckidee, he has been vegetative for three years."

What are you saying? Can't he stay that way?

The faceless doctor shifted the clipboard and blinked nervously. "In the scope of things, Mr. Feckidee—his contribution to society, balanced with his cost—"

Are you really?

"I'm not talking about euthanasia."

Then what are you talking about? This is one of the greatest writers, one of the greatest minds, that has ever lived. And he's my great-uncle.

"Mr. Feckidee, I need not remind you that the patient was diagnosed with alexia twelve years ago, after the stroke—"

He never had a stroke!

"—meaning the patient could not read or write."

He dictated to me, you idiot. He spoke whole novels to me and I wrote them down. Go look them up. They're in the library. They're at the bookstores. He never had a stroke. He disappeared for a few years, that's all.

Then I was waking up. Proton was shaking my arm gently. "Come on, James. Dinner is ready." I roused myself and got up. I hadn't meant to sleep. Uncle Phil was gone, but I heard voices in the kitchen.

"Jim is a poet," said Uncle Phil, eyes flashing at me as he passed the butter. We were all seated and starting to eat.

"I'm not a poet," I snorted.

"What sort of poetry do you write?" asked Ihrel.

"I'm being cruel," said Uncle Phil.

"I write about other people's poetry," I said. "I'm working on a doctorate in literature. My thesis is on *The Book of Urizen*, by William Blake."

Ihrel nodded.

"I'll take the butter," said Sadie.

"My sister writes too," said Matt. "She would never tell you, though."

"Of course not," said Uncle Phil. "Writers never give themselves away. There's nothing to talk about regarding writing. The writer writes, and the reader reads. Preferably, the relationship never comes down to personal interaction, as that is just plain difficult when you're more intelligent than everyone around you."

We all laughed. God, he had always had that arrogant, lovable sense of humor.

"When the reader doesn't read, we hit him," Uncle Phil went on. "Then we go back and rewrite and make it even more difficult to understand. *See what you missed? Should have gotten it the first time!*"

Matt alone wasn't laughing, but rather looking at Uncle Phil with puzzlement.

"I'm being cruel," said Uncle Phil.

"You do that a lot, don't you?" said Matt.

"Watch it, young man!"

Austin burst into laughter, triggering laughter in all the grownups.

"There's no laughing at me!" Phil spoke in a pompous voice and poked Austin in the ribs. "I'm an old man! Humph-da-humph."

"Pass the salad, please," said Matt.

"What do you write about, Sadie?" asked Ihrel.

"Oh dear." Sadie blushed a little. "Didn't you hear what Phil said? There's nothing to talk about!"

"You should read her poetry," I said. "It's excellent." That thing about *reiterant and pliant* was still ringing in my head.

"Oh, Jim," Sadie murmured.

"What happens when a writer *isn't* read?" asked Proton, laying into his mashed potatoes.

"Suicide," said Phil loudly.

Matt frowned at him, then glanced at me as if to check my emotional pulse.

"I'm being cruel," Uncle Phil laughed. "Sorry. That was a bit much."

"Just remember the boy," Ihrel murmured.

Austin grinned.

"But seriously: rewriting," said Phil.

"What do you write, Uncle Phil?" asked Sadie.

"Ha!" He sat back, laughing, chewing loudly. "Nothing, these last four years."

"Before that?"

"Lots of things. Some poetry, some essays and philosophical rants… incoherent babblings, chips-on-the-shoulder against the prevailing worldview. Oh, and memoirs. That's what Jim took on dictation when he was a kid."

Choked on my food—*memoirs?!*

"You all right there, Jim?"

"Get him some water."

Clearing my throat, speaking in a skeleton voice. "Memoirs?! I thought you wrote science fiction novels!"

"Good heavens, no." He was laughing uproariously. "They were all in first person, and they all used my name."

"But… I thought you were making things up!"

He shook his head. "I'm not *that* creative. The only talent I ever had was in passing things on."

We lounged at the table for a long time afterwards, stuffed and half-sleepy, tired of munching on cookies and unaffected by the coffee. The windows were dark, and a fitful wind was trying to get in at the failing seals. Above and around it all, my uncle was not a writer of science fiction, but of memoirs. My uncle was a madman, a genius, a victim.

"So," said Proton, looking at Uncle Phil.

"Right." Phil stirred but didn't get up.

"Maybe he needs to rest, dear," said Ihrel. "He *did* just come back from a long hard fight."

"Oh, I can do this." Uncle Phil stood resolutely and patted where his belly should have been. "Let's get this over with."

I stood up and followed him towards the coat rack and the door. It was going to be a blustery night. Suddenly I couldn't remember if I had brought a coat, and if I had, what it looked like. But then someone handed me a fur-lined jacket that wasn't mine, and I saw my uncle take down a long black coat from the rack, and I remembered laying that coat in the back of the car when we had left his house. He put it on now, black over his brown tweed, forever blind to the rules of fashion.

"Where are we going?" I muttered as he brushed past me.

"To the portal tree," he said, stumping down the hall towards the back of the house.

A flashlight popped on ahead of us, and the carved shadows of the back door turned in strange projection. A form obscured the door, the form of my uncle, I'm sure. The knob clanked and the door opened. A cold wind came in.

We filed out onto the deck. The wind had blown the mists away at our level, and only a few haggard clouds fled the stars. But low on the horizon across the deck, the stairs failed in the first hint of black haze, surely the roof of the indestructible wrack filling the valley below. I was only guessing in the dark, though.

"Easy," said Matt's voice. "How many lamps do we have?"

"Two," said Proton.

"We need more," said Matt. "We're all here. We'll never make it on those stairs."

"I'll see if I can dig something up," said Proton. He went back inside and came out again a few minutes later. "We did have two more." He turned them on and passed them out. I didn't get one, probably because I was carrying Austin. Uncle Phil was already heading down the steps, his lamp disappearing below the deck into the gloom.

We set off down the steps in single file. To think I had run down these in the half-light! Now they were damp and slippery, and the flashlight beams showed new dangers every moment. Of course I ended up between the Gaddos, not behind Phil; Sadie was in front of me, Matt behind me. Each had a light, and the discolored beams mingled into something like gold cutting the black gray, a summation diligent to keep me informed. Now and again, as the steps twisted, I saw the strange halo and globe below at turned angles, bobbing, bobbing, trotting down and down, ahead of the rest of us, doubtless taking two steps at a time: fearless, proud, beautiful old Uncle Phil.

"Daddy, it's dark."

"I know." I held Austin more tightly with one arm, gripping the splintery rail with the other. "I got you."

"Are you going to cry again?"

I stiffened as I felt tears cloud my vision. I *had* failed him. "No, buddy. I got you."

"Your daddy's a very brave man," said Sadie in front of us. "Don't be afraid if he cries sometimes."

"But daddies aren't supposed to cry."

"Oh yes they are," she said.

Good thing it was dark and the mist was already obscuring my vision.

The last time I looked, the farthest lamp, far below, had already stopped moving. It was now the rest of us and our dim train of globes that snaked and turned and dropped down and down. Then finally Sadie was stepping onto the stark gray blowout and shadow of what had been green grass in daylight. I was next, and I was not ashamed to stand still for a moment, relishing solid ground that didn't creak and splinter. But then the lamps were collecting together, a strange constellation of four soft gigantic stars. I had to blunder towards them.

"Everybody here?" said Uncle Phil's voice.

A lamp lifted and turned my whole vision into a white sheet. I covered my eyes. "Watch it…"

"All right." Uncle Phil again. The white sheet dissipated and became a globe. The globe dimmed with turning and struck off into the mist. The other stars followed, then two slowed—the Gaddos—until I was between them again. Matt was bringing up the rear.

"Lovely night," I heard Ihrel say.

"I know," Sadie murmured. The voices were close and clear, as if we were indoors, as if in a small padded room.

"The funny thing is that I know my way in the dark," said Uncle Phil from up ahead.

Matt's lamp made white moving bones of Sadie's heels and shoes. She moved as I moved as we all moved.

"Daddy… are there monsters out here?"

"No, Austin." I held him tight.

"But what if there are monsters out here?"

"I got you, Austin." I held him tight.

"Watch." Phil's lamp had stopped ahead. "The ground is narrow up here."

We collected behind him. The grass bottlenecked between black and formless pools.

"Just walk straight, and you'll be fine," said Uncle Phil.

He was going on again. On the other side, black branches groped down in the coronal flare of the lamps, gathering so close that they formed almost a doorway through which we squeezed.

I was stumbling and shivering in the mist when something began to change. The vapors ahead glowed with the faintest remembrance of an aura, and the grass beneath our feet became composed, laden, reverent. Walking became more like gliding, like floating. The air took on an ancient poignancy, the fragrance perhaps of a time when the earth was a newborn organism circling mother sun.

The glow was all around us now. It was so faint that I only saw it when I turned my eyes away from the flat mist-shapes of the bulbs. Ahead, I saw a shadowy tree trunk at uncertain distance, floating and not passing by as the trunks usually did. Then I realized that it was gigantic and quite far off and not a tree at all, but rather something with the girth of a skyscraper. The ground was still rising, the grass still rejoicing at our passage.

My peripheral vision said there was a dark formation on our left. I denied it, but it would not quit. Rising steadily out of the earth, it soon claimed to be a wall, yet a wall with the old organic defiance that refused Pythagoras and even the faintest gasps of rectilinearity. Having no lamp myself, I could not get a good look at its texture, but knew only its looming and inescapable presence, rising taller and taller in strange undulations as we advanced towards the towering shadow in the mist.

I heard Uncle Phil say "My country," with a melancholia reserved for privacy, with the loudness that the old do not realize they use for their muttered thoughts.

When the black shadow filled our whole view, we suddenly hit a patch of steep ground. We mounted up and stood within a declivity where the wall on the left at last met the dark, towering form. The lamps turned down to our feet. In some strange mingling of that reflected light and the fainter general diffusion, I saw the silhouettes of all the heads.

"Here we are," said Uncle Phil.

I stepped out of the rings of light and ran my hand along the wall, then along the face of the shadow that filled all my vision. I felt the ancient defense, the insect-battling, the cold-repelling, the living leather of a tree. The girth of its trunk blocked my entire view.

Phil handed his light to Ihrel. She shut it off, and the others did likewise. The night became colder and quieter and the silhouettes of their humanity hardened and darkened against the general gray. I didn't know where the diffuse light in the mist was coming from.

I saw Uncle Phil's form turn and mount the steep ground up to the trunk. There, against blackness, I could almost see a darker crevice, a crack perhaps in that gargantuan and ancient tree. Whether by sight or by some other sense, I knew when he had stepped inside.

He wasn't gone more than a few moments before there was a sound—actually the strangling of his voice—and the dim white of his hair came flying out and he was in a heap at our feet. "Good god—good god—"

"What happened?!"

"Phil!"

"Uncle Phil!"

"I can't. I can't."

My hands gripped him. I tried to pull him up. He was shuddering.

"What happened?" I shrieked.

"The portal is corrupted…" He wheezed and rocked. There was wet on my hands, dark warm wet.

"I don't understand," said Proton.

"My words, black. Black terror. You know the lacerations? Good lord…"

"What are you talking about?" said Matt from the side.

Phil stood but collapsed immediately against me. *Now* he needed me.
"The false vision." He shook his head. "Don't ever."
"Let's get him back to the house," said Proton.
"Good lord," said Uncle Phil.

12

IN THE CRAZED BLEAR of the kitchen light, Uncle Phil was a haggard mask drained of all vitality. He was bleeding a little, too, but we could not seem to find the wound. He sat now at the table across from Proton. Ihrel was brewing tea for the intrepid traveler, perhaps for the rest of us too.

"Tell us again what happened," said Proton. "You opened the portal—"

"Yes." Uncle Phil nodded fiercely. "I opened the portal. After a little searching, I saw the fold where I thought Vaulan was. It looked like the same fold I had found long ago. Since it was the last place I had gone before coming home yesterday, its trail was still warm, so to speak. It wasn't hard to find." He stopped, positively gasping for breath.

Proton nodded. "So you willed and entered that fold—"

"I found not the god Vaulan, not our beloved machine, but the printing press I saw earlier," said Uncle Phil, "only now it was black, made of knives, spewing black words of hatred—*my* words, you understand, transfigured again as they were the first time, but now in the opposite direction. They cut me, my own words, my expressions that had become knives."

His head fell onto his arm on the table.

Proton shook his head. Looking across at me, he mouthed the word *arrogance.*

"Phil," said Ihrel as she poured the hot water over the tea bags, "I don't know how to say this, but… I don't think that was Vaulan. He would never spew words of hatred, or knives, or whatever, at anyone other than the enemy, or one who had become *like* the enemy. And he specifically became machine to abandon the darkness he once had as the Great Stone, since now the enemy has claimed darkness for itself."

"I understand that," said Phil. "But I tell you, this is the same fold where I saw Vaulan. I don't know why the vision changed."

"So…" said Proton, shaking his head. "According to you, the god Vaulan, our lover, became machine some time ago. Now, more recently, you found him again. He was still machine, but more specialized, more specific—a printing press, happening to print *your* words as living fire. And now, most recently, this printing press has turned black and has begun spewing destructive words like knives, which, as before, you recognize as your own."

Uncle Phil nodded, face still hidden.

"Phillip, I don't like to say this…"

Uncle Phil's shoulders stopped rising and falling.

"I think your ego has clouded the vision."

I waited. I had never heard anyone say something so bold to my uncle. But Phil sat up and looked at Proton with sad, blank eyes.

"You see what I'm saying?" Proton murmured.

Uncle Phil grabbed the string of his teabag and began bouncing it fitfully, frowning through the steam.

"I suppose you didn't ask Vaulan to return to earth," said Proton.

"You can't ask anything of your own ego," Phil muttered.

"So the portal is corrupted," said Ihrel, looking at her husband. "This really makes things difficult."

"Forgive me," said my uncle. His face was breaking, as if he would weep. "I have ruined the whole operation. I am such an idiot. I don't know where I got that vision, or whatever I saw…"

"When did you first stumble across the fold that you thought held the god Vaulan?" asked Matt, leaning forward with glittering eyes.

"Once in my youth, when I saw in the flesh what I drew on the walls in the other room," said Uncle Phil. "And once, more recently, though that turned out not to be Vaulan at all."

"I know," said Matt. "I meant most recently. When did you see it as the good printing press? How many days ago was that?"

"Oh dear." Uncle Phil thought, sipping his tea. "By earth standards…

see, that's what I was saying earlier. The shift back to diurnal rhythms is difficult to... oh... three days ago, I guess."

Matt turned back to me. "That was the night of the funeral and the night of the attack."

The lights seemed to dim in the kitchen, and the fitful wind came prying again at the rattling frames. Uncle Phil lay half-sprawled now on the table, his face still upright, eyes studying the strange filaments of steam that writhed upwards from his mug.

"My funeral? The attack?" His eyes widened. "Oh dear, when I lost my grip... and now, the black printing press..."

"You failed," said Proton quietly. "The printing press printing your words smacks of ego—the same selfishness by which you allowed the beast to beat you. You have put Austin and James in grave danger."

Uncle Phil turned to me, eyes crazed through lenses, finger jabbing; but he had nothing to say.

In the stillness and the whine of the wind, Sadie spoke, leaning forwards over the table. "Have we considered finding the god Vaulan in the flesh and asking him, plain and simple, to return to earth?"

Proton's eyes fell on her with something like surprise. "That's what I asked Phil to do. But he came back with visions of printing presses printing his own words, and he didn't ask Vaulan anything."

Sadie seemed not to hear. She looked, oddly, at me. My face must have shown the tenderness of my heart towards her, for her confidence grew like the flame of a fanned coal. "Austin senses the echoes. That much was clear from the way he led me in the park." Proton and Ihrel nodded, as if she had already told them that, had told them when I was not there, had veritably told them behind my back. How dare she.

"Only Phil can use the portal to travel," she went on, "and it's corrupted now, anyway. What about another means to the same end? I don't know how we would leave earth, but if we had a way to travel, the boy Austin could lead us to Vaulan. I'm sure of it."

The boy Austin lead us to Vaulan? He's not *the* boy; he's *my* boy. The presumption! As if I am offering my son like some sort of fuel for the consumption of this operation. As if they can make plans with him at the center of a functionality. He's a human being. He's mine.

"I never thought of that," said Proton.

"The boy won't be doing a damn thing." My voice jumped around the room and they all jumped, sensitive cowards. Even my boy jumped in my lap and looked up at me like something was wrong.

"He's not some pawn for your little operation. He's my boy."

Uncle Phil's face wore the patient pain it had worn at the birthday party and at the news of the divorce and at everything else lamentable. "There's nothing to be afraid of, Jim," he said. "Finding Vaulan is the best thing we could ever do. Sadie has a good point. The fact that he led you all to the echo in the park—"

Proton was nodding.

"No way. No way." Again the silence rang for a moment with my beautiful voice, then rang with nothing at all.

"My boy didn't do a thing in the park and didn't feel or sense a thing at Uncle Phil's house either."

They looked at me like idiots, like they didn't know what I was talking about. Probably didn't.

"You're all crazy and I don't care."

Austin, in my lap, pulled away from me. *Don't pull away from me. I'm your father, boy. Don't ever pull away from me.*

"Jim—"

"It's James, goddamnit." I didn't care who said it.

I saw Uncle Phil nod at Proton. I saw Proton nod at Sadie. Sadie turned to me. Her face, cold, hurt, stronger than me, a terror. "Jim. Give Austin to me."

"Ha!" I laughed. "Never. Your plans of world domination, finding Vaulan. It's all atom bombs." It was. "Ha! Never."

Sadie reached in and took him under the armpits. She pulled. He wriggled, my son, my son, and one shoe hit me in the mouth and he was in her arms. Shouting, swearing. Sweeping glasses off the table. Shattering glasses. You can all die you are fools you can die. And die. I am James. I am not Jim do not ever call me Jim again do not ever.

"Do it!" said Phil.

Proton reached across the table. He hit me in the face, in my beautiful face. He did. I fell over.

"And then I pulled Miss Sadie all the way into the woods. I pulled her all the way, until we found it."

I knew the voice of my boy, but it was dark now and I was down.

"What was it like when you found it?" The voice of Proton echoed down the hall. Now a light growing in a certain shape gradually showed a cracked-open door and, by dim reflection, the faded quilts of Ihrel's labor on which they had laid me.

"What was it like?" said Proton again.

They passed my door. Austin said sharp and clear, "It was like birthday and Christmas all together." The sound of their feet passed on and the light faded. I heard Proton open the great carven door that led out to the deck. I vaulted and flopped and blundered in the dark. Head pounding, face pounding, face throbbing. He had hit me. I hadn't forgotten. Had he thought that I would? And now, this. To take my boy. To take him from my presence by force, by force of brute force in my face in a fist.

I went into the hall. The carven door was just closing. The place was dark. I went up to the door and pulled it open and stumbled out into an even colder, wetter, later night. There were three lights on the porch showing three sets of feet: two big sets, one small. The lights swept up and blinded me and swept down.

"Jim."

It was not the voice of Proton, but that of my uncle. Now, in the dark-adapting of my eyes and the gentle ambiance of the lowered beams, I saw the three of them. My boy was holding a flashlight, as if he were one of them.

"Come with us, Jim," said Uncle Phil, motioning with the lamp. Proton turned away toward the stairs. Austin followed him. I followed Austin. Uncle Phil came after me with the light. Again I climbed down and down with them. My boy led me in front with his own flashlight, and my uncle lit my steps from behind.

I did not know what they were doing, but I began to realize. I saw that certainty was the end of investigation. Vaulan was the subject, as Uncle Phil had said—the subject of an ever-changing sentence, or else himself an ever-changing subject. And were we the object, or the verb? Or just the article, not even the definite but the indefinite, and I the most indefinite article of all? And hadn't I been a bit of an idiot in the kitchen just now or whenever that was? Good lord, they had carried me to a bed after Proton had cold-cocked me. And maybe this Vaulan wasn't so bad after all, for Austin had always said it was like birthday and Christmas all together, and he would know.

"Proton," I said weakly into the mist.

I heard a grunt somewhere down below.

"I'm sorry you had to hit me."

"So am I," he said.

We kept climbing down and down.

"Is daddy okay?" said Austin into the mist.

"Daddy's okay," said Uncle Phil, reaching down to pat my shoulder.

"You know, I don't know where we're going," I said, feeling the color rise in my voice as the mist threw back my words, "but certainty is the end of investigation. It's the end of striving. We're never going to *get there*, and we have to accept that."

"Damn right," Uncle Phil bawled into the darkness.

"This is the pinnacle of investigation," said Proton from somewhere down below.

This time, the descent took even longer. It was something like floating, this sense of no certainty, this sense of continual becoming. That constant motion must have been the first stillness I had ever experienced. But at last, after ten thousand steps, Proton glided out over the dark grass of the valley floor, and little Austin glided out after him. I glided out, and Uncle Phil glided out behind me. We were moving across the black mist-land of a dream. When we began to see the glow of organism in the air after untold wanderings, that glow said that our trek was not some bold cutting into the unknown, but a return to an ancient place of belonging, even a return home, a return to uncertainty, to the only place perhaps where our hearts were ever meant to dwell, to a place like boldly jumping off a cliff, to a place like sitting down squarely between the rails.

When at last we stood before the gargantuan tree, Austin kept wandering up the slope until his beam illuminated the gnarled bark and the dark crevice that turned back his light. Before I knew it, he was stepping up to the portal hole to go inside. Uncle Phil ran up and grabbed him and brought him back down. "Whoa there, buddy; we're not going in *there*."

"Austin, what did you sense in that hole?" asked Proton.

Wide-eyed, Austin said nothing but wriggled around in Uncle Phil's arms and shone his beam over Phil's shoulder, back at the hole. His light would not cut the darkness in there.

"Can he see the portal?" muttered Proton.

"I told you, it's that Feckidee strangeness," said Uncle Phil.

"James, can you see the portal?" asked Proton.

"The what?"

He and Uncle Phil turned away. Austin's light spun back around with the turning and stayed focused on the hole.

"Come on," said Proton. "Let's start climbing." His beam swept over another wall of root to the right that I hadn't noticed before. He went first and Phil went after him, carrying Austin. Austin's light was still bobbing over the crevice, now fainter in diffusion. I came last. Before me, the ancient bark of the gigantic root had furrowed over into a gnarled and twisted imitation of steps. I climbed the wet, slick bark after the others.

"Austin, why don't you give your flashlight to your father," said Uncle Phil.

The beam swung over the rising shoulder and blinded me.

"Easy, Austin," I said. "Don't point it at my face."

He lowered it and reached as far down Uncle Phil's back as his little arm could go. I caught up and took the light from him.

I'm not sure exactly where the root met the trunk. For a long time we climbed up over the knobby protrusions, the woody rock gardens, the fantastic tilting world of the tree's base. There was something like a path worn into the living bark. The path seemed to take the straightest way up when it could, and the safest way when it could not. We went slowly, for the bark was wet, though highly textured. Proton's lamp always bobbed somewhere overhead, sometimes to one side or the other, but always up there. I just followed Uncle Phil and said prayers of thanks to no one in particular for the flashlight.

Then Proton's light was still, waiting. Uncle Phil caught up. I caught up. We had climbed the mountainous root to the trunk itself. Proton stood in a dark crack in the tree where the wood must have shivered apart in the swinging temperatures of millennia.

"Watch," he said. "It's narrow and splintery inside." He turned, and his light disappeared into the tree. I swung my light out over the expanse below us, but it was black mist, as if we had never even started on the ground. I swung my light back and saw Uncle Phil's white head and Austin's glittering eye just disappearing into the tree. I mounted the last bulbous formations and slipped into the crack after them.

"We have to climb, by the way." Proton's voice fell dead and hollow from somewhere overhead. I was inches from Phil's back (judging by the smell of wet tweed), and I had no room to swing my lamp upwards. Then I heard Phil huffing and moving and I heard creaking wood. I knew by the sudden space for breathing that he was gone. My light showed a fractured chamber of wood all around, filled in under my feet with packed stones, rising as far as Uncle Phil's moving legs above me. Right in front of me, something like a set of rungs was carved into the shattered wood. I began climbing.

The rest of it was a blind stumbling through darkness and thinning mist. Up ladders in cracked wood, along branches and up makeshift wooden stairs open to the night, we ascended into the heights of the most gigantic tree I had ever seen.

When the trunk above us had begun forking into thinner spreading growth and I was nearly swaying from exhaustion, we stumbled off the last steps of a rickety staircase onto a thinner branch that dipped a little with the wind. We must be nearly at the top, unguessed thousands of feet in the air. Out there, far away, a star or two glittered through the great dome-wall of the foliage. The soft white glow of Austin's face, sound asleep, bobbed on Uncle Phil's shoulder between those winking stars, a young gentle moon not yet heartbroken with the world's weeping.

A shadowy platform began to show itself in the net of leaves. When the branch below our feet had split into separate walkways no wider than grapefruits, we came under the platform and came to the solid wooden half-ladder that would take us up. The branch was dipping now not with the wind, but with our weight. I was ready to climb to the platform. At least then I wouldn't look down at darkness and mist and the waiting, sleeping leaves beneath my feet...

I climbed up after them to something like an observation deck perched at the outer shell of the tree's foliage. At the back of this platform, the low tumbled form of a cabin retreated into the shadow of the leaves. Before us, those leaves fell away like a solid mountainside into the dim and uncertain mists. There, a mile or two away across the valley, one heavy star winked through the vapors at the guessed-at level of the land: perhaps the place of warmth and safety where we had left Sadie and everybody else. So then: *this* was the hill I had seen from the deck. Above and all around was the night sky of a dream, more real and exultant than any I had ever witnessed. I fumbled to turn my flashlight off.

"Austin," Proton murmured, standing by Phil and patting the boy on the head. "Wake up, Austin." For a moment I felt a twinge of doubt, even of terror—this was the same man at the gas station who had almost— but I put it down. Proton would not have opened his home to us, we who were beast-pursued, if he hadn't meant well. Perhaps the disconnect was not in his intent, but in my understanding.

Austin was awake now, rubbing his eyes and turning away from Proton. Good lord, he just wanted to sleep. I almost said the feeling that was welling up, but then I remembered the other times I had said the feeling that was welling up, and I held my tongue and just thought about the feeling. I *was* a pretty good father, you know, despite Molly's protestations to the contrary. I protected my boy from everything I could. I refused to let him be a pawn. I defended his humanity from the whole world.

In that case, I still had to say something.

"What are you doing? Just let him sleep."

Proton's opaque face turned towards me under the stars. "We're testing Austin, as I said before."

"You never said that."

"Oh." He looked at my boy, then up around at the stars. "Well, we're testing him."

"About what? You never asked my permission."

"In the scope of what his ability may mean, your permission is not exactly... relevant."

Good lord.

"This is cosmic work," Proton went on. "If he can lead us, as Sadie—"

"Listen. Listen to me."

Phil cut me off. "Jim, you're just going to have to sit this one out. We're all unified, except for you. Yes, we all hear your concerns; we just come to different conclusions."

"Oh." I backed away, nodding, putting my hands behind my back. "Oh, all right." I could not see them now.

"Are you all right, Jim?"

"Oh. Just fine."

Phil turned back to Proton and handed my boy to him. He handed my boy to the stranger at the gas station who had shown an inordinate interest in the boy's explorations with a dead phone—oh, and the same guy who had been waiting for us in the woods; who, just now, had led me up twenty thousand steps and ladder rungs and branches into the heights of a tree the size of New York's greatest monuments—who doubtless intended to throw my son over the edge of this platform; who was walking towards the railing now, holding my boy to hold him out over the railing and then let go.

"Where is..." Proton's voice, murmuring to Austin, half-lost. "...can you point?"

With an immediate jerk that nearly upset their balance, Austin jabbed his arm at the sky. He did not waver; he did not move. He pointed steadfastly towards the low rising of Orion in the east.

"Let the boy sleep," I said, but a careless breeze struck up just as I spoke. It threw my voice back in my face.

"Are you sure of it?" said Proton. The breeze brought me his voice. The breeze insisted. It said, *You can't talk. You can only listen.*

"Are you sure of it?" said Proton again.

Austin nodded. His pointing arm never flinched.

"We need to get back," I said into the breeze. "He needs to go to bed, and so do I."

Phil heard me. "Oh, we'll sleep here tonight," he said.

"No we won't," I said into the breeze.

Phil watched Austin.

"We need to go back," I said.

Proton turned towards me. But then he walked past me, toward the low form of the cabin at the back of the platform. "There are cots up here," he said. Phil followed him. I followed Phil. The wind was cold, but Proton opened the door.

A flashlight showed a dark little room with a desk on one wall and folded-up cots on the other. At least we weren't climbing down tonight.

We got the cots out and unsprung them. They smelled like summer camp, like the terror of sleeping in a bed that was not your own and was not even a bed. Oh, we'll sleep here tonight, will we? You mean we'll lie down and listen to the inanimate creakings of ten hundred tons of solid living wood. Now this.

I laid the wet pad out on the frame and lay down on it. I sank, feeling the way the springs denied me my complete shape. I was never going to fall asleep on this thing.

The door creaked open. It was later, utterly dark. Someone had turned off the flashlight. I hurt all over. Phil was snoring happily. Against the stars in the open doorway, I saw the black silhouette of large head and shoulders with little head and shoulders. I got up, weightlessly, and followed them.

"Wake up, little Austin," Proton muttered.

Idiot. But I was too tired to feel even that. Now they were out, creaking across the deck. I stood leaning against the door frame, squinting at them.

"Can you point at birthday and Christmas for me again?" asked Proton.

Under faintest starlight, Austin had something like corporeality. I saw him turn, instantly, and fling his arm into the heavens. I traced and traced again. I traced his arm unmistakably towards Orion, which towered now two-thirds of the way to the zenith. It must have been deep night.

13

COMING AWAKE IN that little treehouse was like coming out of a dream of shards. I was incapable, unrested, wedged into a cot, having surrendered to the springs' demands some time in the night, but no better now for the sacrifice. Austin was still asleep on the cot next to me. The other cots were empty and the door to the cabin was open. The diffuse dawn sun had let itself in. It was precisely nothing o'clock, the air precisely the color of goddamnit.

"I don't think Austin is aware of the significance." Proton's voice curved its way around the door frame from the cold outside world.

"He needn't be," said Uncle Phil's voice. "If the test was as conclusive as you say, then he will have the intuition regardless of how developed his other faculties are. And really, we have no idea what his subjective experience is; he's only a boy."

Only a boy. Just any old boy, just any old expendable boy, my boy, the child who slept still next to me. How dare they!

"The only question is whether James…" Proton's voice stopped, and then his face swung around into the open doorway. "Oh. Good morning, James."

I may have grunted.

Proton and Phil came in. Phil had slept in his tweed and looked something of a wreck. "Jim." He nodded at me and smiled stiffly. He never used to act like that around me.

"What were you talking about?" I grumbled.

They couldn't hide the little glance they shot each other. "Let's eat something first," said Proton. "It's going to be a long climb." He took cans of beans and a can opener from a little cabinet in the corner. "Forgive the oddness of this meal." He cranked open the first can. "Obviously, the options for storage up here are quite limited. Oh, I have spoons for us, too."

I lay back on the cot. The springs groaned.

But we ate the beans, and they were better than nothing. I began to feel marginally more alive, although there was no coffee up there, and no way to brew it besides. I would just have to soldier through to the end.

"You know, I'm not sure what they'll think of it," said Phil as we packed up the cots. "I'm not sure if we'll have unity."

"Those who don't submit to cosmic significance will abandon only themselves," Proton grunted.

"Why are we here?" I said. "I know you're talking about Austin, and something else. What's going on?"

"It appears that your son is capable of sensing not only the divine echoes, but the present location of their ancient source—the god Vaulan himself," said Proton as he threw his cot up against the wall.

"What?" I stood there.

"The test was conclusive," Proton went on. "I sighted along his arm both times. He pointed consistently to a patch of sky somewhere between theta and sigma Orionis."

"I don't know what that means."

"Those are names of stars," Phil put in.

"It means that's where birthday and Christmas are." Proton winked and brushed past me.

The rest of the morning, Proton would not talk to me. I asked him the same things again and again, but he ignored me. Phil just said things like, "Give it a rest, Jim," or, "this will all work out; just be patient." But he was not helpful. Starting to climb down was actually a relief, as it gave me something else to focus on.

It was a cold, bitter dawn, and the crown of the great tree was the only island in a rising sea of white mist. I descended into this mist, having no explanation of our little journey and only a shadowy sense of what these people wanted to do to my son. But right now, I just could not. My only goal was to set my feet safely on earth again while still holding my son. Cosmic significance be damned; he was my boy.

I was scratched, broken, bleeding, nerves singing when I stumbled after them down the root to the grass. For a while I just stood under the bulk of the awful tree, holding Austin close and feeling my planet through my shoes. But my daring leaders did not stop to feel the planet. They were already disappearing into the mist, their voices sharing a hushed communion from which I was excluded. As I stumbled after them, Austin wriggled around on my shoulder to stare at the retreating crack in the wood. I could not stop him.

Sadie, Matt and Ihrel were in the kitchen making lunch. It was all I could do to keep from dashing forwards and devouring the half-finished whatever. But the focus was idiotically not on food.

"What did you find?" asked Sadie once she heard us entering the room.

"You were right," said Proton. "He pointed twice at the same place, a bit of sky between theta and sigma Orionis."

"Oh my heavens." Sadie's eyes widened. Ihrel turned from the counter to look at us. Matt looked up from the table.

"Does that fit with your discovery of Vaulan through fold-traveling?" asked Matt, looking at Phil.

Phil shrugged. "Vaulan could very well be in this universe. I never know where I'm going or how my destination relates structurally to anything else."

"The only question is how," said Matt, thumbing his chin.

"You mean how to travel physically?" Phil began, but I had to speak.

"What are you talking about?" This time my voice didn't fill the whole room and nobody jumped and, oddly, my head wasn't pounding and the fibers of my chest weren't tied in a knot.

"We're talking about finding the god Vaulan in the flesh," Sadie murmured. Her eyes were shining.

"We want to ask him to return and cleanse this planet. We want him to dwell with us again," said Proton.

"What does that have to do with me and Austin?" I asked. The sense of peace was so foreign, it was almost alarming. "I've been wondering that since… since the gas station, I guess, and since I saw the photograph and since we met you in the park, Proton." I was not ashamed to speak like a child to Proton, because that was what I was.

Proton nodded and pulled out a chair for me and one for himself. Everyone else sat down too. The lunch was starting to smell amazing.

"This planet is under assault, Jim," said Proton quietly. "You may not see it every day. You may only see it in the wars, the murders, the atomic bombs, but that's only one layer of the fractal conflict. There is not an atom that is unclaimed, either by our lover or by the darkness; and there is not a galaxy where the balance of the struggle is not swinging one way or the other at this very moment. It's a colossal fight. One planet may not seem like much—and yet it is *so* much. This is the planet of humanity; and in this realm of the universe, humanity has the greatest intelligence for good and the greatest capacity for evil of any sentient thing. Don't mistake me; my goal is nothing less than the purification of all that is, the purification of every atom in every fold. But in the scope of the long fight, I focus on one thing: the purification of this planet."

"Our lover used to live here with us," said Ihrel, wiping her hands on a towel and sitting down across from me. What a wild, alien consciousness she was! "Proton and I remember a time when Vaulan dwelt here. That was millennia ago."

I stared at her.

"But Vaulan was not machine then, as Phil reports him to be now—in fact he was not even Vaulan, but a black meteor of titanic proportions that we used to call the Great Stone."

"How do you know all this?" I muttered.

"We saw it in the flesh," said Proton.

Seeing my idiotic blinking stare, Ihrel said, "My dear, we are both over twenty thousand years old… speaking linearly, speaking of *this* time around."

I saw that Phil nodded.

All right. All right. I felt the strangeness, felt it rise to fever pitch, then let it go. I spoke. "And you want to use my son's unique ability, whatever exactly that is, to find this Vaulan thing and ask it to return to earth?"

"Right," said Proton.

I looked at Uncle Phil. "But I thought you found Vaulan in the portal. I thought you knew where it... *he*... was." I was starting to speak their language as if it were true!

"Right, I did find him," said Uncle Phil. "But you saw what happened the last time I went in there. I don't know if my vision is credible anymore."

"Austin's ability is the best thing we could ever have hoped for," said Proton.

"I still don't understand why you think I would be willing to donate my son to your schemes," I muttered. Austin looked up at me with uncertainty.

"Jim." Sadie's low voice broke through my head. I had no choice but to meet her gentle, forceful, inexorable gaze. "It isn't all cosmic, as Proton makes it seem. There is personal value—infinite personal value—in it for you and Austin. Austin's ability is *evidence* of his purpose; evidence, if you will, of the fulfillment of his humanity that will come when he engages his ability. Even *you* were targeted by the beast—"

"Now, *that* I don't agree with," Uncle Phil broke in. "There was never any targeting of Jim. I left earth four years ago on a protective mission because the moment Austin was born, we saw—"

"Jim *was* targeted," said Matt.

Uncle Phil stared.

I actually nodded.

"When I went to his house, he couldn't get out," Matt went on. "The beast beat him to every door and window. We had to trick the monster with some of his blood."

"Well, I don't know the exact metaphysical structure of this," said Uncle Phil, batting his hand. "All I know is that Jim never needed any protection. It was Austin's birth that started it all."

"What I was going to say," Sadie went on patiently, "is that Jim was targeted, at least recently, both at his house and at yours, Uncle Phil—"

"My house is a safehouse," Phil put in. "The beast couldn't have targeted him or anyone there."

"The beast flattened the fields, roaming around the house on the night that I had to leave Jim there," said Matt.

Uncle Phil frowned.

"Regardless, we're not trying to argue with anyone," said Sadie. Her voice was smooth, her smile so curved and delicate that I would have liked to touch it, to possess it. "I'm merely saying that aside from Austin's purpose, Jim may have a purpose, too. The targeting is evidence of that. The beast never targeted my brother. It never targeted Austin—"

"It certainly did!" shouted Phil. "I showed you my scars!"

"—never targeted Austin once it appeared on this planet," she went on, at last getting flushed and bothered. "It only appeared on this planet after your vigilance was broken, Uncle Phil."

He pursed his lips and nodded slowly.

"The point is not to dispute your view of this," she said gently. "The point is just to redeem Jim's experience." She turned to me, eyes shining with erotic and vagabond affection. "Jim. Listen. There is meaning to your suffering—cosmic meaning, because this is a cosmic fight. And if you have cosmic significance that the darkness finds worth destroying, how can you *not* sign up for this journey with us? We are the front line. We may have assembled only days ago, but we have already grown years'-worth as a family. We are already closer to home. Getting home involves leaving this planet to find our lover. Doing that will fulfill not only cosmic purposes, but your *own* purposes—the purpose of you and your son's existence. That purpose is both cosmic and personal at the same time. Do you see it?"

Austin beamed up at me as if he understood what she was talking about.

"Give us your son," Sadie murmured. "Give us yourself. Leave earth with us."

My heart pounded. My eyes fluttered as I looked around the shining room. The faces were expectant, waiting, but uncolored with any fear of my refusal, as if they already knew.

"All right," I said.

Then it was all a flurry of packing. I didn't know what we packed or how we did it. I didn't know what I personally packed, seeing as I had nothing of my own there other than the clothes I was wearing. But at some point I found myself standing in the hall beside an open half-stuffed suitcase, surrounded by things that were supposed to fit inside along with everything else. That was when Uncle Phil came bustling past.

"Uncle Phil," I said.

He stopped and looked at me as if waiting for a statement of some functional weight.

"What are we doing?"

"Going to find the god Vaulan in the flesh." His eyes were shining.

"But... how?"

"Archangelic deïtons," he said, nodding. "That's what I was telling Matt."

Now it was my turn to stare.

"Just pack your things, Jim."

"I don't have any things."

"Pack for a month. A year." He snapped his fingers. "Which reminds me—" And he was gone.

Later, we came together and ate dinner. Proton called it our last dinner on earth. I didn't know what he meant by that, but I believed him. There was a strange levity in the air. It was as if we had all graduated from childish demands for pleasure to something more painful, yet deeper and more peaceful. I felt squashed, even flattened, yet the happiest ever, truly ever.

"A toast." Uncle Phil raised his brimming glass. "To Vaulan. To our planet. To Austin."

We clinked our goblets. Wine dribbled onto the tablecloth. Ihrel started fussing about it, but Proton murmured something in her ear and a smile came over her face. We all had another glass.

When my palate was saturated and the wine had disrobed, Proton got up from the table. "Friends." His solemnity played my heart like a cello bow. "We're about to depart."

"Forever!" cried Austin.

"Not forever," said Uncle Phil. His eyes were shining again.

"For how long?" asked Austin, beaming around at every face with a ripe young questioning gaze.

"This is the last step, and the first," said Proton. He lifted his glass. "To our journey."

We raised our glasses and clinked them together. We tossed them off. The wine flowered; it burned.

Uncle Phil stood up with a clattering of his chair. "I'll lead the way." He reached down and picked up his suitcase, brown dead tweed to match his jacket and pants, and walked out of the kitchen. I didn't know where he was going or why we trusted the leadership of a man who had failed through the weight of his own ego, but we went after him.

Outside, the gray mists were rising from the valley as the retreating sun left space and coolness for them. Only the lowest plane of light through the trees still held any memory of gold; the rest was silver and brown and black. Even as we stood collecting ourselves, the last rays of the sun through the pines surrendered. The crack of the world closed over them, and day was already halfway to dusk.

Uncle Phil was striding off up the slope, swishing aside the pine needles of years. He was a lone itinerant preacher in the fast-coming dark, and we had to strike out after him. As we walked, I recognized here and there a fallen tree or a stone. We were going the same way that Matt and I had gone earlier when I had wished to die. He *was* a preacher, my uncle, my terror.

We hit higher ground. The flock slowed, and I carried Austin along with my suitcase; but the shepherd plowed on through the poison ivy. The mists were rolling up behind us from the valley. The mists said that the coming night would be void.

"Somebody tell him to slow down," I muttered.

"Uncle Phil, slow down," Sadie called through the trees.

He stopped without turning to look at us. After a few moments, when we had almost caught up, he struck off to the right down that same slope of gray grass. We cut after him through the black and silver of the brambles. My feet were all wet.

The mists failed. Looking back, I saw the vapors rising up like a wall glowing softly in the dusk where the pines stopped: collective sentinel phenomena perhaps, guarding that house and that valley at the top of a mountain I did not know in my home country, guarding it from the night and the beast. Looking down, I saw the ruined train tracks at the bottom of the gorge. Night had already come over them. The chair was just a vestige of structure, the poison ivy a pulsation of blood in the dusk.

"Where are we going?" I called.

"To the tracks," said Uncle Phil as he crashed down through the bramble.

Soon we stood at the bottom by the decrepit railway, drunk on the madness of our poet leader. What he intended, I did not know. But now he was mounting what was left of the embankment, now standing between the rails and kicking idly at the remnants of gravel and the straggling weeds, now dropping his suitcase and bending and putting an ear to the metal.

"Nothing." He stood, looking around. "This may not even work. Still…" He looked off down the tracks in both directions, then back at the gravel between the ties. "There *is* ash here. That alone…" He turned and began walking down the tracks to the right, towards the valley, I thought. "Even if these aren't exactly the right tracks, they should get us there," he said over his shoulder. We followed him, of course. I didn't know why; he had failed dreadfully in protecting us from the beast…

We walked and walked. It got dark fast. Soon we were stumbling along over rotting railway ties, guided by our flashlights and the inexorable, unbobbing light of Uncle Phil. The tracks went on and on, curving a little but mostly running straight, straight towards the valley; and yet the valley never came, and there were no signs of mist to the right or straight ahead.

The night had the torturous clarity of January. When I saw the star Capella rise in the sky-cut trees before us like a glass shard of the sun, I knew that it was an unnaturally cold night in October and that we were walking east. But somehow that seemed wrong, for I could have sworn that when we had stood by the tracks before it was fully dark, before Uncle Phil had chosen the way, east had been to the left, the way we had *not* gone. But I must have gotten mixed up.

My heart began to swell with the walk. It really was possible to do good in the world. Here we were, setting out on who knew what adventure, already looking up, already moving. The brisk clarity of the stars, the silent nods of the black nets of trees, confirmed that we were, at long last, not astray in the universe. We really did not need to know it all. We really could live in the uncertainty, as if that constant motion were truly the only stillness. Lord, I had been a fool.

In the rise of spirits, in the growing faith, we had begun to spread out along the tracks and across both sets of rails, feeling the strange masterless freedom of striving individually towards the same goal. Now, I found myself stumbling along near Sadie. I knew her in the dark by her footfalls and her little huffs of breath.

"How does it feel?" I muttered, my lungs moving in an eager cadence.

"Like dying, like living," she said perfectly.

Even Austin had a flashlight. Even Austin walked independently beside me, before me, behind me, whatever and always unchanging. Good god, I did not need to carry him all the time. Good god, he could walk. He even knew how to use a flashlight. Where had he learned that? By his breath, by his eager footfalls, I knew him to be just as much a player in this game as I. And I had been a smothering idiot, maybe even sabotaging the protection and nourishment that I had tried to—

The fact that he would even dare to lead us—

Sadie laughed for no reason. Oh, I wanted her. Not her body, unless as the crowning of some greater consummation; you see, I did not want to marry her, because marriage is a way of tying yourself to what turns out to be a huge block of unloving iron, and Sadie was not that, so I could not tie myself to her in that way. But I wanted a certain oneness with her, something deeper than the false vows and the young idealism of the farce of love. I guess I wanted to deep-marry her. Does that make sense? But how could I not? *Ask yourself, under breath and silver sheening, will you deny it?*

The golden star Capella entered the grand stage again, now floating a stunning distance higher: steady, untwinkling, unbearable. The whole constellation was up now—Auriga, intrepid charioteer of the tilting east—O baptist proclaiming in the wilderness the way of the Lord—O gateway to Orion—

My legs and stomach were weak, ready to demand second dinner from me if I was going to demand *all night* from them; but my mind and my heart rang to a singular melody, a walk towards culmination greater than the needs of my flesh.

The power of Austin's guidance was such that his lamp, like Uncle Phil's, did not bob or waver. He was too strong; he was a god. How they would battle for his strength! How they would battle to own him! Would we win, or would they? This was only the beginning of the fight that would be his life.

Uncle Phil's lamp was not moving. We began to catch up with him. His lamp dropped, and my light showed that he was bending down, putting an ear to the rails.

"Son of a…" Uncle Phil's eyes went wide and white. "No, not that one…" He jumped up and hopped to the other set of tracks, the ones on the left. He dropped down again and listened again. "Oh my Vaulan."

"What?" Proton asked.

"This is it."

"*What?*" Proton barked.

"It's coming." In the stark flashlight beam, Uncle Phil was beckoning.

"What's coming?" said Sadie.

"The deïton train," he said.

We went and stood with him between the rails. I bent down and listened to the metal. I heard a dull *thud-thud* and grinding, the tortured revolutions of some derelict machine.

"Oh my Vaulan," said Uncle Phil.

Austin stood looking back the way we had come, sweeping his flashlight back and forth across the train canyon and the sheltering woods. He shut his flashlight off, but did not turn back towards us.

I looked out into the night.

A light was coming, a towering pillar of luminance still far off down the canyon of the trees. Above the slumbering whine of the crickets, I heard the grindings, the groaning of the earth under unendurable bulk. It was coming fast.

"Better get away," said Sadie. She stepped forwards and took Austin's hand, heading across the right-side tracks towards the trees.

"Hey!" cried Uncle Phil. "Hey!"

Proton and Ihrel turned away too.

"Hold on," said Uncle Phil. "You don't understand."

"It's going to run us over," said Matt. He went across the other tracks, down the embankment, to the shelter of the trees. I followed him.

"That was the whole idea!" shouted Phil. "It's a deïton train—"

"Suicide was *not* the idea," said Matt, running on ahead, down under the trees.

"It isn't suicide!" Now at last Uncle Phil followed us, outnumbered, bawling into the night. "This is our travel mechanism. This is how we find Vaulan."

"Unlikely," said Matt from under the black trees.

The shriek of a lonesome trainhorn tore the air. It went on and on, blaring with organ discord until suddenly it stopped and its flat aftershocks died in the woods. The pillar of light was taller, blinding. The earth was shaking.

We all stood now under the trees at the bottom of the embankment. The brambles and poison ivy tossed fitfully, scraping us. The only clear path was the tracks.

"…appears to be a misunderstanding," Uncle Phil declared blindly into the trees as he came stomping down. "This was my whole idea. It's a deïton train."

"If you want to kill yourself, I pity you," said Matt, and by analogy he was also saying that to the me of earlier today. How dare he. But he was talking to Phil now. "However, I will not kill myself. Just when we're on to something—just when we—"

The screeching, grinding, *roaring* drowned his voice. Everyone turned to look. The light blazed unbearably, as if Capella itself had come down to grace the prow of the dreadful locomotive. In that coming white glow, I saw the rails bucking and shuddering, the rotten ties shattering. No train I had ever seen had screamed so much at the movement of its own parts. Derelict and unoiled, unpowered, it must have been loosed down some distant mountain; and now, in its mad career, no law of friction could ever contain it.

The shrill tremolo of Phil's voice squeaked, "Oh my Vaulan—oh my Vaulan—"

Sadie and Matt restrained him as he tried to dash for the tracks—

In cacophony towering ten octaves high, it swept past, O blaze of sparks and showering light. The exploding wood of the ties peppered us, stabbed us. We ducked down. My light fell and rolled and stopped to show Phil groveling halfway up the embankment, tangled with Matt and Sadie. The groans and wild screaming of the axles, the savage rhythms invented by ruin, the breaking, bucking, clanging of unoiled and misaligned—

"Oh my Vaulan—" His reedy old man's pleas—

I fell on Austin, covering him, holding him.

"Oh my Vaulan—"

The train swept past. The dropped flashlight beam showed the cars, rusted, rotten, breaking. An axle wrecked in the light: grinding: upsetting the car—derailment—the coal cars rolled. We saw their tops, their mountains of coal coming down like avalanches. Phil and Matt and Sadie scrambled. Cars swept past on their sides, trackless, unslowing; serpentining, wrecking—we fell back into the prickers and poison ivy, hit with bullets of coal. The sparks, the blaze, the screaming iron—but it was too fast. Even derailment couldn't slow it.

"Oh my Vaulan—"

They held Uncle Phil down in the thornbushes.

"Oh my Vaulan—"

"It's not your Vaulan!" shouted Matt.

The train went past and past until finally the red caboose came whiplashing through the coal on its side, red light blinking drunkenly, saying, *this is the end of the end.* Then it was all retreating into the night, roarings and wreckings fading quickly until it was all silent and we lay still and the rails sang with silvery sounds. Then even that sound failed. Only the crickets sang, and the night was quiet and dark.

After a while, I heard them moving. I felt around in the dark, but I could not find my flashlight. There was coal everywhere. I was sitting in coal. I dug Austin out. He was not whimpering or hurt at all. I felt his gaze turn in the darkness towards the disappearance of the train.

"I was *not* trying to lead you to suicide," said Uncle Phil. I heard him stand and brush himself off. Someone switched on a flashlight. "That was no natural train."

"Then what was it?" said Matt.

"It was an archangelic deïton," said Uncle Phil.

"Have we missed our chance?" asked Proton.

Uncle Phil shrugged. My flashlight beam showed him now. "Who knows? I tried to convince you to stay."

"You realize it looked like madness," said Proton.

"Of course! Finding Vaulan always looks like madness. You ought to know that by now."

"I still can't believe you wanted us to stand in front of an oncoming train," said Matt. "I appreciate your expertise, but really, we need to start leading this operation by committee."

"Oh, no, no." Phil shook his head. "There is no committee. There is no leading. There is only the path."

"Your idea of the path would have killed us all," said Matt.

"So what? I thought you wanted to travel. I thought you wanted to find Vaulan. Well, sometimes the fold where Vaulan is looks like suicide from the outside. That's when each of you has to decide how badly you want him. He won't be found by sitting in an easy chair at home and contemplating the loveliness of life. He is found in death. I died a little bit every time I fold-traveled, as I said. Hell, I lost the ability to read and write years ago because of it. Jim knows that. My memory is going now, too. So is my instinct for social grace." He laughed sadly. "Don't think I don't feel it."

We stood around in silence in the night. There was nothing else to say. Suicide? I may have longed for death earlier today or yesterday or whenever that was, but now I was different. I thought we were on to something. I thought we were going somewhere important. *Suicide?*

"Let me put it this way," said Uncle Phil. "The resolution to find Vaulan *is* suicide. Therefore, any little suicide within that larger death is harmonious, a variation within unity—part of the best-composed art you could ever make."

He *was* serious.

"I don't want to kill myself," said Matt. "There's too much good that I need to accomplish."

"Oh, you are so lost," said Phil, climbing over the coal up the embankment, as if to keep walking. "All your good works must begin with suicide."

"Hold on," said Matt, but the others started climbing up the coal mountain after him. I hoisted Austin and dug out my suitcase and went after them. But the left-hand set of tracks was wrecked. The twisted rails and shattered ties were too hazardous in the dark. "Let's walk in the trees," I said.

"Yes," said Matt.

"We can walk on the right-hand tracks," said Uncle Phil.

"Absolutely not," said Matt.

We went down the embankment and walked again under the trees. Capella danced higher through the black leaves. It was deep night. Orion's rising couldn't be more than a few hours away.

Where were we going? My uncle was still blazing ahead, unconcerned, unfamiliar. I must have fallen under some brazen intoxication, the way I had followed him and was still following him. We all must have. He was such a failure. Now he was failing again, before our very eyes. You know, we had drunk a lot of wine.

Gemini was rising. With it came the first aura of the moon. The night was getting late. My legs stumped on, willing billets of rubber under a head with no direction. I was a pancake. I was lightheaded.

My flashlight still showed the embankment off to the left. Now the trees were thinning. Their canopy still hid the stars, but there was a wide darkness between their young trunks. My shoes crunched now not on dead branches, but on something gravelly. With a vision like breath, the low moon showed through the trees. The world was silver, glimmering and murmuring with light. I looked down. Moonlight showed not grass, but straggling weeds here and there. All around, moss-eaten piles of railroad ties lay rotting under poison ivy.

"If we're going to find Vaulan…" Sadie's voice was distant. I saw another light bobbing beside Phil's. I couldn't hear his response, only her lilting voice thrown down the breeze.

"Honestly… crazy… believe you."

I don't know why he would tell *her* everything, and not me. As if I was nothing to him anymore! No, I had to stop thinking like that. I had to start giving, even if it was only to give to Uncle Phil in that way by trusting him. I had to start dying.

My feet were crunching on something again. I looked down. The weeds had thinned and we were walking on packed ash, a field of black like the remnant of some gargantuan being who had burned to death for the cosmos.

"Hold up," said Uncle Phil. His light and Sadie's light were not moving. The trees were thicker ahead. The ground showed sunken holes in concrete frames. I thought Orion's Belt was just rising through the leaves, but the moon made it hard to tell.

I stood now with Uncle Phil and Sadie. The others came. Austin was with us. The ground fell before us into a depression. I couldn't see anything through the dense underbrush.

Before I could stop him, Austin switched off his light and began climbing down with a soft cracking of twigs.

"*There's* our real leader," said Phil, shaking his head. "Lord, forgive me. I hope I haven't led you all astray."

"You can't just stop leading," said Matt. "I thought you knew the way."

"So did I," said Uncle Phil. "But look, the boy isn't waiting for me to figure it out."

I ducked into the underbrush after my son, turning off my light too. The moon was bright enough that I could actually see more of the world without the glare of the flashlight than I could with it. You know, it wasn't that hard to follow my boy under breath and silver sheening. I would *not* deny it.

Almost to the bottom, I stopped, walled in with scraggly bushes and the long bur-bearing stalks of dead wildflowers. Austin had already slipped further into the depression. He was standing now in one spot. I could see him in a clear bath of moonlight. Looking around, I saw it: there was a round concrete wall rising some six feet out of the depression up to the level of the ground. I turned. It seemed to run all the way around, losing itself in the flow of earth and bushes down which we had just come. No mistaking it: my boy stood in the middle of that circle, in a spot where the trees failed. I bowed my head and plunged forwards through the bushes.

"What do you see, Austin?" asked Uncle Phil once we were all standing near him. Austin did not respond, but kept standing there, looking up at the graffitied wall and the ground, turning slowly this way and that.

The first grinding sound made me jump.

"Good heavens—"

"What the—"

The night was silent again. But it was not a hallucination, for we were all swearing, even Uncle Phil. Only Austin stood motionless.

The next screech went on and on, a wretched, relentless sawing of iron on iron. It wavered, weakened, whimpered, and at last gave out. Silence came again. That was when my eyes, still dark-adapting after the shutting off of the flashlights, first picked out the low jumbled forms further off in the trees, ringing us in. I saw buildings, dark yawning openings; and in a deeper layer of the woods to the right, something like the Euclidean spire of a ruined factory.

Our iron tormentors loosed themselves in full chorus. All frequencies of sound, every agony imaginable—

"Oh good heavens—" Sadie fell to her knees, covering her ears. Proton spun this way and that, baffled. Uncle Phil went stumping through the underbrush towards one side of the depression, turning now and surveying what was behind us and all around.

"Oh—oh—" he shouted. "Oh my Vaulan—"

Trembling, ears ringing in the cacophony, I mounted up a pile of tires and rotting wood. I looked around. We stood in a ruined roundhouse. We stood where the railroad turntable should have been. Half-hidden in the trees, the locomotive sheds opened out in all directions, all leading along rusted rails to the depression that we stood in. Those rails were shuddering now, every set, every angle. In the dark of every opening, I caught shapes sliding past the windows, showing and hiding the moonlit woods beyond. When the first rusted locomotive showed its yawning and faceless boiler in the moonlight, I was not at all surprised.

"Oh my Vaulan—" Uncle Phil was dancing in circles, shrieking, falling this way and that in the brambles.

Unpowered, unoiled, the rusted sentinels emerged from every bay.

The first was already reaching the end of its rails.

"We *were* on the right track," cried Uncle Phil—

Lonesome, wailing and discordant, a far-off trainhorn cut the night.

"Oh my Vaulan—" Uncle Phil was tearing up through the bramble, back the way we had come. He was already scrambling up the wall. "I knew it!" He stamped on something, but I could only see him vaguely. "Tracks!" He pointed off into the woods. "Oh my Vaulan—"

The trainhorn rent the night.

"Jim—we have to get out—" Matt was grabbing me. "Your uncle is suicidal—"

"Wait!" I pointed at my boy. He was gazing around at the converging wrecks that inched out of their bays. The moonlight played his cheeks with innocence, softness, even femininity. "Austin knows, Matt," I murmured.

The lead wheels of the first locomotive clanked out over nothingness, pivoting fitfully.

"No." Matt yanked my arm. "This is *not* what I was talking about in the woods."

"But it *was* what I was talking about," I said.

The trainhorn rent the night. Louder, closer. The ground was beginning to shake.

"Come on!" Uncle Phil came bounding to us. "Come on!" He herded us. We followed him. I don't know why we followed him one last time, but I'm glad we did.

"This whole thing is—" But no one was listening to Matt.

We cut through the bramble, to the wall. Uncle Phil climbed up the rusted iron spikes embedded in the concrete. One by one, we followed him. Behind us, the first locomotive tipped screeching and crashing into the depression, a ruinous wreck of iron.

I stood on top of the wall. I hauled Austin up. The woods shimmered under a second moon, a towering moon. The rails stretching away before us began to sing a song more silvery than the paeans of crickets. *Gloaming can't hide it, reiterant and pliant. It will come to you.* Oh, I would not deny it.

Behind us, two locomotives jammed their noses together, twisted, and found their way into the basin of the old turntable.

The ground was thundering. I heard the wrecking of trees. *Crosswise and overborne in the brown blowing.* Octaves of trainhorn rang in the woods. Uncle Phil planted his feet firmly between the rails, between the ties. Austin stood behind him, unafraid. I stood behind my son. I didn't touch him. I felt Sadie stand behind me. I imagined the others. *Gloaming can't hide it, reiterant and pliant.* Oh my Vaulan. *It will come to you.* It cracked and flung the trees. It was not even fully on the rails; it wrecked them in derelict majesty. The towering white light, the way tree shadows spun back from it like fast formless weapons. *Ask yourself, under breath and silver sheening.* It let rip, it let roar again. Coming so fast and so beautiful. Oh my Vaulan. *Will you deny it?*

PART II
Events in Space
Year 1945-to-the-side

1

IT SPOKE TO ME in fives. From the first, I knew. About, all around, and coming down. This up, this out, and my cold metal. It was a sense of passage: though constricted and tunnel-through, I was coming out larger, clearer, cleaner.

I do believe I was run over by a train.

How my thoughts swirled like twirling weapons, like trees twirling back from the triumphant charge of archangels in the woods—like they did on the last night, the first night of my life. I still hear the blast of that horn, or else I will never hear anything else again, though I do not need anything else; the sound is still going.

Uncle Phil's flash grin too white, coming into my eyes, into. I am not ready. Thinking dead, had lost contact with the old honesty, I guess. It must have been a dream, because he is standing in front of me now, arms around me, and I am sobbing into his shoulder in the mist in the valley that doesn't exist: sobbing into the scratchy white, into the sanctuary white, into the sanctuary man in the valley that doesn't exist. I am not, am not, am *not* dreaming now.

But he led us *here?*

Here was a thing that spoke to me in fives of fives. *Here* was an offer resplendent with the cold hard logic of process, of function, of machine. My heart said yes; my lungs said yes. I broke diurnal rhythm and I learned, I learned, I slept. I broke diurnal rhythm because the machine had a better idea. It loved me, cold metal telling me death, and I accepted it.

I do believe I was run over by a train.

Austin had carried his own light. The globe of Phil had led us into the earth, but Austin's flashlight had lifted us to the stars. O staircase locomotive spaceship. O glory.

Sadie came into the room that pulsed with larval machine. She came in shimmering like I don't know. That round wave-shock-thing of her almost-blonde hair dropping just below her jaw—and O, how the lamp and the kitchen light told her radiance in a story of universal strings! The gold, the white that is gold, the strings—and they played her cheeks in translucent music. You poet, you dreamer. You visionary, you prophet, you Venus.

Still here? She took another cookie from the plate and felt the carafe of coffee but must have found it too cold.

Still here, I muttered, with all the shame of the hometown hero and the eternal student and the clueless father and the man run over by a train.

She munched the cookie. Her very reciprocations of jaw were perfect.

Reciprocations perfected and divinified spoke to me in fives. My heart said fives, my lungs said fives. They all sang together in harmonic motion. To be a harmony is so much better than to hear one. I no longer had to choose, for it had left me no choice. It was all fives. It was cold, and I rested on hard metal. I felt the rivets, the bolts, but it was fives, speaking to me in fives of fives like food, like sleep. O staircase locomotive spaceship.

Austin carried his own light, but he did not need his own light. He was his own light. At the rim of the bowl of trees, he put his light down and he shut his light off. Inside the bowl of trees he stood, centered and commanding, cognizant and steady: a breath of boy, a straight sharp vision like an endless blade, cutting up like blinding angle into the night—a straight sharp vision like leader, like unknowing poet under madness muse.

You got a pen, Jim? The muse has come upon me.

Yes.

This will be chapter twenty-seven.

All right. Go ahead.

Text begin. I came up from nethers into something I thought I knew.

But it was a blank and formless fold, something prepared and not yet inhabited. Rectilinear blacks took form against white, parted, and took form again. Commas in that phrase, Jim; though I'll probably edit it into a proper sentence later. But going on. I saw angles of mechanism and points of rotation, something of which the steam locomotives of man's design are but a poor imitation. However, I knew that it did not yet exist. It was just now coming to be. It was only black lines on the white of unpreparation; yet in the magnificent fractal structures, I knew my Lord.

Uncle Phil, is this story true?

He always shook his head then. Oh, James.

I do believe I was run over by that train.

If that machine was good, if it's what I saw in the woods at his house and if it's what he saw long ago and if it's what killed us all (which was actually a good thing), how can he have seen it as knives spewing words of hatred? I didn't know his vision could fail. My uncle, my uncle. How wrong was he all around?

It spoke to me in fives of fives. It broke my diurnal rhythm long ago, and it said, *here are fives, here are fives.* It was staircase locomotive spaceship, and *it,* its cold metal, its fives, defined staircase locomotive spaceship. O glory, O rest.

The steam curled up from the mug, up around her nose, parting and avoiding in a gentle margin that revered her form. Surely she repelled all contrary claims. Surely the gentle fold of her cheek was a fold itself, a universe, a *fold,* as Phil called them. Surely she invented in constant infinite new creation about her person. Surely she engendered. Surely as her lips moved, as they parted and formed air and formed harmonic resonance, they shaped and colored and glorified her latest infusion of eternal wellspring. Surely her words were true.

It spoke to me in fives, in shouts of fives, but I wished to sleep. It spoke to me in fives, but it was too loud. I wished to sleep, but it clanged, clanged, banged ridiculously in fives. My sleep was so cold. My metal was so cold. I didn't want to get up, because getting up was too hard and too warm. It shouted, sang, screamed at me in fives, and all at once it stopped. I woke up, O staircase locomotive spaceship.

I lay on cold, hard metal. I lay on a line of rivets. The space was small and dark, a box. Through gears and levers now motionless, I saw one small square window of stars.

If I had died, this was no heaven I had ever envisioned, and certainly no hell.

I moved. *That* was something more like hell. That was my body peeling up from the rivets. I could feel the age-old indentations in my flesh, as if I had always lain there. The indentations of the rivets were almost as natural as my other shapes, like my nose and my ears, except that having them hurt.

I could barely stand in my little box of a room, for most of it was filled with a bizarre network of wheels and gears and pulleys that was nothing but black rust in the starlight. From idiotic instinct, I reached out and touched the nearest gear. It burned my finger, though it was dry and unoiled.

I turned to the little window. The stars were cold, alien, without atmospheric pulsation of any kind. I saw no Orion, no Great Bear, no Pegasus—in fact, nothing at all that I knew; but I was not afraid.

A short rusted ladder coming down out of the ceiling was my only escape. Turning, I grasped the rungs and scrambled up.

I emerged into cold darkness. For a while I sat there on hands and knees, reaching timidly ever farther into the obscurity; but I found only cold, flat, rivet-scored floor and walls on either side. I was in a corridor.

Curiosity overcame my timidity. I started crawling. When the diffuse light behind me had long since disappeared, I began to think that the passage might be infinite. I stopped and stood up slowly, feeling with my hand before my head. But this passage was taller than my little chamber, and I could stand. How long had I blundered along needlessly on hands and knees? Now I walked slowly down the passage, again keeping fingertips on the cold rusty wall.

At last I saw signs of light. At first it was nothing definite, and I swore it was a tremor of my ocular nerve. But when the vision returned and began to insist on its direction, I decided it was not a trick; it was a faint whisper of silver somewhere far, far ahead.

I walked faster, no longer afraid of invisible things. A vision began to dance before my eyes: something like the tiniest horizontal bars of light, maybe seven of them, stacked in descending brightness; vague, formless, the stuff of a dream. If the passage had an end, that was it; if the bars were real, they were perhaps the formations of a cage that would tell me nothing other than the fact of my loneliness in a strange place after being run over by a train. How I hoped they were something else.

At last I saw it: they were steps rising out of the passage, lit faintly from above.

After a long climb up those steps, I found a small platform with narrow walls. There was one small window like what I might have found on a steam locomotive back home, back then. I went up to it. I didn't dare touch it, for I could feel the chill of deep space emanating from it. For a while I studied the sky. I tried to remember what I had seen from my chamber, but I hadn't paid enough attention to notice if this view were any different. Eventually I decided it must be; the platform was brighter than my chamber, doubtless due to three intolerably bright stars that blazed through the window.

I turned away. On either side of the steps I had just climbed, twin staircases doubled back, ascending into darkness. I took the one to the right. My feet crunched on something scattered on the steps. I bent down and felt with my hands. It was ash, or coal, or both.

I soon lost track of the staircases and their relation to each other. One turn in the dark is the same as five, and I found no more windows. I groped up the stairs on hands and knees. I found walls on hands and knees. I did it all by feel.

I was climbing a steep, twisting staircase when I suddenly saw light around a corner. As I climbed up and around, the light got stronger. The staircase ended. In a little starlit chamber, I saw shadowy human forms.

"Jim?" It was Matt's voice.

I went into the chamber. Matt was standing in shadow near a little window to the left. An iron chair sat bolted to the floor directly in front of the window. Another human form lay on the floor in front of a low, round, rivet-scored door. The right side of the room was a crushed jumble.

"You found us," said Matt.

"Us?" I muttered, coming closer. It was Sadie who lay on the floor.

"Austin is here," said Matt.

I looked down. Good lord, my boy, sitting in the chair, staring out the window with eagle vigilance.

Matt put an arm around my shoulder. With his touch, I felt like crying. It had been a long, cold ascent in the dark to get here. Why had I been put so far away from them?

"How are you, Jim?" Matt asked.

"I don't know," I muttered. I bent and touched my son's arm. "Austin, how are you?"

"I'm happy," he whispered without looking away from the window.

I gazed out the window with him. The long battered pipe-snaked boiler of the deïton locomotive, our slayer-redeemer, stretched before us into space. So then: we had been run over, swallowed up, and absorbed into a new life. There was nothing else but the stars heaped and clustered in alien forms. We were going to those stars.

"How long have we been here?" I muttered.

"I haven't slept," said Matt, "but it's hard to measure the time."

I looked over at Sadie. "Is she all right?"

"Oh." He sounded distracted. "She's just sleeping. She'll wake up in a few hours."

"Matt..." I thumbed my chin. The question seemed ridiculous, but I had memories. "Were we run over by a train?"

"Yes." He kept standing over Austin's chair, gazing out the window into deep space.

"Are we all right?"

"Apparently."

No one spoke after that. In the long silence, I began to feel a faint rhythm in the floor, the murmured dreaming *thud-thud* of some distant machine. But this rhythm said nothing to me. It was completely unlike the gears in my chamber that had sung me lullabies in fives. It was something alien, a rhythm for somebody else; and though I knew it was not for me, I suddenly hungered to find its source.

"I'll be back," I muttered, patting Austin on the head.

"All right." My boy did not look away from the window.

I turned back to the staircase—but the darkness was tricking me, or else I was walking in a lawless world. I could not seem to find the descending stairs that had led me up to the chamber. In the indistinct, twisted metal, all I could see was one narrow chasm of stairs going *up*. I looked back at Matt and my son, but they gazed through the window.

"These stairs are wrong," I said, gesturing.

They gazed through the window.

I shrugged and began groping my way up and out of the chamber.

I had not gone far up this steep and twisting staircase when I realized that the sounds I had intended to find had already faded. There was nothing around me but the deep silence of gargantuan slumbering metal.

Soon I came to light. The breath of stars was spilling down the stairs from a small window. There was no platform here, but I stopped and gazed out. I've always been good with orientation, and I swear to you that I had twisted around in the staircase such that I should now be seeing the long boiler of the deïton locomotive stretching out below me; but I saw no metal structure at all, only the unrecognizable stars.

I was about to go on, when the faintest echo of a song stopped me. I held my breath, listening.

Chickens are crowin... mountain... hi-oh, hi-oh, diddle-eye-day...

The murmuring music came down through the darkness of unguessed iron shafts. In the silvery sibilant of *sourwood*, amplified in the reverberant corridors, I heard Ihrel's enunciation and her childish sing-song.

...crowin on souwrood mountain...

I crept on up the steps, pausing to listen whenever the tune grew too faint or my foot came down too hard.

In utter blackness, I came suddenly to some sort of hole in the wall. Ihrel's voice floated right out of it. I felt carefully around the edges of the rusty metal.

"Ihrel?"

The singing stopped. "Yes? Who's there?" I had startled her.

"It's James."

"Oh good! Come in."

"Come... *in?*"

"Can you hear me? I'm in here."

I ducked and began to worm my way into the shaft. It was large enough for me to crawl into, but I couldn't see a thing.

"In here." Her voice was close, only a few feet away.

Suddenly her soft hands touched mine. My ears told me a larger space was right in front of me. Groping, I found air.

"Let yourself down. Be careful."

She guided my hands down to the floor. Tilting a little, moving carefully, I wriggled my way out of the passage and turned over into a sitting position. We were in abject darkness.

"Are you all right?" she asked.

"Quite all right," I said.

"How did you find me?"

"I heard you singing."

She laughed. "I didn't even mean to! I guess you have to do *something* to keep your sanity in here." She sighed, but it was one of those sighs that leaves anxiety unresolved.

"What's wrong?" I asked.

"Oh dear." Her voice moved side-to-side, as if she were shaking her head. "I'm so worried. I don't know how to care for them all. I couldn't even find you at first. Proton won't wake up. He's been sleeping for so long. Your uncle…" Her voice was breaking.

"What's wrong with my uncle?"

I heard her shake her head again.

"What's wrong with Uncle Phil?"

"He's… falling apart."

I nodded, though she couldn't see it. *Falling apart.* That summed up what I'd been seeing in him—what I'd always seen in him, starting even with the dictation and the fact that he had lost the ability to read and write—

"I'm sorry, Jim."

I didn't say anything.

I heard her move in the dark. It sounded like she had stood up. "Come with me."

"Why?"

"I need to show you."

I heard her clothes swishing. I heard her grunting.

"Where are you going? I can't see you…"

"There's a ladder." Her voice came down hollow from above. "Stand and reach. You'll find it. Be careful; don't hurt yourself. I'm almost up…" She was grunting again. "All right, you can come up now." Her voice was boxy, coming down out of a narrow place. I stood carefully and moved my hand around above my head until I found the lowest rung of the ladder.

"Are you all right?" she called down.

"Just take me wherever you're taking me," I said.

"All right." I heard her move on again. "You know, I should take you to the prow. Have you been there yet?"

"I don't know."

"I'll take you. You should be reunited with Austin anyway. But it's a long, long climb from here."

"Wait, I did see Austin and Matt and Sadie."

"Oh good! Were they all right?"

"They seemed to be. But they're *down* from here, not up."

"There's no *down*, James. We'll get back up around to them. But first, I'll show you something else." She kept climbing.

After a while I noticed a change in the sounds of her movements. They were still close and small and right overhead, but now there was a sort of hollow ring after them, like something on the radio. Along with that, I began to hear and feel something else in the metal all around: a low, murmuring *thud*. It only came every few moments. I heard no regularity in it, though doubtless it held to some sort of intervallic pattern.

"We're almost there," said Ihrel. Her voice rang in a vast cavern. I felt her body exit the shaft in a rush of air. Up a few more rungs, and I was exiting, too, climbing out onto cold flat metal.

We were in a vast space of total darkness. I knew its size only by the way the thuds filled it with quiet thunder.

"Come here," Ihrel whispered. Her hand groped for mine in the darkness—but no, it was my wrist she wanted. She put my hand on something soft and warm.

"Is it Uncle Phil?" I whispered.

"No. It's Proton."

I felt the body for a long time, trying to detect any signs of breathing. Every time the dull thud came, it upset the steadiness of my hand. Or so I thought: but then I realized my hand was not moving at all with each thud. Rather, the body was convulsing weakly, taking perhaps one teaspoon of a breath precisely in step with the vague reciprocations.

"He's been like this forever," she said. "He never wakes up." I heard strain in her voice, something desperate which would have been panic had she not mastered it long ago.

"He isn't dead," I whispered. "He's breathing to the rhythm."

"But why?"

I couldn't answer her.

She sighed fitfully. "Ugh, there's nothing we can do. Come on, I'll take you to Phillip."

Slowly I withdrew my hand.

"Follow me." She took my arm again and guided me. I groped across the floor until my hand found a hole.

"I'll show you the way. But listen: you have to go in headfirst. It will feel horrible for a moment, but then it will be all right."

The space was too dark, and everything else too strange, for me to be afraid.

I heard her moving into the shaft. I heard her grunting. Then the sounds became muffled and her voice said from under the floor, "All right."

I groped and found the shaft again. It was madness. "Headfirst?" I called.

"Headfirst," she said from far away and far under.

I began to drop my head, my arms, my upper body into it. I felt rungs, but they were going down, and I was preparing to climb down them upside-down. No one could do that. But I trusted her. I would try.

When I was perhaps halfway in and my head beginning to pound, everything spun. I was weightless. "Oh—"

"Just climb upwards," she said, almost from above.

I groped farther into the shaft. Suddenly I was dangling from a rung by one hand. "Oh—"

"Climb!" she cried from overhead.

I kicked in empty space and swung my other arm until I found the rung. I hauled myself up and up. Then my feet found the first rung, and I rested for a moment.

"Come on," she said from somewhere overhead.

I began climbing headfirst up the shaft.

At last we came up and out. We were in a corridor of sorts. Brilliant starlight lit one distant end through a huge cold window, but the other end was lost in obscurity. The starlight showed massive riveted doors lining the hallway on both sides. In the center of each door was an iron wheel for cranking it open. Some of the doors were open or half-open, and under them, coal lay spilled and spread on the floor. It was the strange tilting place of a nightmare, and a distant rhythm unlike any other was throbbing in the floor and rattling the coal.

"My uncle is… *here?*" I murmured.

"Yes." Her shadowy form moved down the hall. But she wasn't moving towards the starlight.

I followed her until she stood in coal before a door that was almost lost in the gloom. She began to crank the iron wheel of the smaller door. I helped her. At the first shriek of the metal, something like a voice rang out from deep inside.

"He's all right," she said quickly.

We cranked the wheel. The voice went on shrieking with the metal from deep within, answering the disturbance with deranged theories. Finally the last thread of the screw emerged, and the door fell open. Shards of coal hit our feet. I could barely see.

"Visitors must sign in at the front door. Pie, and pipe. Whatsit?"

I stood gaping in the dark.

"Overcast boundaries spells comes from within. I know it. Said we had to watch. See? Same as my chest."

The voice of my uncle.

"This was the second one. I know it death, and not you; but wasn't lying. Wasn't."

"Uncle Phil?"

"That's Phillip Feckidee to you. Make no mistake."

I couldn't see anything through the dark little hole.

"Phillip... Feckidee?" I tried again.

"Didn't think it could lacerate. Didn't think it could infiltrate. Well, look. And all that for nothing. If he, I'll. I will. Then you'll all."

I reached a hand into the darkness. My uncle's claw grabbed me and pulled. I fell through the hole and came sprawling into the chamber on hills of coal.

"Boilerroom. Titanic power here, but careless. Guard! Guard!"

His vicegrip cut off the blood to my hand.

"Uncle Phil—"

"*Our* responsibility, and look what. Look what."

He dragged and flung my arm. My hand hit the metal wall. He wiped my hand back and forth as if washing a window with it, though he was strangely gentle. Still, I felt the surface: metal impossibly scored with parallel grooves.

"And this? After all I. After all I."

He dropped my arm. I flopped face-first into the coal. I heard the coal moving, heard him shuffling farther into the darkness. "Look what," he muttered. "Look what." I floundered and tried to lift myself out of the coal.

At that instant, a strange song of fives began. In perfect temporal harmony, it fit the rhythm already going, though it was not quite the same. The intervallic relationship was beyond my interest. My poor, poor uncle. Oh well. The new song called me.

I turned around and wormed my way out. I spilled out into the corridor.

"I'm so sorry, James," said Ihrel.

"I have to go," I said, feeling the intrinsic beauty of the new music.

"Oh, is that yours?" Her gaze followed me as I went down the hall towards the distant starlight.

"I have to find it," I said. "It's just the prelude, but I have to…"

The booming was louder overhead. We were closer to the starlight. I stopped and looked up. I saw a hole in the ceiling.

"I have to go," I said. My stomach was growling terribly, as if I hadn't eaten in ages. My limbs were getting weak.

"Climb up the wall," said Ihrel.

I climbed up the wheel of one of the doors. There was some sort of hanging pipework in the gloom just below the high ceiling. I swung out along this. My body ached and stretched out. I was not strong enough to hold myself. I came to the hole. I grappled upwards and found the first rung inside. My favorite song came down through the shaft.

"Are you all right?" Ihrel called up after me. "Can you manage by yourself?"

"Yes," I said.

I climbed up into the shaft. My music rang all around me. The thuds, the bangings. No, it was not as close as I had thought; it was just so different from silence. I climbed up the shaft. I was so hungry. Oh, I had never eaten. I had years' worth of hunger bursting in me. My head was spinning now. I wanted to sleep. That was what the rhythm whispered to me: *food; rest; sleep. Come.*

The corridor of coal was far below me when at last I emerged into the black riveted hall. My bangings were louder now, and straight ahead. I stood up without having to feel for the ceiling. I began to walk, then to run, in the dark. Soon the open hatch of whispering starlight began to dance ahead of me. My machine was singing to me. My machine was singing me home. My starlight was a mirage in the floor. The music was so loud. Shaking, I stuck one foot down into my hole but missed the rung. I couldn't wait, so I let myself fall through. I hit my head on this and my arm on that. O, my little starlit chamber. The unoiled gears spun in sparking whine. O, my deafening glory. I crawled across the cold rivets. I was fading. The prelude was ending. And even as I watched my machinery, one lever groaned and moved and one still gear came down and meshed with the others. The cacophony tripled, and I collapsed under the first few bars of a grand statement of fives. I slept then.

I CAME UP OUT of fives again. It was not strange this time, but familiar;
it was me. I knew when my song of iron was ending. I opened one
eye and saw the lever move. I saw the gear rise out of mesh and freeze
instantly, red-hot, seized. Straightaway, the further banging stopped and
the machinery rested: *tap tap, tap tap.* I was alone in my box of metal.

I moved and felt myself. I turned over. I did not mind the rivet sores.
I had sores because I had been where I belonged. I had been with the
music that was process-formed for one whose organs had always longed
to live in fives. I felt myself live. I was well-rested; my fluids pulsed
in fives, now remembering and honoring what they had learned—now
turned loose, now reverberant, now jubilant. I was not even hungry
anymore.

I sat up and moved over to the window. I looked out at the ice-cold
stars.

Good god, Phil had brought us here.

Surely this was not the end. Surely, in his pulsing, pounding, insistent
knowledge, Uncle Phil had seen beyond this. Surely he had not failed us.
Could he fail? He had led us to the stars; he had let us get run over by a
train. He was the madman whom I had always seen, had always dictated
for, had always revered, but had never known. And now this: staircase
locomotive spaceship.

I tried to remember those dim times on earth. I remembered a house
in the mists. There had been people there—these people, my people, the
ones who were in metal with me now. Were they here? Was Uncle Phil
here? It was almost as if he had died, and not for the first time. Why was
he always dying?

Phil, you idiot. How dare you. How absolutely dare you. It didn't matter to him what other people thought. It was always his vision, his book to dictate. He'd done it again, only this time the story was real, and we were *all* taking it on dictation. In taking it on dictation, we were living his madness for him. He *had* to use other people, because he was losing it himself. This was not my life; these were not my fives. These were the fives of his derelict machine, his idol. The thing wasn't even oiled.

Why had I thought this was me? I had sacrificed everything for their bullheaded obsession. What had I gotten for it? The whole thing was for some function about which I simply didn't care. Vaulan? What? Cleansing the planet? What? How about James Feckidee? A planet is a concept. I am concrete.

But my metal bed had dented my body with the heads of rivets. So the horror was real.

This is your life, Phil. This is your goal. Do whatever the hell you want, but don't drag me into it.

But his goal had always been the protection of Austin. It didn't get any more selfless than that. Uncle Phil had gone under for four years, the entire scope of the boy's life, to protect him. Now Austin was some sort of guiding light, some messenger of the divine grace that I said didn't exist. So I *was* dragged into it and I always, always, would be, just as he had always been dragged into my life.

"James, you are a son to me. You know I never had one."

Am I not more like a grandson? I asked.

Uncle Phil thought for a moment, studying the snow that drove against the wrought-iron-framed and barred window.

"No, really; you're a son. I am too young in disposition, and you too advanced, for us to have that joviality and that distance. In fact, sometimes I feel that you are also the brother I never had."

I allowed myself to feel warm when he said that. The fire, mounting up in the grate with the collapse of the mounded wood, fought the gray storm with glorious god.

"You do realize, James, that she will always be your wife. There is no erasing what you promised her at that altar, nor what she promised you. You may be divorced, but she will always be your—"

She filed for divorce, not me!

He looked at me then as if I had broken another window. Was I to be blamed for being blamed too?

Enough. I had put all that behind me. We were traveling to the stars, to a new life, *in* a new life.

I scuttled across my little chamber like some sort of beetle. I mounted the low ladder and wormed my way up and out into the dark hall. Turning dizzily, I imagined the endless hallway before me and struck off. I ran into the wall and fell on my bottom. I was going to say whatever I always said when I did stupid things, but the word was strangely unavailable to me; so I picked myself up and felt the wall and went off slowly. I soon forgot my anger in the compressing terror of staircase locomotive spaceship.

I expected the hall to lose some of its awful psychological length, since I had been this way before; but now it was longer than ever, or else I was insane. When the ethereal bars of the stairs appeared at last, I was much closer to them than when I had seen them the first time. But instead of mounting up them, I stopped and looked at a low dark doorway beside them which I had not noticed before. Listening, I heard a scratching sound coming out, the gnawings perhaps of some hibernating rodent troubled with dreams of cats. Curious and unafraid, I crouched down and ducked into the opening and felt around. Small uneven steps called me down. I turned myself around and descended, feeling with my feet.

At the bottom, I crouched in a small space. Before me, the steps went straight back up, short and steep, cut with brilliant starlight from somewhere out of sight beyond the low ceiling. I had to find the source of that gorgeous starlight, and the source of the scratching.

I ducked under the low ceiling and climbed up the steps on all fours. I gasped: before me, I saw a gorgeous window of crystalline perfection, and beyond it the vast and delirious throbbing of diamond and interstellar dust. The whole room was ablaze with the sky's white light. Reclining before the window on mats and cushions, her back to me, was Sadie, her right shoulder twitching furiously, her gaze bent not starward, but on something in front of her.

"Sadie?"

The scratching stopped and she looked over her shoulder. "Jim! Good to see you." She jerked her head, as if too preoccupied to invite me verbally. I climbed all the way up and crawled across the floor and sat cross-legged next to her on one of the mats. Oh heavens, the stars, the galaxies. Why did she have captive use of this view? My window was so small. It showed me nothing like this.

She started scratching again. That was the sound of pen's declarations blazed onto paper.

"What are you writing?" I murmured, almost afraid to interrupt her.

"A poem, of course," she said.

"Of course."

I studied the stars. I had never seen this. They were now too bright to look at; not mere points of light, but perfect globes like suns, though solar winters distant. Even the glass could introduce no aberration to their forms. Eternal, brutal, slaughtering, they were lords of the black night. Beyond them, tunneling into the deeps of infinite space, galaxy upon galaxy receded, as if every eonic iteration of the whole universe lay that way in sequence.

"Can you show me your poem?" I murmured.

"I'd rather not." She kept writing.

Rather not? Really? I looked at her. Naked starlight ravished her eyes into superhuman radiance. Her cheeks, once quivering perfections, were now as hard and brilliant as her stars. Had she ever had any sort of tenderness in her heart for me?

She put the notebook down. "Sorry about that. You know how it is when the words are all right there." She did smile at me.

I thought about it. Yes, I knew what it was like. I remembered when Uncle Phil had poured forth rivers of verbosity for my child's hand to jot down under the relentless and magisterial terror of his vision.

"How are you, Jim?"

In turning towards me, her face took on an almost lunar phase: left cheek, left eye blazing with cold silver, right side lost in inky shadow.

"I don't know," I said. "My body seems to have changed."

She nodded. "Do you have a rhythm?"

"Yes."

"So do I," she said. "It *is* different than the old life, but I feel healthier than ever."

I nodded.

She studied me again. For a moment I locked eyes with her, but then I could not stand the piercing refraction of the sum of the universe's light that pinpricked me out of her left eye.

"Are you writing anything, Jim?"

I snorted. "No. How would I do that? And why?"

"How?" she laughed. "With pen and paper. Why? Because it must be said."

"I don't really say things of my own."

"But *someone* has to tell our story."

"That's my uncle's job. He's the novelist."

She shook her head. Her universe-eye glittered in strange shards of color that could destroy me. "He's broken, Jim. He'll never write again."

Why would she say that. Why. I am not Phillip Feckidee. And no, don't ever say that again. Broken. Good heavens. I am not Phillip Feckidee.

"You should tell our story, from your perspective. It *is* about you."

"It's about Austin," I muttered. "He's the reason my uncle disappeared. He's the reason we're in space."

"But the beast attacked *you*."

That was hardly relevant. This was not about me and never was. In fact, that had been the problem all along. No one understood my importance. No one realized that they made me far too much of an accessory. About me? Psh. Come back when you've started to make it about me, as you should have.

But a calm came over me. I was borne down to the earth and made small. O gargantuan terror, O staircase locomotive spaceship.

"You know, I had no idea what would happen when you and Matt came to the old red-roofed church," she said. "But look where we are now. Look how close we're getting."

"Sadie…" The stupidest question had come to my mind. "What matters to you the most?"

She laughed. "Starlight, at the moment."

I closed my eyes to give them a little rest.

"How about you, Jim?"

"Normalcy."

She laughed again. "Then why are you here?"

"Because you all insisted," I muttered.

"What, and you have no desire to find Vaulan?"

"If I had, I would have found him long ago."

She shifted on the cushions. Her hair fell in a new way—a distant, beautiful way. "You're such a downer."

What the hell. I looked at her. What the hell.

But her face turned to me, and the lunar smile, the starlit eye, showed curves of affection. "Don't be alarmed, dear James. It doesn't mean I don't *like* you." Her hand rested on my arm and rubbed gently back and forth.

"You like me, huh?"

"Of course! Everyone likes you. You're unique. No one else cares about his son like you do. No one else is writing a thesis about Blake."

"*Was* writing a thesis." I winked.

"Right!" Her silver laughter thrilled.

"So you like me."

"Who wouldn't? We all like you, Jim."

"What do you like about me?"

"Austin adores you for being his dad. Matt respects you, of course."

"I meant you singular." I stared at her, heart thumping. She had suddenly become the most beautiful starlit girl I had ever seen.

She looked down, blinking, reflecting. "You're a good man, Jim, in spite of your impossibilities."

I kept staring at her, but she turned and looked out the window.

After a while she sighed and pursed her lips and spoke again. "What happened to you and Molly? If you don't mind me asking."

"We got a divorce," I muttered.

"Why?"

"Why didn't you ever get married, Sadie?" I blurted out.

She glared at me. "At least give me the respect to answer my question or tell me directly if you'd rather not."

"What?"

"Don't dodge my question!"

"What are you talking about?"

"Ugh… you're impossible."

Impossible? *Impossible?* I looked at her, but she was a blur. She was a washed-out starlit paste. At least give me the respect. She was a blur. I was impossible.

> "You're impossible, James. I've tried for three years now. If you were going to change, you would have already."

> *If you had intentions of changing me, then why the hell did you choose me? Why didn't you choose someone you liked?*

> "Am I allowed to like you, Jim? Am I allowed to say 'I like you, and when you scream profanities at me, it isn't the real you, and it needs to change?' May I beg you to become something better?"

> *I'm not perfect, Molly.*

> "And I'm weak, Jim."

> *Oh, that's great. Where the hell do we start?*

> "See? If I still thought you had any adoration left for me, any sanctuary in your heart—"

> Her tears, her face in her hands, bursting out of the room, running running running.

"I'm sorry, Jim. I'm sorry." Sadie's hand squeezed me.

"Don't be sorry," I burbled. My voice was a broken wind instrument. "It's not your fault."

"Do you remember me now, Jim?"

O Sadie, your tender voice; and you put your arms around me and my head found itself against your soft warm neck and I sobbed, I sobbed, I sobbed.

Her adaptive organic love was nothing like the cold hard reassurances of my iron bed, my rivets. I bore no tattooed signs of my allegiance to her. I did not have to pay; she paid, and yet it cost her nothing to give of herself, to give her clothed shoulder and her soft warm neck, boundlessly and forever, to the most wrecked piece of the species. I tell you, I *remembered* her.

When a dull *thud-thud* struck up in the iron all around us, she pushed me away with both arms and held me there, listening. "Oh," she murmured, and I saw a wave of weariness dim the coronal glory of her face. "Oh. I am *so* tired."

The rhythm said nothing to me. "Is it your song?" I whispered, my voice hoarse from the draining fury.

"Oh, I have to go." Both hands squeezed my upper arms—strong, feminine hands, soft but firm—and released me. She half-stood, teetering before the frigid window. "Oh, Jim—" She sat down again, fumbling as if with eroded focus. "Where is it." She found her notebook and pen under a blanket. "Take these." She thrust them into my lap. She was pale now, but pale from within, not from without. "Write our story. Write it from your perspective."

"No!" I threw them into her lap.

"Do it—" She threw them back into mine.

"See, Sadie, that was my uncle. Not me. *He* was the one—"

"Didn't you take novels on dictation? Didn't you learn anything from it—anything at all?" She got up and went past me, shaking. She began climbing down the stairs. "Your uncle is incompetent now, so it's your turn. Oh, my head…"

I took her notebook and pen and backed down the stairs after her. The little space and the ascending steps beyond were so dark after the stars.

"Oh, I have to go…" Her voice rang down off iron and iron.

"Wait for me," I said.

Back in the dim hall, I saw her shadowy form mounting the broad starlit steps that led up to Austin's cabin, to the prow, as Ihrel called it. The wide slow ruminations murmured in the walls and floor and ceiling all around. Sadie was running up the steps now. I ran after her.

I didn't get up to the little platform in time to see which way she went; but trusting my memory and my gut, I bounded up the staircase on the right, into darkness.

I came up into the prow. Sadie was already curled before the firebox door. A dark form stood behind the iron chair, gazing out the window. I came and stood beside the chair. I looked at my son and at Matthias

Gaddo. My son's face wore an impossible and radiant serenity. He was doing what he had been made to do. His glittering eyes, as precisely focused as when I had seen him last, were unwearied, sustained perhaps by a power available only to those who submit to shake the universe.

Matt's troubled brow was cast in darker shadow. Noticing me, he turned his gaze away from the window, though he did not remove his arm from its resting-place on the chair.

"How did you sleep, Jim?"

"Very well." I thought about the hard metal of my chamber versus Sadie's soft neck, but I could not sort out my warring allegiances.

"Sadie just lay down to sleep again," he said.

"I know."

"It's her time."

I studied him. "Have you slept at all?"

"No." He gazed out the window. "I don't seem to need it. I'm not tired, and we've been traveling for weeks."

"Weeks?!"

"I think; but it's hard to keep track."

I looked at Austin. "How are you, son?"

"Wonderful," he murmured. His eyes were glued to the window.

"Have you slept at all?"

"If I sleep, I won't be able to see where we're going," he said. He didn't even sound like my boy.

"He can't sleep," said Matt. "This is his job. Besides, he doesn't need to."

I might have argued with Matt if Austin didn't look the happiest and freshest I had ever seen him.

"Jim."

The gravity of Matt's tone brought my gaze back. He was looking at me with long sad eyes.

"I'm worried about your uncle. Sadie told me he's losing it."

"It looks that way," I muttered.

"She said he's down in some ancient coal-room in the bowels of this thing. She said he prefers the dark—that he won't come out—that everything he says is angry and incoherent."

"Yup."

"What do you think we should do?"

I shrugged.

For a while he studied the stars again. "My only hope, which may just be my own wishful invention, is that Vaulan will heal him."

I held my tongue. *Vaulan.* That name? What a joke. And coming all this way!

"Otherwise, and until then, someone else has to step in," said Matt.

I looked at him again. Then I noticed the finality with which he rested his arm on the iron chair. It was functionality, not ego, that led him to lead. Were I to assume that role, it would have been from ego. That was where he was a better man than me. His gaze, too, was as resolute as Austin's, as if he could see it, too—though I knew he had sensed nothing at Uncle Phil's house, nor again in the woods at the park.

"I confess, I have some anger." His eyes followed Austin's out into the universe. "It was your uncle who led us to the suicidal tracks. It was your uncle who got us... *here,* wherever we are. Now the last bit of him snaps, and we're on our own. What am I supposed to do? I have no idea where we're going."

"But I do," said Austin's silvery voice.

Matt said nothing, but his hand removed itself to pat my son's head. And even as the boy's skeleton sprang with the gentle blows, his eyes remained fixed and unblinking, as if somewhere out there in his unclouded vision he saw a pinprick of Christmas and birthday all together.

It became my habit to return to the prow. Though I must pass Uncle Phil's chamber to get back to my own in the strange upward circle of the staircases, I wouldn't even let myself think about him. The prow was the only place where I found any solace. The angular rhythms of my machinery had begun to take on a flavor not of benevolent guidance, but of domination; and though I couldn't fight them when the reciprocations struck up again and called me back to sleep, at least in my waking hours I could have the company of Matt and my son (and sometimes Sadie) in the prow.

I don't know how many of my sleep cycles had passed, but I do remember that I was standing there beside Austin's iron chair, staring out into the glittering void. Matt's and my son's vigilance was unbroken. Sadie slept before the low iron door, as usual. It was somewhere around nothing o'clock in that cold iron spaceship.

A hesitant footfall announced someone's presence. I turned to see Proton half-emerging in the gloom, one foot on the top step, the other leg lost in shadow. It was too dark for me to see his face, but I knew him by his movements.

"Proton," I muttered. Matt turned to look.

"Friends," Proton mumbled.

Matt shot me a glance.

Now Proton came and stood behind the iron chair, resting both hands on Austin's head, gazing out into the endless night. "I've slept so long… ah, well." He squinted, as if he saw something of interest in the void. I watched his eyes move along the locomotive boiler that stretched before us into space.

"Matthias…" He was squinting again, one-eyed. "Is that protrusion aligned to our trajectory?" He pointed down at the boiler.

"More or less," said Matt.

"Yes," said Austin.

Proton squinted again, then raised his arm in a straight salute as if heiling that Aryan lunatic back on earth. To this gesture he added some cryptic positions of the other arm, as if performing some sort of kung fu or, perhaps, an ancient technique of astronomical calculation.

"Well, I'll be." He was still squinting and aligning.

Matt shot me a glance.

"Why would Vaulan return *there?*" Proton muttered.

"Would you mind explaining yourself?" said Matt.

Proton pointed. "See that dark spot? We're heading toward it."

I squinted, scanning the sky. I suppose, beyond the bright stars, I did see something like a black puncture in the silvery fabric of the deeper starfields.

"What is it?" said Matt. Fear was nothing more than a murmur in his voice.

Proton sighed. "It's a field of blackened planets."

"Blackened?"

"Burnt."

I squinted out into the night again. No, I couldn't really resolve the spot into anything. And how did he know anyway? Had he been there before? If we were really billions of miles from earth (*that* notion was still sinking in), how could a little black blotch out there possibly be anything he had ever seen before?

"That's where I came from," Proton muttered. "Therefore, that's where you all came from, too."

"Oh, yes," I said. "Oh, certainly. We all came from that black spot."

"James." He turned to face me. One side of his face was lit with starlight just like Sadie's had been, though these were different stars, somehow. "Don't try and start something. Just don't. You're traveling inside a deïton—an extension of, a feeler of Vaulan, if you will; largely inanimate of the god's all-seeking fire, perhaps, but a deïton none the less, for that is the very definition…"

I raised my eyebrow at him. *Lecture me? Really?*

"…and if you violate the peace of this spaceship, the machinery will shut you down, just as it does when you need to sleep—for your own good, and for everyone else's."

Matt gave a strange little start and looked at Proton as if he had just thought of something.

"In other words, keep your sarcasm to yourself," Proton went on. "I can tell you the story if you want. It's all true; I don't have the gift of fiction. But I won't tell it to your mockery. I need you to trust me."

I breathed deeply. Staircase locomotive spaceship whispered to me, to my pulsing fluids, in gentle fives. Harmonics and multiples of my pulse died down to a fundamental, to a clear and steady rhythm.

"I do believe I may have overreacted," I said.

Proton nodded carelessly. "Then I'll proceed. I did not originate on earth, James."

I stared at him. My fluids throbbed in quiet fives.

He pointed again along the line of the locomotive boiler beside the window. "I originated out there, on one of those worlds."

"You… came from out there?" I murmured.

He nodded.

"Tell us the story," said Matt quietly.

"All right." In the gloom, I saw a certain hardening of his jaw, the only emotion his face had yet displayed in all my time with him. "You're going to meet Vaulan, and apparently he has returned to that place, so you should know." His voice got quieter.

"Though infinite in extent, the universe is finite in texture. Of necessity, then, an infinite being who wished to act on such a universe would find itself fractured into a kaleidoscope of forms as its boundless essence entered curved space. Thus it was that He Who Is Deeper found resonance as the million, million gods." He pointed out into the jeweled chaos. "Every star is a body of one of those gods. However, all gods are unknowable to us, save one—save Vaulan Sonapétpik, our lover and maker. But I'm not there yet, am I?"

I drank in the magisterial night and let his words flow over me.

"Regardless, there was a time when the stars were not yet invented," Proton went on. "In a dark universe, the greatest god-shard, if you will, sought innovation of form and expression of the function of love. Out of nothing, this greatest of the divine fragments built a gargantuan orb of fire. He went into it, animated it, and sustained it with his essence. It became his body. It was the first star, the first artwork; and it was larger than galaxies.

"The other god-shards, sharing by intrinsic network in his boundless imagination and seeking externally to imitate him as well, built lesser bodies to orbit his. There were stars upon stars, and this corner of the universe blazed in eternal day."

I studied that little black negation of the star-fields.

"If they built stars, they built worlds," Proton went on. "If they built worlds, they built races. You should have seen the diversity, the color, the modes of being lost to us and unimaginable now." He shook his head.

"Did you see these things?" I murmured.

"Oh, yes. Even before I was fully formed in the flesh, Vaulan gave my mind vision. I remember it all."

"What happened?" asked Matt.

"Do you see a great star in that void?" said Proton.

I looked out again at the little disk of blackness. "No."

"I was only half-formed then," he mused. "I remember my mother, Vaulan—well, Vaulan Orvestra, as we called her then. She has had so many names in the endless spiral of time." He shook his head. "I remember looking out through her fingers at her face that was the day. Hers was a beautiful face: those eyes like blue suns, that golden hair a constellated dawn…

"But you see, the greatest god-shard fell. I don't know how, but a canker of pride entered him. He delighted in his own work above that of his fellow gods. I always thought that he must have lost his divine nature, somehow, for this to happen. True divinity must be incorruptible, I thought. So perhaps he never had true divinity. But why was he the most powerful of them all?

"Regardless, there is one god I know who never corrupted himself. Vaulan, our lover, has remained pure in function through the ages, though he has changed form countless times to meet our new philosophies. Think about it; there is a reason he is machine now."

"So that we can figure him out?" said Matt eagerly.

"No, no," Proton laughed. "Because we are so bent on building machines ourselves. There was a time when earth was mostly fields and forests, mountains and streams. There was no need for him to be machine then."

Silence fell in the little cabin. I looked down at Sadie where she slept before the firebox door. Her shoulders rose and fell with the slightest heave, as if sleep had rendered even her breathing difficult.

"What happened to the big star?" The little voice was Austin's.

"It exploded," Proton murmured, squeezing the boy's shoulder. "The great god released it in his heart, for its processes required his continual intervention to keep running. No one knows why he abandoned his star, but he did. The fireball scorched the million worlds to death, slaughtering all the sentient races created therein. Vaulan Orvestra saw the tragedy coming. She took me up in her arms and fled with me through deep space. But she could not escape the titanic fireball. She was burnt black on the outside, black as death. Her piteous weeping still fills my head. She landed with me on earth. She was a charred and blackened orb, a great black stone, and I was encased within her. In fact, for a while after that, we called her the Great Stone, and we stopped saying 'she' and started saying 'it,' because fire and sorrow had blasted all personality out of her, we thought. In reality, she had only hidden it, but anyway…"

"I'm scared," Austin whispered. "I don't want to go there anymore."

"Keep your eyes on our goal," Proton murmured smoothly, rubbing his head. "This is for the good of everyone."

"If my son is scared, can't he take a break?" I said.

"No one else can sense Vaulan's location," said Proton.

"My boy hasn't slept at all since we left earth."

"This is his role," said Proton.

"Listen." I grabbed Proton by the shoulders and spun him.

"James, I warned you," he said, facing me, one eye glittering, the other lost in shadow. "The machine will shut you down if you disturb the peace on board."

I felt staircase locomotive spaceship whispering to me. I felt the quiet pulse of those fives. My expanded throbbing brain shrank and pulsed gently, meekly. I released Proton.

"I'm sorry," I said. "I believe I may have overreacted."

4

"Jim, are you in there?" It was a voice I knew, something from back then, back there. But it was not my time. I was sleeping in my metal box, with my gears, and I was not to be disturbed. But then my fives released me.

"Jim?"

My machinery stopped. The gear raised itself out of mesh and froze instantly, red hot and unoiled.

"Jim?"

I sat up, stiff and rivet-scored as usual.

Suddenly, feet came down my ladder, into *my* chamber. The body appeared, more and more, until I saw the back of Matthias Gaddo's head. He climbed down gingerly, crouching under the low ceiling. He turned to look at me. "Sorry to wake you, but I have an idea."

"You didn't wake me," I said, motioning toward the silent mechanisms under which I slept. "My machinery stopped and I woke up naturally."

"Exactly." He snapped his fingers and pointed at me.

I raised an eyebrow at him.

"That mechanism controls you, right?"

"I wouldn't say *controls*. That makes it sound like a bad thing."

"It *is* a bad thing. We aren't working as a team. Come on." He turned back towards the ladder. He looked ridiculous, half-walking on his haunches and reaching for the rungs with over-long arms.

"What are you talking about?" I said without getting up.

He turned back to me, one hand on the ladder. "The mechanisms control you all. They decide when you wake up and when you go to sleep. They change with clockwork regularity. Your particular cycle is simple: you sleep for five hours and wake for five hours. I've kept track. I still have my pocket watch." He patted his shirt pocket. "But no one is aligned to the same cycle. You each have a different whole number, and for most of you, your sleep length and waking length aren't the same."

I felt the fives pulsing in my fluids. I felt my rest, the satisfaction of my stomach, my energy, my physical state perfect and cheerful but for those rivet sores in my side.

"Me, I don't even have a rhythm," he went on. "I've been awake since we started, and I haven't eaten a thing. But I don't feel tired or hungry."

"What do you want to do about it?" I muttered, feeling a little flutter of fear in my heart. I was quite used to my fives.

"Unify the phasing," he said. "Then we'll all sleep and wake at the same time. It'll bring us together as a team. We'll be better friends, and we'll be better prepared to deal with anything that happens on this journey."

"What's going to happen?" I said, a murmur of fear swelling in my heart.

"*I* certainly don't know; I'm just trying to make this work better. I'm trying to lead."

I squinted at him. I couldn't read his face in the faint, diffuse starlight. "Matt… don't you think you might be trying too hard?"

"Of course not." He frowned. "This is my role, Jim. Your uncle is incompetent now, and Proton is always asleep. He sleeps for twenty-one hours, in fact, and wakes for three."

"You don't think Austin and the spaceship itself might be our true leaders?" The words seemed to move through me from another source.

"Doubtless, doubtless." He was nodding like some sort of corrected professorial fop. "But I *do* seem to have a role to play. There must be a reason I wasn't given a rhythm. If I had slept at all, I never would have figured out the phasing of your sleep cycles."

He had a point, whatever it might mean. "All right," I said, shrugging and rising onto my haunches. "Lead the way, O leader."

He gave me an annoyed look but turned and climbed up the ladder.

"I don't understand these staircases and corridors," he said as we walked down the dark hallway. "When I was leaving Austin's area to come find you, I was looking in the dark for the top of the stairs by which you've always come up. I couldn't find them. Ihrel was there, luckily. She told me to go up. 'There's no *down* in here,' she said, 'only up.' So I took the staircase that went up."

"It's circular," I said. "You won't understand it."

"I'm realizing more and more that Uncle Phil was *not* wrong," said Matt. "I keep thinking of what he said when the first one went by and no one believed him: *that was no natural train.*" Matt sighed. "It's too bad that now... he..." I felt him glance at me in the gloom. "How are you doing, Jim?"

"What?" I squinted, imagining I could almost see the distant glimmering staircase that would take us to the prow.

"With Uncle Phil, I mean."

"I'm not doing anything with him now," I said.

We kept walking.

"I mean, how do you feel about it?" His voice was awkward, like he knew he should ask but didn't want to.

"Like I've lost him twice," I muttered.

We stepped off the last stair into the starlit prow. The softer silhouette of a woman stood behind Austin's chair. Sadie was asleep on the floor before the firebox door. Ihrel turned. Her gracious voice floated across the little space with a mother's concern. "Are you two all right?"

"Of course we are," said Matt. I thought he was a little too gruff. She meant no harm by it. But she wasn't offended.

"I have to ask, you know." Her voice was smiling, comfortably self-knowing. "I *am* the oldest lady on this expedition. Someone has to check up on you silly children."

I laughed. I actually laughed.

"Did Proton talk to you about this?" She was pointing out the window. We went over to the chair. I gasped. The sky was almost wholly obliterated. The stars had died before a vast canvas of black, something like heavy smoke from an oil fire. Only at the cloud's ragged edges did any stars show.

"Yes," said Matt quietly.

"We're going back to where it all started," she said.

"I know," said Matt.

"I guess it makes sense that Vaulan would return here," said Ihrel. "I wonder if he's on the same planet."

"We'll find out," said Matt, patting Austin's head.

"I must confess, I *am* a little concerned," she said. "If Vaulan fled our world from weariness of our evils, why would he return to the site of the greatest tragedy in all of time and space?"

No one said anything.

"Austin," she said, "are we still heading towards Vaulan?"

"Yes," he said, without blinking or looking aside.

"You mean towards birthday and Christmas all together," I said lovingly.

"I know what Vaulan is," he piped.

Ihrel laughed. "You certainly do, young man." Her smile turned towards me. "You must be so proud of your son, Jim."

I *was* proud of him. He was surpassing his father, just as he should. If this at four, what would he be at twenty-four, at forty-four? I felt myself let him go.

"I told Jim about my idea," said Matt after a while.

"Oh dear," said Ihrel. "I don't know."

"It would be better if we could all talk together," Matt went on.

"Yes, you said that before."

"We can't do that now, because the rhythms force you all back into sleep at different times. You and the others can't stop them from controlling you."

"And I somewhat doubt that *you* can, as well," she said. "Not to mention that I doubt the safety and the necessity of any such attempt."

"The necessity—"

"Austin is guiding us. Staircase locomotive spaceship is taking us." She knew the name I had given it in my mind! "I think we're doing just fine." She smiled at Matt.

"That's what I said," I muttered, but Matt was already talking.

"See, we need to work as a team. We need to be able to sit down and say 'what does everyone think of this?'"

"What, are you planning some sort of new decree?" I said. "Some new command?"

"Please, Jim." I heard his controlled frustration.

"I just don't see how you're going to do it," said Ihrel.

"There's a station down in the bowels that controls the phasing of your mechanisms," said Matt. "I counted the hours of your sleep cycles, each of you, and I counted the ticking seconds in different parts of the mechanism at this station. The whole number ratios are identical: there's a gear system down there that matches each of your cycles."

Ihrel shrugged. "All right. If you have some mechanical insight into this whole thing, I trust you."

I wanted to say *I don't*, but I knew that would be disruptive.

"Let's go," said Matt.

"Now?!" I cried.

"I want to unify the phasing."

"But we can't leave Austin here alone," I said.

"I'll be fine," said Austin in his little voice.

"Come on, Jim," said Matt. "Sadie's there. She'll wake up the moment we've accomplished it. Besides, I need your intelligence."

"I thought you had this all figured out," I said. He was turning away towards the staircase that ascended into the gloom. "I thought you were leading."

"I am," he said. "That's why I need you to follow."

We climbed up through the staircases and passages. These and their strangeness were familiar to me now—even the one in Proton's vast chamber, the one that seemed to flip everything and complete the cyclicism of it.

At last we came out. The rusted godforsaken corridor, the bowels of our iron prison, tilted before me. I knew the place was level and stable, but my head could not seem to agree. My heart said, "Here? *Again?*" For whenever I came here, I avoided Phil. Whenever I came here, I walked straight to the place where I could climb up and find the shaft that took me to the hall where my chamber was. I had taught myself that Phil no longer existed, that this was not his corridor, that one of those iron doors was not his.

"This is where Phillip is," said Ihrel.

"I didn't know that," said Matt. "Show me."

She moved down the hall. Stray lumps of coal scattered before her. In the gloom, she stopped before a door that I said I didn't recognize. Joining her, I heard the muffled shouting from deep within.

"Phillip!" Ihrel called. Her voice fell dead and close, without reverberation. The monologue beyond the door ceased. She grasped the iron wheel and gave it one screeching inch of a turn. "Help me," she said. Matt was by her side before I could step in, but it didn't matter.

When at last the door clanked open, Phil actually came out. "I'll weasel and thenwhat. You know. Over edge. Because of all that hogwash in the backwater. Can't."

"Uncle Phil," said Matt.

"Wondering what you thought. Complacent no more? And where?"

"How are you?" Matt reached out a hand, but Phil didn't offer his.

"At first, was a bad thing, thinking. But quite possible. The escape, the journey. All of it, without it after all, if."

"I have no idea," said Matt patiently, composing himself to start his speech. "Uncle Phil, you know how you're always waking and sleeping to the demands of that mechanical rhythm?"

"Of course," said Phil.

"Each of you has a different rhythm, meaning you're never all awake at once. I know this because I don't have a rhythm, and I've stayed awake the whole journey, counting and calculating your rhythms."

"Of course," said Phil.

Matt turned and gazed toward the dark end of the corridor. "At the end of that hall, there's a mechanism that controls all those ratios. I've studied it, too."

"Of course," said Phil.

"I want to unify the rhythms. I want to bring them into phase and change their ratios as necessary so that there will be only one rhythm. Then you'll all wake and sleep at the same time."

"Gods of the heavens! That, oh, oh no. No understanding. And contained—but it won't be. See me? Oh, I would know. And all these marks! You won't stop it."

Matt glanced at me and Ihrel.

"From the first, I have always. Shocking to me, that you would even. But of course, you youngsters. I, having spent four—and how could you forget? But what about what *I* say? Beyond it, strength. Power. Oh, and cutting. I told you my, chest. My walls. Everything. And now you won't."

"I don't know why I tried," said Matt to Ihrel. He turned away and began walking down the corridor away from the light.

Uncle Phil leapt after him and tackled him.

"Whoa!"

"Hey there!"

Ihrel and I jumped on him and pulled him off of Matt. I tried not to hurt him, my something-like-uncle; but though he was old, the tenacity of his muscles was undiminished. I found myself folded up in scattered coal, my mouth smarting from a wild kick.

"Please restrain him," said Matt, rising out of the coal and walking on down the corridor.

But Phil needed no more restraints. He suddenly gave up and lay forward on his elbows, head raised, gazing intently after Matt. In the sudden stillness, I heard muffled bangings beyond the wall at the end of the passage—sounds moving in a rhythm too irregular to be that of machine. As my eyes adjusted, I saw there, not far off, the last and towering iron door; and before it, a strange throne of gears and wheels clicking and moving quietly.

"If he even…" Phil whispered.

Matt stood now before the altar of machine, head slightly bent, form lost in necromantic gloom. He began to grasp and shift the corroded levers. He began to turn the rusted wheels. With each shrieking clank of a control, he changed the pattern of clicking.

"If he even *ever*…" Phil whispered.

At every pause in the grinding of the levers, beyond the steady clicking of the gears, I heard the muffled bangings beyond the door: sounds like heavy flesh seeking escape.

"The last lever is stuck," Matt grunted.

"Don't," said Phil. "Just don't."

"Have to," Matt grunted.

He heaved with his weight on the last lever. It gave with a shriek. He fell across it and hit the floor. The gears changed to a single slower *tick-tick*. With a muffled bang, the vast iron door opened a few inches. *Tick-tick, tick-tick.* My body scrambled, lost. My fluids scrambled, lost. Where fives? Gone. Another bang, less muffled—the sound of a massive body hitting a door, a sound like the worst night of my life—the door inched open again. Here, I could not stop it. He had unlocked the door, just as I always thought. Here, paralyzed, I could not even try. So we had failed: I had kept it out on that dreadful night, but now we could not keep it in.

The iron block blew open and slammed the wall on screaming hinges. Shaggy, coiling and writhing, the tentacles came first like a blown dam's river. They swept Matt against the wall in the coal. They swept out and pinned Phil to the floor. Behind them came their bulk, a sinuous head bobbing and looking with agile intelligence.

"Good god—" My own voice, my scream—

Claws came down from under the bulk and worked Phil. He screamed. I saw blood, more blood than I knew a body contained.

Satisfied with slaughter, it sprang away. Its musky hair threw me against the wall and threw Ihrel against the wall. It stood for a moment beneath the shaft that led up and out—how did it know?—and then began to drain itself up the shaft, tentacles and coiling appendages first, until only the eyed head remained and the claws hanging down out of the shaft, and then those were gone too with a sucking and brushing sound.

I rose from the coal mounds, now fiveless, stumbling and drunk with no direction. I fell against the wall.

"Phil—*Phil*—" Ihrel, herself bleeding, on her knees and Phil in her arms and she rocking back and forth clutching, clutching; and blood, oh blood, the blood of my uncle, my brother, my fellow conspirator with white hair, was upon her.

"Austin!" Matt rose out of the coal and bounded past me.

Good god, my son.

Matt was already climbing up the wall and the pipework, reaching into the shaft. As if he could do anything at all about it! I jumped out of the coal. I may have lost my fives, but already I began to sense the new rhythm. I could run; I could jump. And my son, my son. But would it know where?

Of course it would—

No. It shouldn't. At my house, the boy had opened the door. At my house, it had tried to kill *me*.

But now it had bypassed me completely. Something had changed.

We fought up through the shaft. Matt's feet kicked and crushed my hands, and I grabbed his heel for a ladder rung. The musk smell, the stench of fur that had lived forever without bathing, hung rank upon the lightless iron. The beast's groanings and breathings echoed down through the small spaces to our ears.

Then Matt stopped kicking my hands and I stopped grabbing his feet. I looked up as I climbed, but I couldn't see anything. The shaft was pitch black.

"Matt?"

"Come on!" His voice came down from overhead. He was beyond me.

I heard scuffling. He was fighting it, alone. I climbed faster, but the sounds were gone. I climbed faster. Suddenly my hand struck space. The iron lip of the shaft cut my arm. I flailed, felt, and climbed out.

The long corridor stretched before me. In the murmuring gloom, I saw Matt's form far away, bobbing. Nearby, a strange new unity called to me out of my trapdoor in the floor: no longer my fives, no longer. I ran down the hall. The new rhythm steadied my head.

"Come on!" Matt's voice rang down the corridor.

I squinted. I could see the stairs materializing in silver tumbling starlight. I shouldn't have. I should have seen the beast. Where was the beast?

"Come on!" This time, Matt's voice was all rebound. He hadn't even turned to call to me. He was running fast. I ran. The musk smell was heavy in the darkness, and under my shoes, I felt the long brown hairs that it had shed. My son, my son.

Why was it going for him? Why not for me? At my house—

Matt was bounding up the faint steps. Even in the whisper of starlight, I saw the long brown hairs scattered there.

A woman's strangled shriek came down the stairs.

"Son of a bitch!" Matt shouted.

I dashed up the stairs after him. At the landing he stopped, heaving, squinting perhaps into the dark at the twin diverging staircases.

"Go right!" I said. We ran up the stairs. It was all such a long fight, and the gloom, the endless gloom—but we climbed wearily off the last step.

Tentacles filled the cabin. Starlight showed where the tentacles had pinned Sadie against the firebox door. Starlight showed where they cradled Austin: dark virgin and child, the thing virginous of his blood perhaps, and preparing. My boy's arms and calves swung limp from its swaying tentacles. Sadie couldn't breathe. I could hear it in her soundlessness and see it in her weak struggling. I would have loved to save her, to save any woman; but she was not Molly and never would be, and what could I do? So I stood there.

Matt stood beside me, breathing. Something was dripping from Austin. *Drip-drop, drip-drop.* Sadie was dying. They both were.

The ceiling groaned. I thought the beast was bursting the room by expansion, but no; the ceiling was getting lower, now turning, now churning. The walls groaned. I heard inanimate bangings and ruminations, the power of machine self-summoned out of rust and uselessness, something prepared forever for this. I heard the staircase behind us break and clap shut. I heard the firebox door crumple to receive Sadie, making a depression where her flatted diaphragm could work again.

The ceiling was breaking open, a little black doomsday sky. The last trumpet sounded as the disrobing gears struck up their whine. The tentacles swayed. The frontless backless head spun and the opaque manless eyes looked, looked, uncomprehending. Then down out of the ceiling they came, gears spinning like blades, processes unified to a single drive speed. The dancing machine-field over our heads came down and Matt grabbed me and flung me on the floor beside him. The gears came down and their rusted teeth did not hesitate at beast-flesh. They spun and tore. The beast raged and moaned, but the cabin shrank upon it, armed and awake, old metal. I covered my face with my arms. I blocked my mouth and nose from the flying gore, the stuff black as iron and cold as mud. My fives, absorbed, one rhythm, one purpose: to cut, to kill, to rescue, to save. The cabin was its bloodbath. We all bathed. It roared and roared, but the screaming song of old machine roared louder. No one, nothing could stop it. We all bathed in shreds of beast.

IT WAS LONG AFTER the unoiled machinery had stopped screaming that I lifted my face and uncovered my eyes. The cold gore of the adversary covered me, but it really was just mud, just old earth and water smelling of clay. It filled the crushed cabin, here shin deep, here waist deep. There was nothing resembling beast left. The chipped and rusted gears, salvific saws, hung still and silent from the deformed ceiling. Across the space, I saw Sadie half-buried in the mud, now beginning to stir. Matt was beside me, beginning to rise. Where was my son?

I staggered to my feet and waded through the gore. Everything was off balance, as if we were on a boat tipping continuously over a waterfall. But I found my sea-legs and made it to the iron chair, that one steadfast formation.

"Austin?" I breathed. "Austin?"

I carved through the gore around the chair with my feet and hands, but I could not find my son. Stopping, listening, I heard a quiet whimper. There, in the corner under the window, my fighting eyes saw something, a curled form doubtless thrown there in the struggle. The gore was shallower there, even absent. He could breathe. He was on the floor, whimpering.

"Austin!"

I waded around and fell on my knees beside him. I scooped him up and turned him over as I rose. Starlight blazed on his pale face and unseeing eyes.

"Oh, Austin—"

Matt waded over. "Is he all right? Is he alive?"

"He's alive," I said, "but he isn't all right."

We held him and examined him. There was blood on his clothes, though we could not seem to find the source of the bleeding.

Matt cleared the chair, then took off his outer jacket and laid it across the seat. I lowered Austin and set him down. He was so far away, so small, so pale.

"Help me take his clothes off," said Matt.

We undid his little clasps and buttons. He was so tiny. At last he lay before us, a pale miniature of man with short limbs and an over-large head—bloodless, though his clothes were damp with blood.

Matt rolled him over. His back was covered in blood.

"Oh god—oh god—" I breathed.

Matt wiped it off with his sleeve. We hunted up and down his little form, but there was no cut or bruise or anything on his backside that might have been bleeding. So Matt turned him over.

His front side was covered in blood.

"Oh god—" I think I fell over into the gore.

Matt was crouched in front of me, slapping my cheeks with the gentle sincerity of a friend. "Wake up. Stay with me. Come on, Jim, be a man. Wake up."

I stood again. He had wiped Austin's front side clean. There were no wounds to be seen, and no new blood. But I knew what we would see if we rolled him over again.

"He's bleeding," I said. "He's dying."

"I have a scalpel," said Matt. "If we can find the spot, if we can sterilize the knife, we can do surgery."

"Surgery?" I stared at him.

"If we can—"

"I'm not a surgeon, and neither are you!"

"He has a claw lodged in him," said Matt. "We have to get it out." He produced something from his pocket. Under a plastic cover, a blade glittered in the starlight.

"No," I said.

"We should dress him again," said Matt. "It's cold in here."

Sadie came and stood beside us, weeping quietly. "Oh, Austin… oh, Austin…" She was shuddering.

"He isn't dead," said Matt as he buttoned up the boy's shirt and threw his own grownup jacket around him. "He's injured."

"But he's just a boy," she whispered. "Austin? Can you hear me?" She bent and looked in his little face. He did not respond. "Oh, Austin…" She wept again and reached down and took him out of Matt's hands. She held him and laid his head across her shoulder. She turned slowly back and forth, shaking with sorrow. He stirred at the compassionate squeeze of her arms, nuzzling his pale face against her cheek.

"He's so cold," she whispered. "Jim, can you spare your jacket?"

"Of course!" I nearly ripped it pulling it off myself. We got it on Austin. Sadie sat down in the seat, still holding him. The dark space was so cold.

"Oh dear." She was swaying as if with dizziness. "Something doesn't look right."

"What?" cried Matt.

"Or else it doesn't feel right. But that would make sense, you know?"

"What?!" cried Matt.

"He isn't guiding us to Vaulan anymore," she said sadly.

Matt leapt to the window and began sighting along his arm as Proton had done. "Do you really think—oh good god." He spun and stared at us.

"That's why it's so hard to walk in here now," she said. "We've gone off course."

I jumped up. I had to tell Proton. Where had we left him? He must be asleep still in his chamber. No, not asleep, because Matt had unified the phases. I waded through the gore towards the stairs. Of course there was no downward staircase, but I could not even seem to find the upward one.

"Where's the staircase?" I called over my shoulder. Sadie looked around the seat, and Matt came wading over.

"What do you mean?"

"I can't find the staircase."

We stumbled around at that end of the room. It was just dark enough to keep us thinking we simply hadn't found it yet. But the wall was all crushed and twisted, and things were shaped differently and smaller now.

"It doesn't exist anymore," Matt murmured.

"Doesn't exist? Good lord…" I kept feeling the twisted iron walls.

"You would have found it by now," he said.

There could be no doubt that our trajectory had changed. As I stood for hours behind the iron chair, one hand hanging over it to rub Austin's head on Sadie's shoulder, I watched the slow upward rolling of the sky. The dark granular formations obscuring nearly all the stars showed that we were still in the midst of the blackened planet field. But the sky no longer displayed the ongoing central magnification that it had; rather, it rolled slowly up like some apocalyptic eastern tilting of the night. We were dipping endlessly towards something, and we couldn't do a thing about it.

The rhythms were different now. Perhaps it was still too soon after the unification, but I hadn't felt any sort of call to sleep. I could feel my fluids pulsing, but it wasn't the old familiar, and they were forced to align to the new beat unnaturally. I was tired, dizzy, hungry.

Standing there, I realized it: even if the rhythms ever invited me to sleep, I wouldn't be able to get back to my cabin. I wouldn't be able to get to my gears, my metal, my rivets that used to dent my flesh and remind me where I belonged.

I felt Matt's presence beside me. He too was standing in helpless idiocy, watching the inch-by-inch, minute-by-minute rolling of the sky. His was idiocy, yes, but less helpless in retrospect. He could have prevented this—my fluids being forced, my chamber being lost, my son being injured—if he hadn't pushed his glorious new vision upon us.

"We seem to be heading toward a point," Matt said, extending a finger about a third of the way up the sky. "It's been climbing up with the other stars, but in the last two hours, our curve has leveled off. The point, and the whole sky with it, has moved up much less in the last two hours than before."

This time I didn't say anything. There wasn't a room to storm out of, so I wasn't going to start something that I had a possibility of losing. But this false friend—this philosophizer, this intellectual dandy of a stand-in-leader—burly-elbowed, storming in with purpose because the old guys were done for—

"I don't understand why it went for Austin," said Matt. "All along, it went for *you,* as if you were its only target. Yet Phil always maintained that Austin alone was the target. So why did it go for you at first? Why did it suddenly lose interest in you and try to kill Austin again? What changed?"

As if that mattered! He had *caused* my son's injury and my uncle's injury or death or whatever it might be, through his own arrogance—

"Maybe you broke the bond of love that you had with Austin. Maybe that was what covered him at your house. It always wanted *him,* but your love made the two of you one in its vision."

As if that had anything to do with anything. Now the rhythms were off and I was being forced to align myself to something that was made for someone else—doubtless, made for *Matt*—and when the rhythms called us all to sleep, he would be the first to lie down in this, the chamber once rhythmless; and he would rise the most well-rested and well-fed, while the rest of us grappled with a cycle not tailored to our organs as our old rhythms had been—

"Phil told me that Austin could see the portal back on earth. He said it was some sort of Feckidee strangeness… but something that you didn't inherit. He said that was why the beast tried to kill Austin shortly after his birth. It was the whole reason Phil left to protect him."

Did it matter now? My son was still bleeding from an invisible wound, with beast claws invisibly lodged in his body. My uncle lay, if he still lay anywhere at all, in some bowel of the deïton train that the machine's reconfiguration had rendered inaccessible.

"That's the only explanation," said Matt. "When Phil failed, the beast broke through into this fold. But now, seeing the metaphysics in the flesh, it mistook *you* for its target, through the work of your covering love. But your love must have broken down, judging by *this*. It finally saw Austin again."

My fault? *My fault?*

"It's tragic, really."

My uncle, my friend, my brother-fellow-conspirator with white hair—

And my boy—

Murderer. Murderer. God damn son of a—

I spun and punched Matt in his fat face. He flew back against the iron wall. His head hit the wall. He buckled forwards and fell in the mud. He deserved it, traitorous son of a bitch.

I said nothing.

He rose out of the mud, blinking, bleeding a little. Yes, I had caused it.

"You aren't helping," he mumbled around a fat lip.

Sadie was crying again. She didn't have to look now. She knew. I had broken everything.

"I'm tired of your arrogance," he went on. "Your whole ego doesn't fit inside this ship. You can't even conceive of the common good."

"You wrecked the common good," I said. "We all had our rhythms, and we were happy, and apparently the beast was on board all along behind a door that you unlocked."

"I had no idea," he went on. "Had I known, I wouldn't have done it."

"What the hell did you think those sounds were?"

"What sounds?"

"Behind the door!"

"I just heard machinery."

"Something was slamming against the door while you were fiddling with things."

"I just heard machinery."

"It was organic, Matt. You could hear the… the… *body*-ness of it."

He just shrugged. No, *he* had broken everything.

"You deserve to die," I said.

"Jim!" Sadie gasped, jumped up from the chair, spun and stared.

Matt shook his bloody head. "I wouldn't, Jim. I wouldn't."

I heard iron creaking behind me. I knew in an instant. I knew what I had done and what I had become. And I knew what it did to any incarnation of beast.

Creeeak…

Staircase locomotive spaceship hit me in the back of the head. I was gone.

Waking up, I found the back of my skull pounding. If we had been tipping over a waterfall before, now we were flying down the infinite descent itself. I was not on the ground, not in the mud, but floating in the air. The iron chair seemed to have fallen on its face, and with it, the floor had at last stood up for itself. The window, something like a little crystal floor, admitted an almost earthly twilight to the twisted iron cabin. Matt was floating nearby, clinging to the chair. I had hit him. I had hit my friend. What was I? Sadie was curled in front of the chair, sort of on it, sort of floating. She had wept when I had hit her brother, the man whom I called my friend. But there was no changing it. I grabbed the chair and pulled myself over and looked.

It was no starry sky out there, but a tapestry of muted greens and golds curving gently away out of vision. It was a world, a planet.

My head pounded again with the impossibilities. I gave up.

When I woke again, there was a sense of almost no motion. I felt earth beneath us, but far beneath us; and between us and it, I felt the creaking reciprocations of tired wheels, as if we were moving at walking speed over bumpy ground in a carriage with no suspension. I was on the floor this time—ah, gravity—and piled in a heap. I got up, stumbling and sore, and looked around. Matt lay unconscious against one wall. Yes, I had hit him. Sadie sat half-slumped in the chair, still cradling Austin. Her face bore the dried signs of tears. My boy's sickly eyes were open, watching me. The beast-mud was gone, all gone; and the firebox door against which Sadie had always slept was unlocked, grinding slowly open and shut on weary hinges.

I staggered to the window and looked out. I saw a vast plain of twilight, flat as concrete, pure weathered stone. Far ahead, sheer black heights rose like some geological metropolis lost in gathered gloom. The sky was partly starry, partly wracked with gutted cumulus the color of nothingness. The creaking and distant shuddering of the machine went on, but from this height, my eyes could not tell if we were really moving.

I turned from the window and surveyed my son. He was pale and tired-looking, an old man of four years. I bent and reached gently into Sadie's arms and took his weight in my hands. Her sleeping arms clung to him somewhat, but perhaps her intuition recognized the father's touch. She let him go. I lifted Austin and straightened the jackets around him and held him close. I could feel his chill radiating even through the many layers. "There, there…" I muttered, patting and caressing him. At least it was warmer in the cabin than before.

I went and stood with him by the window again. He tried to turn himself in my arms. I realized he was looking at the firebox door. "Outside," he said in a hoarse little whisper. I hugged him tight and bent and examined the door. Pulling it back with some difficulty, I found a dim chute of some sort and a waft of the strangest fresh air I had ever smelled. The chute went down at a sharp angle. It seemed to extend beyond sight, though it was hard tell in the gloom.

"Outside," he whispered again. "Come on, daddy, outside…"

I blinked away my tears and angled myself and stuck a foot into the chute. It was sheer, but the surface seemed smooth. Gravity would take over once we were in it. I had no idea if it would be smooth all the way down, but I sat on the floor and began to scoot into it.

"Outside…" His little voice, his poor little voice, so much weaker than the time at Uncle Phil's house when he had said the same thing while pulling on his little baby shoes, the same thing while running through the grass with airplane arms, the same thing as we'd struck off to meet our first machine as the voices on the dead phone must have truly told him to do…

We were off. The texture of the old iron kept us from sliding too fast, and there were plenty of overhanging pipes and broken levers for me to grab to slow us down. We slid through remnants of beast-gore. Perhaps the door had opened for that purpose, to drain the cabin.

We had gone far when, wonder of wonders, I saw a small porthole of moving stone at the bottom. It was just then that the chute took a steeper angle and the texture of the iron became smoother. Before I could do anything, we were racing down the last stretch—hitting sides, swinging back, hitting sides—and the stone view was growing.

We dropped out of the chute onto cold stone. I took the impact on my side and shoulder, shielding Austin from it. I lay gasping for air. The end of the chute was already ahead of us, moving on, dribbling beast-gore onto the stone. Overhead and in all directions, not more than three feet above the ground, a vast iron underbelly was passing over the stone: creaking, shifty, dripping oil from broken seals, dragging hoses and twisted pipework. Far out on either side, dim wheels held up its gargantuan bulk, groaning in slavery to its inertial demands. We lay under it, little ants waiting for the chance stabbing of some knifeblade of broken conduit.

It was slowing, but we had to get out from under it. Clutching Austin to my stomach with one arm, I began to crawl across the cold, slaty stone towards the distant glimpse of twilight beyond one side of wheels. The thing was enormous. My arms, my knees, everything ached. But I kept going. We would get out. We could do this.

We got near the edge. The wheels were attached to random structures: some turning as they should, some dragging from broken axles, but all arranged without pattern or clear design. Yet even in the gloom, I recognized them: they were the drive wheels of steam locomotives, as diverse doubtless as the many machines that had fused as one in that ruinous roundhouse in the woods. Some were pistonless, while others dragged shattered pistons across the stone; but none was driving the machine forwards. They simply bore its bulk under gargantuan momentum.

Still stooping and crawling, I dodged out between the wheels, past one and then another, until at last I lay panting on the hard stone with an open sky above me.

After a while, the stark loneliness of that alien world hit me. I got up, holding Austin close, and began walking, then trotting along the side of the machine. The front of it was far ahead, lost in gloom. I had to stay near the chute. I simply couldn't get separated from the others. I should have woken them up before I left the cabin. If only I had known where that chute was going to take me.

After a minute or two, I realized that the machine was slowing. It was grinding to a halt on groaning wheels. I slowed to a walk but found myself still outpacing it. I got down on hands and knees and peeked under its belly, but I could not seem to see the end of the chute.

Now the thing had nearly stopped. Still it inched forwards, shrieking, rasping, shrieking, its wheels cutting cracks and furrows in the stone. Now at last its wheels gave one last dying scream and stopped. The whole thing was silent.

There was nothing else. There was nothing I could do. I sat down heavily on the stone and closed my eyes.

"…can't believe it."

Voices.

I spun around. Figures, far off down the length of the machine, up near the front, coming towards me across the twilit plain.

"There he is," said someone.

I spun the other way. Figures approaching from the back of the machine, too.

"Is Austin with you?"—Matt's voice, from the front.

"Yes," I shouted.

"…have Phil."

I spun around. The figures coming from the back were carrying something long.

At last they met me beside the cold iron. Everyone was there, even Uncle Phil. He lay on a long straight piece of metal. He was pale and ancient-looking. Proton and Ihrel had been carrying him but had set him down now. They were breathing hard.

I looked at Matt. He had a fat lip. He glanced at me and nodded stiffly. Then he turned to the others and addressed them. "We're alive, but where the hell are we?"

"Austin is injured," said Sadie. She was not looking at me. Doubtless I had lost any chance of having good relations with her. I had hit her brother.

"Let me see the boy," said Ihrel. "Oh dear..."

Proton and I regarded each other but said nothing.

I bent and looked at my uncle. Like my son, he was alive, but white and shriveled and sickly. His open eyes seemed fixed on some distant and invisible point of regret.

Proton drew close and murmured in my ear, "Those attacked by the beast are dying. We have to do something."

I stared at him. "Dying?"

"Don't you think? You can see it in their eyes."

My heart, rising like a panic tide—"What can we do?"

"I don't know," he said.

I looked at Ihrel. She cradled my son to her breast and patted him. Her moist eyes looked out at me and pled for a solution.

"I don't know what to do," I said. "How should I know? I'm not a doctor. I don't know this stuff."

Just then everyone froze. There was no denying the odor. It was faint, but unmistakable and growing.

"Do you smell something?" said Matt.

"Yes," said Sadie.

Matt sniffed again. "It smells like food."

6

THE PLAIN EXTENDED for miles all around us. There were only two landmarks: the massive formations of stone that I had seen from the window, which now lay ahead and to the left; and similar (though more jumbled) formations, which looked a little nearer at hand, lying ahead and to the right. When a gentle breeze from that way occasionally cut the quiet air, we smelled food again; so we set off in that direction. Whenever I looked over my shoulder, our silent iron sentinel stood motionless behind us. Perhaps we could still get away.

A line appearing across the plain soon became a startling reality: a low wall was approaching us. Getting over it or through its openings would be no problem, but more disconcerting was the fact that it was there at all. With its straightness and its remnants of doorways, it was clearly the product of sentient design.

At last we stood in the wide doorway, pausing to breathe and wonder at the existence of the wall. It was no more than a few feet high, covered in something green like moss. Beyond it, strange blocks and plies of stones lay scattered, likewise covered in moss. I stood by the wall and peeled back the moss. Underneath it, the stone was blackened and weathered as if long ago blasted with fire.

"I sure hope that's food," said Ihrel. "The machine's rhythms were feeding us. I'm terribly hungry now."

"Let's go," said Proton. He and Matt bent and picked up the makeshift stretcher again. We set off, wandering between the moss-eaten ruins. The black cliffs were not quite so distant now.

When the cliffs were towering over us, dark and straight and inorganic, I began to see ruins of architectural stone beneath them: walls, windows, doorways, all covered in the same green moss, all roofless and open to the sky. The smell of food was stronger now, and in one doorway, I caught a glimmer of yellow light. Soon I could distinguish flavors in the smell—the mingling of strange ingredients which I had never tasted before. As the firelight illumined our bodies and murmured in our ears, we began to walk more slowly and more reverently.

At last we stood before a high moss-covered wall. Through empty windows and the doorway in front of us, I saw something like the bombed-out ruins of churches in England that they had always shown in the papers back then, back there: a shell of structure with no roof, shrouded in a twilight of moss, shrinking under the infinite black cliffs. Firelight flickered on its inner walls, but I could not see the fire directly.

Matt and Proton set Phil down. Matt stepped past me and went through the doorway and stood looking at the fire that I could not see. Shifting Austin in my arms, I followed Matt through the empty doorway.

A girl sat on a low stone before a fire, stirring something in a crude pot. She couldn't have been more than ten years old. Her garments were rags, and her face, focused on her work, was lost in her raven black curls. All around her, the inner walls of the spacious ruins were filled with moss-covered shelves. The shelves held uncountable books, but the books were not covered in moss.

"Hello," said Matt.

She looked up and surveyed us with her green eyes. Finding nothing of value or interest, she looked back down at her pot and resumed stirring.

"We come from far away," said Matt again.

She did not look up.

"She can't understand you," I said.

"Obviously," he muttered.

Ihrel stepped past us and touched the girl on the shoulder. Ihrel pointed at her mouth and rubbed her stomach and then indicated all of us. The girl seemed to think for a moment, then smiled and put up a finger. She stood and walked across the open space and disappeared into another doorway lost in the gloom under the cliff.

"I think she's going to cook for us," said Ihrel. "At least, I hope so."

"Who is she?" muttered Matt. "How on earth did she end up *here?*"

"Who knows?" Ihrel laughed.

In a few minutes, the girl came back out, clutching an armful of moss to her body. She dropped it into the pot. It hissed and steamed. She sat down again and resumed stirring. I glanced at Matt. He gave me a look of trepidation, but needlessly; the concoction didn't smell bad at all.

I began to explore her library, examining the books. The older volumes were partially buried in moss, but those more recently used were not. The etched, gilded spines in strange scripts meant nothing to me—until I caught a golden Roman A peeking out between curled fronds of moss. I peeled back the growth and mumbled the title to myself.

A History of Fold-traveling. By Phillip Feckidee.

"Good lord," I muttered.

I pulled the book out of the moss and flipped open to the first page. The study rang with his voice and the merciless snow piled against the window. I read aloud. "I have lived a long and strange life, and even now I know not whether the tale of my strangeness is complete. This writing may be premature. But at the least I will start at the beginning and tell as much of my story as I may. My life changed forever when I met Proton, who is called the Hiding Man, in that faded cornfield at the end of day."

So what am I writing for you? I asked. *Truth or fiction?*

I do remember that he always laughed right then. "Oh, James. Oh, James."

"My god," I said aloud.

"What?" Matt's voice drifted to me.

"My god."

Clutching the book to my body with both arms, I stepped through the moss, back towards the others. Matt was staring at me with a look that said, *what have you got there?*

"Look," I said. "My uncle. My terror."

He met me halfway to the fire. I set the book down on a large moss-covered stone. He examined it.

"I took this on dictation," I said. I couldn't say anything after that.

He looked up at me, white-faced and wide-eyed. "How did it end up *here?*"

I couldn't say anything. I couldn't see, either.

Matt stood and glanced over his shoulder at the others, at the girl. "But how did she…"

This wasn't supposed to happen. I had had my time with his memory, my time to kiss it goodbye. I *had* kissed it goodbye. You don't understand. I lost him twice. As if once wasn't bad enough—then to get him back, unexpectedly, to lose him again, to get him back again in the form of him lying on that makeshift stretcher beside the fire, again and again, alive, dead, alive, dead—

Matt stepped past me back towards the shelves. I didn't know what he thought he was doing, but my uncle was dead and dying.

"Look at this," Matt was saying. "Another one."

As if it mattered. As if a book could bring my uncle back. The book was part of the reason he was dying now, because that insatiable spirit that had driven him to write was the same that had driven him to fold-travel and thus waste himself on infinity.

"My god, Jim, they're *all* his!"

But he was dying. It didn't matter. Oh, but I had taken them all on dictation. I didn't know how they had gone from manuscript in my child's hand to bound and printed volumes on an alien world, but they had. And it was *my* hand! I had joined with him, veritably become one with him in making these things. Were it not for me, these books wouldn't fill these shelves. The branching causal tree—the titanic weight of our work in that study—was he truly read *cosmically?* And I'd had a hand…

Matt was hurrying now to the next block of shelves, muttering, "Jim, they're *all* his!"

Now the others were taking notice, getting up, following him to the shelves, seeing the books, peeling back the moss just as I had done first, reading the spines. But no one read the scribe who had made it all possible; no one read me where I sat in the study on those bitter and glorious winter days, or where I sat now on the mossy stone and wept. No one, unless dying Phil by some nervous tremor jerked his head on the stretcher in my direction, so that one failing eye glittered joyfully at me.

The moss of that planet makes a comfortable meal. The taste is not what you would expect. It is very alive, but very heavy, very fortifying, like those greens they eat in the South back then back there, but heavier and darker. I didn't know how the deïton had sustained us; but that was the first material meal I could remember eating in a long time, and it was wonderful.

We were all sitting around on the moss-padded stones, digesting, not thinking much. Matt was trying for a third time to communicate with the girl. Despite her library of English books, she understood nothing. Matt turned to me, frustrated.

"Jim, do you have that pen and notebook that Sadie gave you?"

"Yes." I pulled them out of my pocket.

He took them and began writing. I craned my neck and looked over his shoulder, but he wrote too fast; before I could get a glimpse, he had torn the sheet out and handed it to her along with the pen.

She looked it over as if reading it. Then, wonder of wonders, she spread the paper on her knee and scribbled something there. When she handed it back, I saw Matt's writing: *can you read this?* Below it, I saw her strangely precise imitation of some bookish font: *yes.*

Matt looked at me. Gears of wonder were moving behind his face. Sadie leaned in, and Matt showed her the note. She gasped. Ihrel said, "Let me see," and she and Proton looked. Even Phil stirred fitfully, and Austin burrowed deeper into Ihrel's shoulder as if the strangeness were too much for him.

"I'll be," Matt murmured, turning the note over. He looked now at the girl. She was smiling at him, her green eyes glittering in the light of the fire.

The rest of our communication with her took the form of a silent interview, as each of us, one by one, wrote questions for her as they popped into our minds.

What is your name?
Stella Orgetorix.
Does anyone else live here?
No.
Do you know anyone who can help us?
Only myself. [She wrote with a precociously developed style, doubtless due to the pedigree of her reading.]

The man with white hair and the little boy have been mortally wounded. They have the claws of a beast lodged in their bodies, but the wounds have disappeared. They need surgery. Can you do anything for them?
Not that I know of. I am sorry.
Can you feed us?
Wait, are you hungry again?
How old are you?
Old enough to know that I am a child.
Where are you from?
Here.
Who are your parents?
I don't know.
Tell us about your past.
I'd rather not.
Where did you get all these books?

Here she took some time responding. But once she started writing, she pointed out towards the plain. Looking that way, I could just make out the distant dusky form of the deïton train rising mountainous against the sky. Then she was handing the note back to us where we all sat huddled together.

A machine like yours came down out of the sky and gave the books to me.

"Vaulan," said Matt.

Stella started at the name.

"The printing press. Phil's vision. Remember?"

Proton frowned. "You mean…"

Matt began writing furiously. This time he let us all read the question before he gave it to Stella.

Do you know Vaulan the machine?

She wrote back immediately: *Yes.*

Now a flurry of questions and answers commenced. No one could have gotten the slip of paper from Matt. He had all the questions.

What is Vaulan?
It is complex, ancient, incomprehensible, and good.
Where have you seen Vaulan?
Here.
Is Vaulan here now?
No.
We're looking for him.
I can see that.
Where is Vaulan now?
On the steel planet.

After writing that and passing it back, she got up, beckoning to us, and led us out of the library, back onto the plain. The titanic sky came down all around, shrinking even the distant hulk of the deïton into insignificance. For a long time she stood, watching the clouds, waiting perhaps for them to break. At last she pointed. One by one, we came up and sighted along her arm. On my turn, in a fleeting hole in the cloud, I saw a faint star that did not twinkle.

I WON'T SAY IT was night, because it never got any darker on that planet; but we all lay down in the moss. It was surprisingly comfortable material for sleeping. I felt none of the heaviness that I generally feel. Though I never entered a deep sleep, I awoke well-rested, with a general sensation of floating in my mind.

Stella was cooking us breakfast. I knew by the smell that it was the same moss stew. Otherwise, there was very little to prepare. We had no belongings. I had nothing on me other than my clothes, my pen, and my notebook. The sky and the general level of light were no different than before, and this, combined with our lack of bedding and possessions, made this morning nothing but an unfolding of the previous night. Our stay on the planet was beginning to look like a moment of memory.

I began to wonder if Stella would come with us. After breakfast, I saw that she would. Something about her body language, the way she faced the doorway rather than turning to the side to usher us out, told me what she intended. Indeed, by the square setting of her shoulders, I thought she could have led us herself. When we got going, it was no surprise that she walked up front with Ihrel and Sadie.

But there *was* a surprise out on the plain: the deïton was gone.

We began to run, even Matt and Proton as they carried Phil. It just couldn't be. We had come all this way. Without the deïton, we were nothing but lost, little children.

We had gone a good ways out across the plain, running hopelessly towards nothing, when something appeared: a line somewhere between us and the horizon, traversing the expanse. The others slowed to a walk, but I kept running, bouncing Austin on my shoulder as gently as I could.

I came upon it much sooner than I had expected, and now I slowed in reverence. No, it was not a line; it was two lines, two rails stretching from right to left across the plain, with countless rotting wooden ties beneath them.

I stood before the tracks. I turned back towards the others, looking into the gloom for their faces. They were coming up slowly behind. They didn't see it yet, judging by their hopeless expressions.

At last they stood beside me and all around me. The silence of shock fell between us all.

Then a sound cut the air—a sound which did not belong on that alien planet, a sound distant and piteous and forever mourning. Matt looked at me and gave me a strange smile. Still holding his end of Phil's stretcher, he jerked his head. He and Proton stepped through the ties and stood resolutely between the rails. Against my will, my smile came out, too. Remembering again the meaning of surrender, I joined them on the tracks.

*

Deep river,
My home is over Jordan.
Deep river, Lord,
I want to cross over into campground.

It was Ihrel's voice that woke me. She sang with the kind of murmur that intends no audience but itself. She sang like one seated cross-legged, like one with palms turned upward.

Deep river,
My home is over Jordan.
Deep river, Lord,
I want to cross over into campground.

I sat up then. We were all lying on the cold hard metal floor of the prow. We were all jammed in there together, like we belonged. I felt, but there was no pulse in my fluids other than my own. I was dreadfully hungry. Ihrel sat cross-legged before the window. She must have gazed and gazed. The black and crystalline night was all around us, out beyond the window.

> *Oh, don't you want to go,*
> *To the gospel feast;*
> *That promised land,*
> *Where all is peace?*

Yes Lord, I did. O Lord, I did. I got up and stood behind her where the metal chair used to be. I looked out. Dead ahead, glowing faintly with an inorganic bashfulness, a metallic disk hung in space. Whatever starlight got through the droves of blackened planets lit a dull silver flame in its surface like the glittering threads in stainless steel panels in elevators back then, back there.

> *Oh, deep river, Lord,*
> *I want to cross over into campground.*

*

I awoke again to strange clicking sounds. Blinking at the ceiling, feeling the stillness, I realized that Ihrel was no longer singing. There was no sound but that clicking. I sat up and looked around. Near the wall of the cabin, Uncle Phil lay still on his stretcher. Now the same gears and mechanisms that had slaughtered the beast had come down over him. However, their motions had turned delicate and gentle: a click here, a click there, with only a little blood on them. I could see, too, that his chest was rising and falling slowly, in a steady rhythm of peace. But I couldn't see his head, for the machinery blocked it.

The others were sleeping nearby. Proton, Ihrel, the Gaddo siblings, they were all there. Hanging down near the wall was more machinery, likewise bedewed with a little blood. But where was Austin? I squinted in the darkness, looking for him; but he was gone. Then I saw that the firebox door was open again. I stood: through the window, I saw the still Euclidean curve of a flawless steel planet.

I stepped over the others and crouched and wormed into the door. This time there was no beast gore to contend with. I slid and groped my way down in total darkness.

At last I fell out onto the ground. The planet was truly steel, truly perfect. Even under the girth of the deïton, starlight found its way in and played the metallic threads that lay buried at impossible distances in the planet's metallic perfection. The nearest locomotive wheel made not even the slightest indentation in the planet's surface. In fact, it was the lip of the wheel itself that buckled under the bulk of the machine.

For a while I lay there, listening to the silence. The deïton was not moving at all. It rested, perhaps, from its long labor of space conveyance. It was silent, and I was silent, and the world was silent. Nothing had happened on this planet for a million years, and nothing *would* happen, for there was nothing here but the tired old deïton and us, its hapless wards.

Then I heard a scrape. One razor drawn slowly across the perfect steel of the planet could not have made a more nightmarish sound. I listened: it came again and continued.

I began to crawl towards the front of the machine, vaguely in the direction of the sound. There, somewhere out beyond the foremost wheels, I saw a human figure.

When at last my sight was cleared of obstructions, I lay under the front edge of the machine, watching, gaping. It was my boy. It was Austin Feckidee. He was crouched down, drawing something across the smooth steel, backing up as he went. He was moving; he was whole; he was alive.

I crawled out and got up and walked towards him. I stopped partway and simply stood, watching. Before him, a long, straight incision stretched into the distance. Only the planet's perfection allowed me to see it, for it was no more than a hair's breadth wide. Crouching, Austin

backed up step after step, drawing a glittering tool across the planet—
the very scalpel with which Matt had proposed surgery. They boy had
found a use for it at last.

"What are you doing, Austin?" I asked.

"I'm unzipping the planet," he said.

He passed me, still making his cut. A strange *thud. thud. thud.* began,
a rumination deep in the planet's core perhaps, carried up to the surface
by the unbroken perfection of solid steel. Now a groaning sound joined
it, as if the whole planet were birthing a muted agony. The surface on
which we stood shuddered.

"What have you done?" I said over the growing noise—but I spoke a
genuine question, not a reprimand.

"It wants to go outside," he said, standing beside me and beaming
up at me.

His miniscule cut was splitting. Far away, however many miles distant
he had started, I could hear the steel breaking. The planet quivered with
expectation. The pulse was getting louder, a profound thundering, as if
the whole world were machine just under that steel crust. All around
the pulse, young blaring rhythms sprang up, striving against it, blending
across mathematics in strange fractional balances of primes over primes:
incongruent, striving, warring, yet in totality, adding up to an infinite
harmonious noise.

The ground shook. A golden-orange light colored the air above the
far end of the cut. The air warmed to a dancing mirage. To each layer
of mechanized thunder came new fractal divisions of tone and beat.
A billion bells clamored for clarity. Horns of tugboats and whistles of
locomotives fought screaming out of the crack. The steel rippled with
heat.

Before us, the crack widened into a ravine, then a canyon. Warm red-
yellow light gushed out like a wound that sought to give. The cacophony
became its own placid stillness in my ears. I had heard all frequencies at
slaughtering volume, and my ears were done. Like the time in the woods
back then, back there, I would never hear anything else again. One
ridiculous smokestack, like that of an oceanliner but glowing gold all

over, rose tottering out of the canyon. After it came a swinging derrick
of the most ridiculous and convoluted design. A golden iron arm, not
humanoid in the least, in fact indescribable, came out and set its gigantic
base on the steel ground and heaved. It lifted the source itself: the thing
which I had glimpsed, which Sadie had glimpsed, which Phil had seen
born and which he had drawn in graphite all over the walls—the thing
that was now glorious gold, now throbbing, now living.

I fell on my knees. Austin did too, throwing his little arms as far
around my torso as they would go. I held him close. This time there was
no need to go outside; we had gone outside, about as far outside as you
could go, and we had found it at last. Now it was the machine's turn to
go outside.

The thing just kept coming and coming: red wheels within wheels,
golden piston housings, titanic boilers, swaying cabins shimmering with
the blast of atom bombs. Its girth split Austin's cut far beyond where
he had stopped, and it drove the walls of the canyon farther and farther
apart, presenting analogously its incremental infinity, until we could see
nothing beyond it in either direction and it had blotted out half of the
dark spangled sky. Still it rose and sang.

I felt a hand on my shoulder. Turning, I found Matt behind me, and
with him Sadie and Proton, Ihrel and Stella. Speech was impossible, and
even smiling would have denied the gravitas of the machine. There was
nothing to do or say, because *it* said everything.

The machine was spilling out of the canyon now, spilling onto the
steel, an infinite mountain-range of glowing mechanism. I turned back
again, looking for Uncle Phil. A last and lonely figure was approaching
us from the deïton, but it had black hair—

Now the deïton was grinding towards the glowing machine; around
us, perhaps, for we stood in front of it. It was elongating, changing
shape as if its logic were liquid rather than solid. Now its first tumbling
wheels met the shimmering mountain and melted into it. At that touch,
golden red coloration infused our gray and unoiled staircase locomotive
spaceship with eternal wellspring. The color flowed in from the point
of contact, accelerating the melting-in, drawing the tired finger of god

back to the one source of indomitable essence. The deïton had come home, and it glowed like atom bombs, like Christmas tree, like lights.

Another hand on my shoulder. I turned. The brown eyes of genius blazed out at me, but they were set in a face like the one he had worn in the old sepiatone photograph with the gas station drunk called Proton. Above those eyes, his hair curled in madness; but like the old derelict deïton, his hair had taken on the stain of something more alive. He was young, even *my* age, brown-haired, at last truly my brother-fellow-conspirator, at last truly my brother.

On seeing him, I felt a great shift inside me like when your stomach turns in sickness—except my soul turned in joy. I was at once like him: young, fresh, weightless in spirit, and fully cognizant of the eternity of the state in which I had just been set.

"Welcome home, James," he said, embracing me. He was the strongest man who ever lived.

From the endless corridors of that reflection, we gathered again before the machine, as we knew we must. Out from the form that blocked the stars, there stretched an operation of spinning rollers, swinging levers, moving plates, reams of golden paper flying. It could be none other than the printing press that Uncle Phil had described long ago in a distant shadowy world—none other than the press that had made Stella's books in her strange library. Whether Phil had seen a false vision or not when he returned to earth in that hazy story, I am sure that he and Vaulan have rectified the matter; but I can tell you now that the machine we saw was good, and it was making books.

The first book that fell into the output tray was gloriously bound, its spine writ with gilded letters: *The Task of Sadie Gaddo*. Seeing her name, the prophetess went forward with reverent steps until her form quivered in mirage under the pounding morphs of the machine. She took the book, heedless of the heat. She opened it and read slowly. I could not see what was written, for I was too far away; but when she came back, her face wore a placid joy that she could not share with us.

The press had not been idle. Still spinning, screaming, whirring, shredding reams into pages, it had already cranked out another book. The tome that crashed into the output tray bore likewise a spine with gilded lettering: *The Task of Proton and Ihrel*. The couple went forward and took it and came back. They began reading silently together, standing near us but not showing the page. Then Proton began to read aloud.

"No, dear friends, I will not return to earth. Your labors were great, but it was not for you to bring your visions to fruition. If that shall ever be, it will fall…" He paused and looked up, straight at Matt. *"It will fall to Matthias Gaddo."* He closed the book. "That's all it says. The rest is blank."

Matt's wide eyes drank in the machine, and his mouth hung open a little.

Another book crashed into the tray. Titled like the rest of the series, its unique name blazed out in golden letters. Matt walked slowly towards the towering machine. He turned wavelike in the heat as he bent and lifted the ponderous volume and brought it back to us, reading it already. But his face was troubled.

"What is it?" I said.

He handed the book to me. I opened it. The first page bore the title, *The Task of Matthias Gaddo*. Below it was a subtitle: *Or, Go Back To Earth*. I turned over the first page, but saw nothing. I turned some more. Nothing. I flipped pages and pages. They were all blank.

"But he gave me this too."

I looked up. Matt held a tiny clown-colored box, some childish carving of a pirate's treasure chest no larger than a pack of cigarettes. Things rattled inside when he shook it.

Another book had already dropped into the tray. I saw my son's name in the title. I let go of his hand as he walked forward unafraid. I watched him shimmer in the heat as he heaved the book down to the steel ground. I watched him sit with legs in a W and flip the book open with both arms. But he was puzzled. Perhaps he couldn't read well enough, having but lately learned the alphabet and a few words. Perhaps I would have to interpret his story for him. So when he brought the book back, I gladly lifted its bulk out of his arms and opened it and prepared to read to one who could not read, as I always had.

The title page was the same as the others: *The Task of Austin Feckidee.* Below it, the subtitle: *Or, Go Back to Earth.* I turned page after page. I flipped madly through the gigantic volume. The whole thing was blank.

Another book had already fallen into the tray. Stella went forward and took it and came back and showed us all the title page and the blank pages. She would return to earth as well.

When the next book hit the tray, I squinted and read the gilded spine: *The Task of James and Phillip Feckidee.* I looked over at my uncle, my brother, and we set out towards the press together.

Standing in the midst of the mirage, I knew the heat was dangerously strong, but I found in it an overwhelming expression of love and comfort. If I were to melt into it right then, I would have been the happiest ever.

Our book was massive, far larger and thicker than the others. Phil took it out one-handed, but offered it to me. "Read to me, dear James." His smile was forever. "My soul is starved for words."

I balanced it across my straining arms and turned to the title page. *The Task of James and Phillip Feckidee.* There was no subtitle. I turned the page and began reading aloud to Phil, as I always had.

"I am your god. I am your Vaulan, your machine. You two found me again at last. Now you will live forever with me and write together the book of the universe, which is never finished. From the seeds of your work, a garden, a planetary flowerbed, will grow. It will cover this steel planet with green life. Your friends return to earth; from the seeds of their work, a garden will grow which will likewise cover that world in green life. But they will only discover it by trying to accomplish what they do not know—what you cannot tell them."

I looked back at the others, but they were too far away to hear my reading over the roar of the machine. I looked at Phil. He smiled and pointed into the depths of the spinning, swinging, glowing forms. In the shimmering haze, I saw shelves and shelves of volumes extending in incomprehensible directions without end.

Phil pointed to the page. "What does it say? I still can't seem to read the printed word."

I found my place and began reading again. *"Here, as you accelerate upward to join the eternal spiral of my time, you see the books which you have always written and will always write together."*

The text ended there.

I sat beside Phil. Behind us, the rhythms and processes of the great glory throbbed without change. Before us, the planet stretched in a perfect curve into infinity, where the dark sky came down. From the machine beside us, a single set of train tracks stretched across the curve into the untold distance. Above where the tracks bent out of sight, a lone star twinkled brightly as if receding into the night.

"Here we are, James," said Phil.

"How did we get here?" I asked.

"I do believe we were run over by a train." He grinned at me.

"What did you see, back then back there, when you came out of the crack in the tree? You were talking about a printing press…"

He shrugged. "I saw a false vision, but one with a basis in truth. Turns out it was my words that were gray, and the machine itself that is fire."

I said nothing.

"But the words are still needed, and again, it falls to us," he said. "So, take pen and paper. Take this on dictation."

I waited, holding the implements.

"Are you ready?"

"Of course," I said.

I waited, but he said nothing.

He shook his head. "No; I can't. You have to start it, Jim."

"Me?!"

"Didn't any of that practice count for something?"

Didn't it? Oh, it did. I set pen to paper—but I did not write yet. As the pen rested there, the flowing ink infused it with a dark and growing cloud. I swear to you that, by some power which I did not yet know (but which I have since come to know better), a white fleshy root and a young green stalk sprang from the ink blotch. A young plant was growing from the spot where my pen drained ink into the paper. The white root sought downward for soil, the green leaf upward for light. I could not see how it would survive, but it had begun: my garden, my flowerbed. We would write this. We would grow this.

I began to write. *You see, I first discovered William Blake, that man sent by whomever God thinks God is…*

THE END

READ THE WHOLE

VAULAN CYCLE

by g. t. anders

The Feckidees would like to be normal, but generation after generation—first great-uncle, then father, then son—gets sucked into a hidden struggle of cosmic proportions. It turns out those strange abilities are no coincidence after all: the Feckidees have been gifted for a reason.

VAULAN CYCLE *book i*

A t Uncle Phil's funeral, James Feckidee notices a curious old photograph. Uncle Phil looks a good forty years younger, but the man next to him in the picture, who pumped James's gas that evening, looks the same age as he did earlier today. Add to that the stranger's odd interest in James's young son, Austin, and things couldn't get any more alarming. Or could they? Only if a monster staked out James's house…

James is about to learn a few things. It looks like there was a lot more to Uncle Phil than James ever guessed. It was no coincidence that the monster came for James on the night of Uncle Phil's funeral—and it was no coincidence that James ran into that ageless stranger at the gas station.

ISBN: 978-0-9856522-1-0

read a sample now

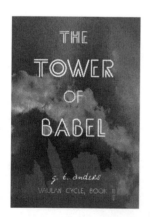

VAULAN CYCLE *book ii*

A ustin Feckidee wants to make it as an artist. He has the talent, the grant, and the studio space in the city. If only he could shake his past— the strange work he did with a few friends at an abandoned church in the countryside.

Now, that past is staring him in the face again. Stella, the ringleader of the old operation, has sent him a letter begging him to return to the work that failed utterly three years ago. Should he answer her call to be a servant, or should he stay and pursue the heights of his own artistic genius? His decision might just change the world, or show him who he really is—or both.

ISBN: 978-0-9856522-0-3

read a sample now

V⋀UL⋀N CYCLE *book iii*

On a virgin world, Vaulan offers them all the ultimate transformation: to become gods of infinite stature. The transformations will only come with great sacrifice, perhaps with great reward.

But can Austin, Stella, Gaddo and Israel put the past behind them to find new identities? More importantly, can they handle the truth about Israel's daughter Miranda?

COMING SOON

For updates, join our mailing list. Newsletters are sent out infrequently—only when there's big news.

sign up here ☞

or visit:
http://www.gtanders.com/free-short-fiction/

THERE'S MORE!

coming 2015

We're All Singing Now

Making Art In The 2010's

G. T. ANDERS

We're All Singing Now will look at the stories of individual artists in all media—music, writing, visual art, film, and dance—and connect these stories to the larger cultural and technological shift that's upon us. In the age of a crowded Internet and thousands-of-bands-you've-never-heard-of, the book asks where we came from culturally and where we should go from here artistically.

for updates, sign up
for our mailing list ☞

http://www.gtanders.com/free-short-fiction/

I'm always up for a conversation, and you can connect with me in a variety of ways. I publish a blog at my website, and I respond to comments as much as I can. You can also connect with me on Facebook or through email.

 Website: http://www.gtanders.com/

 Facebook: https://www.facebook.com/gtanders.author

 Email: author@gtanders.com

Acknowledgments

This book never would have become a reality without a lot of help.

To my wife, Danae: Thank you for your enthusiasm, your encouragement, and your sense of balance across all areas of life.

Matthew: Thank you for your honest critiques and your hard work on the Kickstarter video and Victorious Airborne master. You know your stuff.

To my parents, Ken and Sue: Thank you for your lifelong encouragement of my work. I couldn't have done it without you.

Anna, Ashton, Lucy, April: I'm indebted to you for your willingness to read the book beforehand. It would have been a flop without that.

To Those who made this Book possible
with their Generosity:
THANK YOU!

Kathy	Matthew
Robin	Brian
Mom & Dad	Michael
Lucy	Craig & Alison
Aunt Jenna & Uncle Mike	Mark & Charlotte
Dr. Howard	Saran
Dennis	Dave & Judy

23533517R00136

Made in the USA
Charleston, SC
27 October 2013